Savitar

Ron Mueller

Books by Ron Mueller

The Savitar Series-Science Fiction
- Journey's End
- Savitar
- Confluence

Bram Nielson Series-Science Fiction
- The Fold
- The Message
- Fold Wormhole
- Negative Fold
- Ripples in Time

The Alex Evercrest Series-Detective
- The River Front
- The Girl on the Grill
- Missing
- Maggot
- Racist
- Votive Candles
- Windy City
- Country Road
- Pool of Blood
- Sins of the Daughter

The Taelo Series-Prehistory America
- Taelo: The Early Years
- Taelo: The Golden Feather
- Taelo: Journey of Discovery
- Taelo: Dangerous Passage
- Taelo: Condor Clan Slingers
- Taelo: Circumvention
- Taelo: The Journey of Sages

A Taelo Story
- The Name of the Child
- White Swan and Quiet Pheasant
- Broken Spear
- Floating Cloud
- Quiet Rabbit
- Busy Bee
- Little Otter& Talking Wren
- Burley Bear & Meadow Flower

A Feather-in-the-Wind Story
- The Eastern Elk Clan

The Door Series-Science Fiction
- The Door
- Delivery
- Journey Beyond

The Problem Solver Series-Secret Agent
- The Beginning
- Drug Lords
- Broder Crosser

Current Past and Future-Science Fiction
Event Survivors-Science Fiction
The Door-Science Fiction
Viajante 7-Science Fiction
Imagination - Courtney Huynh & Chloe Parker

Savitar

By: *Ron Mueller*

Around the World Publishing LLC
4914 Cooper Road Suite 144
Cincinnati, Ohio 45242-9998

This story is a work of fiction. Names, characters, places, and incidents either are products of the author's imagination or are used fictitiously. Any resemblance to actual events or locales or persons, living or dead, is entirely coincidental.

Savitar by Ron Mueller, Copyright © 2012.
©2023

All rights reserved, including the right of reproduction, in whole or in part in any form.

ISBN 13: 978-1-68223-305-4
ISBN 10: 1-68223-305-7

Distributed by Ingram
Cover Design By: Ron Mueller

Savitar

Table of Content

Ron Mueller

Dedicated to:

Rosemary, a dear friend, she is now among the Stars.

Savitar

Chapter 1: Discovery

The threat of Earth's total destruction startled and confounded Zack. He worked through his initial comprehensive analysis several times to confirm his conclusion.

He thought through how to get verification from his analysis support team.

The disappearance of the asteroid he had been following came as a surprise and at first, he had assumed it was data error.

He had used three additional reliable sources of the data and the result was the same.

He had he discussed this with Craig, his partner. Craig assumed some sort of error in the calculation and had discounted the finding.

Zack left shortly after the other team members. He went about his normal workout still chewing on the problem as he ran laps. He showered went home and went to bed.

By three in the morning, he gave up trying to sleep. He decided to get up for an early morning breakfast and went to a nearby all night diner that he often frequented.

"Hi Arlene, let's start with a cup of coffee and then I will see what else I get," Zack said as he sat down at the counter.

He took in the rest of the diner. There was an old man sitting over a cup of coffee but otherwise the place was empty. This was just a small hole in the wall place. He wondered how they made enough money to stay open.

After his breakfast, Zack left the diner, crossed the street, and went down into the subway. The walk to his office took him by a lush rose garden and tree lined park where he often went to eat his lunch. This early in the morning it loomed grey and more foreboding than usual. He figured it was the early morning hour and his state of mind.

Once he reached the office, he gathered his material for the normal morning analysis planning meeting. He was trying to figure out the best way to get the team to verify his findings.

When Craig came in, he sat down at his desk and looked over and declared that he had a miserable night and was upset about the analysis.

He came into the meeting in an ugly mood. He had reached the conclusion the team had made an analysis or observation error.

Zack knew Craig had come to the wrong conclusion, but he decided against arguing.

"How the hell can we lose a ten-mile-long asteroid?" Craig barked at the observation and analysis team.

Zack observed that Craig was talking to the team but looking directly at him.

"I want you to find out where we went wrong and I want you to find that dam asteroid," he continued

Zack knew what they would find but he decided to keep his mouth shut. There was no use arguing with his partner and mentor when he was mad.

He had now worked with Craig for almost ten years. Zack knew his own conclusion put him at the freaky fringe of scientific theory.

He needed independent verification and Craig's demands would accomplish that.

Zack decided to spend his time putting more detail to a solution his sleepless mind had come up with. He took his computer, a drawing pad and pencil and headed out to see if the rose garden in the park would help his thinking. He hoped it would provide the grounding that he felt he might have lost.

Until a few years ago, Zack had been Dr. Craig Garrity's sole assistant. He and Craig had spent six years using land and orbital telescopes in radio, light, and infrared technology to look back in time.

They studied the specific location of Earth in space over its billions of years of life and correlated these positions with the various periods of the extinction of life.

They found evidence of bombardment from debris fields in space leading to the periods of great extinction. Their work received wide recognition and Zack got his PhD in Astronomical History. This was a unique PhD that Zack with the support of Dr. Garrity had designed.

Zack remembered the day he, Dr. Garrity and a NASA representative met to discuss the possibility of getting funding to look ahead to where the Earth was going.

Dr. Garrity connected looking ahead to NASA's research in how to protect the Earth from another asteroid like the one that had killed off the dinosaur. He made an outstanding business arrangement.

He and Zack set up a firm to search ahead to the space into which Earth was heading. The government would provide the computing, analysis resources and office space. Together with NASA they set up a program they named "Pathfinder." Dr. Garrity enrolled his, across the world, network of acquaintances in the effort. All the major observatories were linked to Pathfinder's data banks. All orbiting telescopes were engaged. This was a winning arrangement for everyone involved.

Zack came up with the idea to enroll home PC users to help in the analysis. He designed and had an Analysis App programmed that could be downloaded to a personal computer. It could be activated and then do analysis in the background. This was a big hit with the general public. Junior high and high school students seemed to especially like the App.

Many used the App on their i-phones. There were enough users that it provided a big chunk of the required data analysis

Since the Earth rotated around the Sun and the Sun traveled on the outer edges of the Milky Way, and the Milky Way was itself speeding away from the center of the Universe, determining where and how to look was a challenge for a host of astronomers, physicists, and mathematicians.

It took almost a year to develop a model for Earth's journey with enough detail to enable them to analyze the potential threats coming at them through space.

It was a multi-dimensional time and space analysis.

Zack new how easy it was to get lost when doing the analysis and then putting it to practical use to visually look ahead through a telescope. He and he network supporting him were doing this visually, in infrared and with radio signals.

Zack quickly recognized the necessity and the depth of the government financial pocket as they hired hundreds of data processors.

The data displaying a specifically defined signature was quickly processed.

Other, less-promising data was put in a large database and was slowly fed out to all the App users. These users downloaded small segments of it to their PC's or their i-phones. The analysis program chunked away. The chunks showing promise, from this second level of analysis, were highlighted by the apt and passed back up to the program analysts for more detailed analysis.

The disappearance of one three-mile wide by ten-mile-long asteroid slated for a close pass of Earth affirmed the value of all the tedious analysis that had been done.

The previous day Zack had reviewed the data and the visual record being made of the asteroid. He watched as the asteroid changed course, then seemed to stop and disappear.

He sat and did an initial sketch of his idea. Taking his work to the park had been a good idea. He was able to do an initial drawing and then put together the equation that he would complete to determine if he had any hope of making his idea real.

He walked back to the office and as he entered, he was immediately face with a still upset partner.

"How in the hell can we lose a ten-mile-long asteroid?" Craig asked again in consternation.

He commented that his confidence in the team was taking a beating at the moment. He was sure some mistake in data analysis had occurred.

Zack decided to continue to develop and work on his own analysis. He had come up with his own alarming conclusion and was quietly working on its proof and a potential solution.

Craig and the analysis team were focused on the period leading up to the disappearance. They requested back up data from all participating observatories. Craig ran through the analysis himself and reviewed the visuals. He pointed all telescopes to the last location of the asteroid. He had data collected in all the frequencies possible.

His analysis confirmed the disappearance. The asteroid began going off its course and then it seemed to stop. Finally, it slowly began to disappear. Infrared data showed the asteroid give out its last signature as it disappeared.

It was the dying signature of an object being consumed by a black hole!

Zack had been waiting all day for Craig to reach the point when he finished his analysis. He had meanwhile researched the conclusion he had reached the night before. He had found reference to his specific conclusion. Albert Einstein himself had predicted the existence of what he had found.

"What is your conclusion," Craig looked up and asked from across the office they shared?

"You seem to already know. When did you figure it out," Craig asked as he turned away from his computer and looked at Zack across the room?

"I figured it out yesterday before going home. It kept me up all night." Zack replied quietly.

"You find a black hole in the path of the solar system, and you keep quiet," Craig said with a shake of his head?

Sometimes he wondered about his young partner. He was brilliant but sometimes he was too polite.

"Would you have done anything differently since this morning if I had argued that it was not the analysis but a black hole," Zack said standing up to get another cup of coffee?

He asked if Craig would have accepted the concept of a small black hole waiting ahead in the path of the solar system. You know as well as I that small black holes are supposed to have ceased to exist at least a billion years ago.

After some discussion he and Craig decided they would need the independent confirmation of at least three other independent global teams. Craig would contact the teams and asked for their independent analysis of the missing asteroid

He sat down took a sip of his coffee and pulled up the analysis he had spent his time on.

"We not only have found a black hole. We have found one directly in the path of the solar system. More specifically it is one with which Earth is on a collision course with," Zack said as he put his analysis up on the large flat screen the two shared.

He had developed a rough drawing of the situation.

"How long do we have," Craig asked as he looked at the sketch?

"We have roughly four years until the edge of the solar system reaches the black hole and about seven years until it intersects Earth's orbit," Zack replied

I am ninety nine percent sure that Earth will be direct hit on this black hole. The hole is stationary. The solar system is approaching it on a collision course.

"Is there anything else you know that I should know," Craig asked?

"Yes, but I'm not talking until after our dinner. Emily made us promise to be on time and personally I love her cooking and don't intend to be late," Zack replied as he powered down his laptop and put it away in his briefcase.

Craig followed suit and the two walked out to his car.

"Welcome, I am surprised you two are early. There is beer or wine in the fridge. Go in the den. I'll call you when dinner is ready," Emily said as she greeted them.

Zack always made sure to be on time for Emily's dinners. She had trained as a chef and always served the most delicious dishes. He could not understand how Craig kept himself in such good shape. He figured he would be one hundred pounds heavier if Emily was his wife.

They had just finished the Modelo when Emily called them to dinner.

It was a rule that they did not discuss business at the dinner table, so the talk was about Emily's day.

Zack did share that the roses in the park were blooming and that there seemed to be several new types that had been planted.

"Emily that was another one of your marvelous dinners. We were early because I declined to engage your husband with any business when I realized we might be late for this treat," Zack said in praise as he sat back and sipped the coffee that Emily had served.

"You two go into the living room. I will bring in some more coffee and a few cookies," Emily said as she got up to clean the table.

Both Zack and Craig carried their dishes over to the kitchen sink before going into the living room.

Afterwards they sat in front of the gas fireplace with a cup of coffee and some of Emily's cookies.

He had tried to think of a more persuasive way to say it, but he just blurted it out.

"I have a way to capture the black hole and move it out of Earth's path," Zack said.

He stopped and sipped on his cup of coffee and watched for Craig's reaction.

"Capture a black hole. Even if you can, what are you going to do once you capture it?" Craig asked with a chuckle as he contemplated the impossibility of such a task.

He really enjoyed the creativity that his star pupil and friend would periodically display. However, this was a little beyond the normal, it was a little on the crazy side.

He figured it was probably the caffeine from all the coffee Zack drank. He knew it was not drugs, but he would have believed so if he had not known his partner for so long.

"I am going to use the blackhole as the center of a giant spaceship. It will provide the gravity and the power for this spaceship," Zack replied quietly.

He was aware of Craig's skepticism, but he was sure of his idea and that he knew how to build the spaceship.

He had spent the day on the analysis of the power of this small black hole. He had concluded that it could be contained in a magnetic bottle.

He knew Craig was not yet understanding or accepting this as a serious suggestion.

"Tell me more," Craig said as he leaned forward to see if Zack was serious.

And by the tone of his voice, Craig thought Zack was serious.

"Here, let me show you," Zack said as he powered up his laptop.

He showed Craig his power analysis and a potential way to bottle the black hole.

They got into some serious and deep discussion.

Zack was surprised when he realized it was past two in the morning.

"Its lucky tomorrow is Saturday we should probably go to bed," Zack said.

He realized how tired he was. He was sapped.

"You're welcome to use the guest room." Craig said as he too realized how tired he was.

Emily had said good night when she brought in the coffee and cookies. That had been more than four hours earlier.

Craig was now hooked on Zack's idea. It would take a lot of additional analysis and design work, but the idea seemed plausible.

He once again was humbled by Zack's uncanny ability to cut through a monumental problem in a simple direct approach.

Zack accepted using the guest room. He made quick work of getting asleep.

It seemed that having someone accept his discovery and his solution as plausible had released his anxiety and he did not wake up until he heard Emily's call for breakfast.

He looked at the clock and it was past nine-thirty.

"I let the two of you sleep in this morning.

I must be the only woman jealous of a former male student, for keeping my husband out all night.

What were the two of you talking about for so long," Emily joked.

She had taken Zack under her wing and thought of him almost as a younger brother. She had hosted Zack's parents on the ribbon cutting ceremony when Craig and Zack opened their current business.

"Well in all truthfulness, if I or Zack were to tell you, we would all have to be shot," Craig said giving Emily a good morning kiss while giving her pat on her behind.

He was not ready to tell anyone about this situation. Emily worried about threatening rainstorms. He was not about to mention Earth's potential doom idly or casually.

"Zack and I are going to have to work this weekend. We have a situation needing immediate attention. We need to prepare some presentation for this coming Monday or Tuesday.

The two left after a quick breakfast and went into the office.

Craig and Zack sat in their office reviewing what they had learned. The blackhole was not a collapsed star. The black hole was much too small. Instead, they theorized that it was material compressed by the original big bang formation of the universe that had made this relatively small black hole.

They wondered how it could maintain itself. Theoretically it took a much larger amount of mass to form and then maintain a black hole. This small but deadly one had absorbed or sucked in an asteroid almost ten miles in length and three miles wide. It seemed that it sustained itself by taking in these smaller chunks of matter.

Earth was too large to be sucked in, but an encounter with even a small blackhole would create havoc and have a dramatic impact. They theorized Earth's atmosphere, and its water would be stripped, and the event would likely disrupt the planet's orbit.

Zack postulated Mars might have experienced this same black hole in the distant past. He also pointed to the debris out past the orbit of Mars where a fifth planet should have formed.

The cycle around the edge of the Milky Way was roughly once every two hundred fifty million years. Perhaps the Solar System had previously had multiple encounters with this blackhole.

Or perhaps there were other similar black holes in the galaxy. If his theory proved to be true, it would solve the long-discussed mystery of why Mars lost most of its atmosphere and its water.

"If we want to survive this encounter, we need to martial Earth's resources and take immediate action. How are we going to pull this off," Zack voiced his concern as he sat looking at the screen?

"I will contact the President and set up a meeting to brief him," Craig said.

Zack knew about Craig's friendship with the President. The two had grown up in the same neighborhood, attended school together and had both graduated from MIT. Craig had been an active campaigner for the newly elected President. Even so he was still surprised to see Craig calling the President on a Saturday.

Zack found it amazing that Craig could just dial him at a moment's notice.

"Yes, please tell him it's Dr. Craig Garrity and I have information critical to the well-being of the nation." Craig spoke into the phone.

He hung up.

"Let's see if Dan call's me back. He told me I could call him at any time." Craig said as he looked over and smiled at Zack.

A few moments later the phone rang. Craig put it on the speaker phone, but he put his finger to his lips and pointed to Zack.

"Well, I just left my daughter's swim meet. How are things with you and Emily," the President said in friendly tone?

"Emily is fine.

However, I really am calling about a very serious threat to the Earth. I want to review it with you this coming week. Please listen to me personally. Afterwards you can unleash all of your technical resources to verify what I tell you. Can you get me on your agenda," Craig replied more seriously?

"Yes, I will see you. Let's make it Monday at lunch. You know you have ruined my weekend with this. Should I pray in church tomorrow," the President replied?

"Thank you and yes several prayers would be appropriate," Craig responded.

"Wow, I never would have dreamt it would have been this easy to get to talk to and see the President," Zack said in amazement after Craig hung up the phone.

"Well getting Dan to listen will not be the issue. He just got sworn in. As you know I attended his inauguration.

Getting him to take immediate action and making it stick may be more of an issue. However, Dan has a history of making things move and getting things done. Let's get our presentation outlined and fleshed out. We don't want to blow this presentation," Craig said quietly.

Zack spent the rest of the morning working on his concept and preparing a draft of the presentation he had wanted.

Craig was reviewing the slides and adding the verbiage in the notes section of the presentation.

It was late Saturday afternoon when a of limo stopped in the parking lot of the office. Two black vans were parked on either side of a long stretch limo car.

Zack was shocked when he looked up to see two very serious men enter the room with their badges out.

"FBI is there anyone else here?" he asked looking around.

"We are the only ones," Zack replied thinking it was obvious no one else was in the room.

"How can we help you," Craig inquired.

"It's clear," the second agent said into his phone. The two stepped forward and to the side.

The President walked in.

"I couldn't wait until Monday. I know you wouldn't call me on something trivial. You are tracking a close encounter asteroid. Is it on a collision course?" the President asked as he came in.

Craig looked at the two agents.

"Are they cleared for all information," Craig inquired?

"Gentlemen, please give us a few moments alone," the President said to the two agents.

Once the door closed Craig stood up.

"Dan thanks for coming. Let me introduce you to Dr. Zackary Milton. He made the discovery we are going to tell you about. He has also proposed a solution to this problem. I am relieved to be able to put this in your capable hands. Zack, you tell the story," Craig said as he shook hands with the President.

Zack was a little unnerved.

"Mr. President...

"Please call me Dan," the President interrupted as he accepted a cup of coffee from Craig.

"Dan, there is a black hole directly in the path of the Solar system and it will be in Earth's orbit in about six years. Thursday, we witnessed it swallow the near pass asteroid we have been tracking," Zack spoke slowly and clearly.

He was trying to be as clear and as direct as possible. He wanted the President to understand the critical need for immediate action.

"You don't pull any punches. What kind of damage are we talking about," the President inquired?

"Well, this is a small black hole. It theoretically should have ceased to exist several billion years ago. Our solar system seems to be one source of its sustenance. It is too small to ingest the Earth but that won't do us any good.

It will likely leave Earth in the same condition we find Mars today. It will strip away the atmosphere, our oceans, everything on the surface," Zack replied.

"Here let me show you the pictures we have of it swallowing the asteroid," Zack continued.

"This is going to take more than a prayer in church. What is the solution you have come up with," the President inquired?

This time Zack pulled out his notebook.

"I was getting ready to put this into a graphics package. You're about a day early for anything more than my hand drawing. My calculations are all in my computer and of course they will take additional checking, but I am confident I have the right scale for the size of this solution," Zack said as he turned to the page with the sketches of the capture device.

"Dan, the dimensions of this capture device are at the limits of what is feasible with our current technology. It is doable but it will take the concerted effort of all the resources of the Earth. The inner sphere is fifty miles in diameter and the outer sphere is two hundred miles in diameter. The inner sphere will need to withstand a nine G force trying to ingest it. The outer sphere will be at one G. It is simple to make but will need to be assembled in space. Do you have any questions," Zack said as he stopped to let the information sink in?

"This just seems to be getting tougher as I learn more. You said this was the only solution. Don't we have some other weapon at our disposal," the President said looking at Craig?

"There is no weapon known to mankind strong enough to eliminate this black hole from our path. I initially thought Zack had fallen over the edge but when I reviewed his notes and proposed solution, I realized it indeed was the only possible one. This is a problem with only one very difficult monumental solution," Craig responded.

"How much time do I have before I must take action," the President inquired?

"I called you because we are already very late in taking action. We must be on our way toward the black hole in the next two years. You need to understand, accept, and implement this proposal immediately," Craig replied.

"It seems clear to me. It truly is a monumental undertaking. I can see we have the technology to make it happen. I am not sure we have the time and the resources. I agree immediate action is required. I will have my cabinet called together for an emergency meeting on Monday afternoon. I will send over some resources to help you prepare a presentation. You are planning to work on Sunday while I pray?" the President said as he stood up?

"Yes, we were planning to work tomorrow. Any help we can get would be very useful. Make sure one of them knows all the idiosyncrasies and quirks of your cabinet members. Please apologize for me to Lydia for disturbing her family on the weekend." Craig said as the President got up.

"Craig you always were a pain. I can't say this meeting was a pleasure. This will be a weekend I will probably never forget that I was at Cathy's swim meet when I learned the world was coming to an end," the President said as he opened the office door.

Zack stood looking at the door in disbelief. He had been expecting a long-drawn-out discussion about alternatives. Or at least having the President dig into the details of the discovery.

He looked over at Craig and saw that he was smiling.

"He is that direct and he is very smart. He may be smarter than both of us," Craig said as he commented that they needed to get back to work.

Zack and Craig made an outline of their presentation. They decided to call it a day. They agreed to meet at eight in the morning.

The next morning, Zack was surprised by the number of cars in the parking lot. It was Sunday morning, and the lot was at least half full. He saw Craig's car and parked next to it as usual.

"Good Morning. As you can see, we have lots of help. I have coffee brewing and I have found places for this group from the White House to be able to do their work. I almost left when I drove in and saw all of them here." Craig greeted Zack as he walked in.

"How many are there and what are we going to do with them all," Zack said as he plugged in his laptop?

"There are six of them and they have instructions to prepare the entire presentation. I thought you and I would review what we outlined late yesterday afternoon and then let them go at it. We can do some more work on your design while they get the presentation ready. They can ask questions for clarity and later today we can do the final edit. Tomorrow morning, they can finalize the presentation and make final copy," Craig replied.

"Sounds good to me, I wasn't sure how detailed to make the presentation. They will know exactly what is needed. I am going to introduce myself, get a cup of coffee and then I will be ready to go," Zack replied as his computer came to life.

Monday morning Zack and Craig arrived at the parking lot in the back of the White House. They were stopped at the entrance and asked for identification. Zack was surprised to find their names were on the list. He parked and Craig and he walked up to the entrance gate. Here they were met by one of the team that had worked with them on Sunday on the presentation.

"Welcome to the White House. I'll take you to our office area. We will finalize the presentation and get it ready for the cabinet meeting. We are in the process of finalizing the changes we agreed to yesterday afternoon. Everything is on track. This has personally blown me away. I sure hope your idea takes immediate traction," Jerry the leader of the Presidents team greeted them.

Zack sat down and went through the presentation with Craig. It really was of professional quality.

"Wow, I wonder if this team does any work on the side," Zack commented as they finished the review of the presentation.

The President's team had prepared a simple animated slide presentation showing the black hole, the disappearance of the asteroid, and some education on a black hole. They followed with how the capture and movement of the black hole could happen.

"We should have had this kind of help the last time we were trying to raise money for our studies." Craig commented.

"I agree. We should be able to make a convincing presentation with this slide deck," Zack replied

"I would like you to do the presentation. I will chime in if you miss any critical points, but I would like you to be up front," Craig requested.

Craig was aware that several of the cabinet members did not like the fact that he was a personal friend of the President, and he figured the best course of action was to put Zack out front.

The President walked in and thanked and welcomed everyone for attending this special meeting. He set the stage by asking everyone to allow the entire presentation to be given then afterwards the group could go back to any point and ask questions.

He pointed to one of the clerks and said that after the presentation ended a paper reference copy would be handed out.

He then introduced Dr. Craig Garrity and Dr. Zackary Milton. Zack stood and gave a brief introduction of himself.

He then let them know about the discovery of a blackhole that the solar system was approaching.

The presentation went smoothly. The entire room seemed to be at attention and their faces showed no emotion.

The paper copies were handed out as Zack ended the screen presentation.

The President then clarified that he would lead the discussion portion of the meeting.

Zack and Craig listened to the reaction the concept was eliciting from the cabinet members. This was what Zack had anticipated from the President.

"What's the big fuss? Why don't we just send several nuclear missiles and blast the black hole out of the way," the secretary of the interior spoke up loudly.

"Well Lawrence, a black hole can suck in stars and stars that explode with the force of millions of our nuclear missiles. We need to do something very different than to try to apply our meager force. I am also not sure we can be as accurate as we would want from this range," the Secretary of Defense replied.

The response surprised Zack. He sensed the Secretary understood and was supportive of the capture concept.

The discussion which followed allowed Zack to answer additional questions and to share his general approach to capturing and utilizing the black hole.

After, what seemed a redundant and circular discussion the cabinet agreed capturing the black hole was the correct tactical action.

The meeting ended and they followed the President into the oval office.

"The two of you have stepped up to help the world, and I want to thank you. I'm afraid you are in for an experience you did not imagine. Your leadership and guidance are of such critical nature I have asked each of you be assigned personal bodyguards. You will be taken from here directly to FBI headquarters to select them. You may not have noticed but you were being watched since our meeting on Saturday," President Lansing said after the cabinet meeting.

This came as a surprise to both Zack and Craig. They asked whether such action was necessary.

"Please accept this in the spirit of friendship. I have no choice but to ensure your safety. You give me the news of the end of the world and you two are the only ones with the plans to save us. Of course, I have to ensure your safety," the President said as they walked back to his office.

There was no farther discussion on this topic.

"We will need to enroll the leaders of all the major economies. This will be followed by enrolling the entire UN membership. I will arrange for this to happen.

I will have the presentation team, work with you on any tweaks that may be needed. You may need to simplify a few points. I will also need to take part in these next presentations. They will coach all of us on how to best present this concept to ensure getting the global support we need. We are going to have to sell, cajole, beg, sweet talk and threaten. We will need to do whatever it takes to get the key leaders to support us," President Lansing said.

Soon after, Craig and Zack were escorted out to their cars. Two FBI agents got into the back seat and drove home with them.

Chapter 2: Project Savitar

The President stood looking out of his office window. He understood the gravity of the situation and would act with speed and urgency. He had a strong political team, but he had been in office for less than a month and they had barely moved into their offices. He knew that he was taking unprecedented action. He would need all the help from his friends and allies to pull it off.

"Well, I wanted to make a difference. I guess I will need to be careful what I wish for in the future," he thought to himself.

"Mary, come in and let me work with you on some meetings that will need to be immediately scheduled," he said while he held down the speaker button on the intercom to his desk.

Please set up an emergency meeting with the leaders of the Industrial Seven. Set it for Wednesday. Stress, urgency of a global nature needs to be addressed and the requirement for top leader representation.

Tell them I understand this is very unusual, but it is of such a monumental nature that this action is required," Dan clearly instructed.

A week later the leaders sat around the table. By this time the President, Zack and Craig had rehearsed the presentation multiple times.

The President's staff had analyzed each country's most probable objections and the political currency to make alignment happen. One hundred percent agreement was critical. The President knew he needed every leader to be in total support.

"Welcome. Thank You for responding to such a sudden request. I have been as stunned as I believe you will be by what you are going to learn. I have asked Dr. Zachary Milton to explain a serious and very threatening situation. He and his mentor Dr. Craig Garrity have made a startling and grave discovery affecting all of our well-being. I will now let Dr. Milton describe the situation," President Lansing said as he sat down.

"Gentlemen, six months ago, astronomers and scientists verified a small black hole lies ahead of the Earth's path. Our only hope is to capture the black hole and move it out of Earth's way," the Zack said as the picture of a black hole was projected on the screen.

"What is the threat of this black hole on the well-being of the Earth?" President Lansing asked his rehearsed question.

The three had practiced this as means of keeping the discussion moving forward.

"The projected path the of the Earth is so close to the black hole that all surface objects will be stripped off the Earth's surface. The air and the oceans of the planet will be sucked in. The actual planet will pull away and go on its orbital path," Zack replied as the next set of slides animated the words being spoken.

"Is there anything we can do about this situation," President Lansing asked after the buzz had died down?

"Yes, we can move the black hole out of our way," Zack replied as he followed the careful rehearsed script.

"Do you have any idea on how to move a black hole," President Lansing continued?

"Yes, we have a basic design of a cage in which to hold it and then move it out of Earth's path," Zack replied. "In fact, this capture offers a potential platform for long term space exploration."

"Would you please give this group a simple description of how this would be done," the President continued.

Zack turned on a prepared animated video. It showed the black hole, the conceptual capture sphere and simple animation slowly moving the capture sphere around the black hole. Then it went on to show the entire structure being moved out of the path of the Earth.

"The basic idea is to surround the black hole with magnetic fields. We will form a magnetic bottle around the black hole. Then we will slowly push it away from Earth's path.

This will require the construction of a sphere with a fifty-mile inner diameter and an outer shell with a diameter of two-hundred-fifty miles. It will be built it in two halves. These two halves will be closed around the black hole. Giant electromagnets mounted on the sphere will provide the magnetic bottle to hold the black hole," Zack replied.

"My heavens, this will require the total resources of all our countries. Why don't we just blast this thing out of existence," the President responded in mock surprise as he watched several country leaders nod in agreement?

He was now asking the same questions posed during the cabinet briefing. These questions were being asked to allow the leaders around the table to develop a better understanding and some level of initial acceptance.

"Yes, this was our initial reaction until you understand the nature of black holes," Zack responded smoothly. "No matter what we would send in, nothing would ever come back out of a black hole.

Nothing escapes.

Black holes pull in stars. Huge explosions thousands of times more powerful than all our combined weaponry have been documented. The black holes take everything in and actually increase in power and size.

This black hole pulled in a five by ten-mile mile asteroid. The total energy of the asteroids mass is equivalent to all the energy of all our nuclear missiles.

"Our only hope is to capture and hold this small black hole and make it work for us," Zack replied.

"It can be the fire Prometheus gave to man. Harnessed it can make us powerful," Zack orated as he took in the faces around the table.

They were listening. Some were nodding in the affirmative.

"I just hope we are able to move its mass once we capture it," Zack thought as the conversation continued.

None of the scientist on the team was sure as to the mass of the black hole and what power it would take to move it.

The discussion went around the table with questions about the certainty of the observation, of the intercept path, of the amount of time before Earth reached the black hole. It was a repeat of the previous meeting with the cabinet.

"The world has seven years to capture and move this black hole out of Earth's path or we face extinction. We have developed the initial plans of how to build the structure to capture this black hole.

The peoples of Earth have the technology, the capability, and the resources to accomplish this feat. However, it will take all the space going resources our countries can collectively muster," Zack said looking around.

"It will also take the help of all other countries as we essentially built a small city in space," were his final comments.

The muttering and discussion went on for hours. Every objection was discussed and refuted. The mood would swing to agreement and then another objection would be voiced, and the cycle would once again begin.

In the end the President agreed to host the experts from each of these countries for further discussions. He won the concession that the experts would discuss and contribute to initial plans on how to capture the black hole versus debating whether or not to do so.

The meeting came to an end with everyone in agreement. They also decided they would not attend the press conference.

The President sent his press secretary to brief the press and let them know that more would soon be shared. The current line was that a new era of working more closely together had been discussed and some additional time was needed to formalize the message.

"Great job, we will have to thank our staff of coaches. I am exhausted. Let's call it a day and plan on meeting tomorrow morning," President Lansing said to Zack and Craig as the meeting came to an end.

Zack and Craig went home and collapsed. It had truly been an exhausting week.

The next morning, Zack sat across from the President in the oval office. The two were quickly reaching the status of friends. Zack was becoming more at ease in the environment of the White House.

"What should we call this endeavor," asked President Lasing looking over his morning cup of coffee.

He was still feeling the tension of the previous day and the morning coffee was helping to calm his nerves. He was beginning to like this young, brilliant scientist.

"Well, I have thinking of calling it Savitar after the Vedic sun god who urges man and beast to act," Zack replied as he looked back at the President and then glanced at Craig.

He had not discussed the name with Craig. It had come to mind last night on his way home. He hoped Craig was OK with the name. He should have asked before blurting it out.

"What do you think, Craig," Zack quickly asked hoping his mentor and friend would not have a negative reaction.

"Do we really have a chance at capturing this thing and moving it out of our way," the President asked as he intently looked back and forth between the two men?

He sensed Zack's tension and was not sure what the cause might be. He had to have full confidence in these two. They had to be in total agreement. There could be no hidden issues.

"There are no technological barriers in building the needed magnetic bottle. The biggest obstacles will be the monumental logistics of getting everything out into space, assembling our future space exploration platform and having enough time to do it. Time is what we have the least of. To pull it all together will take every rocket, every space launch, thousands of people in space and hundreds of thousands on the ground," Craig replied.

"It will take unprecedented ground resources to gather, assemble and organize all the materials. And all of it must be done in record time. My biggest concern is whether all of this can be kept on track. We need the best project management team Earth can muster," Craig went on.

"The high level of radiation exposure is another formidable obstacle. It will make this journey a death sentence for many of the crew. We need the best radiation shielding possible. However, there will be a great deal of critical external work to be done on the way. I don't know of any way to get around this monumental life-threatening issue and the mortality rate we will experience," Zack spoke up.

He had waited until acceptance to his idea was final before identifying the overwhelming issue on his mind.

"Yes, this issue has been brought up by some of my science advisors. It is the reason we have not yet gone to Mars. They predict a fifty percent or greater fatality rate for a one-way trip out to the black hole. We have no choice. We will need to undertake this journey in spite of this issue," President Lansing said with concern in his voice.

"We need to break this effort into multiple projects. These projects need to converge smoothly a year from now. Each project needs to have a top-level project manager. There needs to be a central super project manager to keep it all on track," Zack continued.

"We need to focus on getting material into orbit, in building the sphere out in space, in building the living quarters and other facilities needed to sustain the crew and the structure. We need to build the equipment to make the magnetic bottle and we need to select and train a crew.

I would like to see Dr. Garrity, and the project management groups coordinate these projects. I will focus on refining the capture scheme, work to see if we can address the radiation issue and in training the crew," Zack spoke quietly.

He had gone through the entire process in his mind and concluded the effort would need a tremendous amount of guidance and discipline if it were to succeed.

"The two of you make it sound like an adventure. I suppose it is the greatest adventure to ever face mankind. My role will be to see the world gets aligned, resources keep coming and the public gets enthused about this venture.

Heaven knows we will spend trillions on this endeavor. I already have my best people developing the PR. Since we will need total commitment, and we cannot afford any misbehavior of either our people or of any country in the world, I will be asking for special powers. Congress must authorize the overall expenditure, but I will use my Presidential power to get this going immediately.

My team is already working to define a way to forge a global alliance. I have already talked privately to the leaders of China, Russia, India, and the EU. We have been aligned in our war on terror. Now it is time to focus on the war of survival. The politics of this will be overwhelming. We are at the center at this historic activity. I am pleased to have a part in all of this," President Lansing replied in an oratory fashion.

It was clear to Zack the President had his heart in the right place and his mind on history and the political opportunity this presented.

"I will have the NASA director, Benjamin Ben Samuelson, come speak to you. He is my choice for overall coordinator of the project. I have communicated this to the other countries, and they agree to work through NASA. NASA will manage the project and set up the training for all personnel going into space and on this journey.

If you intent, on, being a member on this mission, you will need astronaut training. Since you are young and in great shape this will get you ready to lead this expedition. That is what you seek isn't it, Zack," President Lansing asked?

Zack was stunned and was unable to give an immediate reply. He had not thought about leading the effort.

"What about you Craig? Are you planning to go as well," the President continued?

He knew Emily, Craig's wife, and the close relationship the two shared and wondered whether Craig would want to go.

"I will take the training, but we are going to need an anchor here on Earth to ensure everything science can learn in the next few years about managing and handling a black hole gets learned.

I see Zack as the right person to be in charge of the expedition. Savitar is a great name for this project and the space vessel," Dr. Garrity replied with a twinkle in his eye.

Craig appreciated Zack's sensitivity about picking a name without discussing it with him first. He was not surprised at Zack's inability to answer the President about leading the effort. The subject had not come up until this moment. He was pleased Dan saw in Zack what Craig already knew was there.

"I imagine every country will fight for a spot on the crew. You will need to determine every crew member's role and how many you will need. I don't think you will have a shortage of volunteers. You will probably need to limit the number and select the members to ensure the countries participating all get represented. NASA will also serve as the recruiting center. You should concentrate on the volunteers and on determining if the persons offered fit. NASA will provide you with all the psychologists, screeners, and clearances," President Lansing continued.

"Things will take off very fast. I am sure there will be times you think you have totally lost control. Let's plan to meet every other week. In this way you will be able to share your firsthand observations and provide me some critical insider calibration. I will provide you with influence in the coming circus of events. Ben Samuelson will contact you in the next day or two," President Lansing said as he stood, indicating it was time for them to leave

"Events are really skyrocketing along. Did I just get put in charge to lead this effort?" Zack asked as he and Craig were escorted out of the White House.

"Yes, Zack the President did make the selection. He recognizes the project will continue well after the Savitar leaves the Earth," Craig replied with a chuckle.

Zack was thrilled by the fact both Craig and the President agreed he would lead the project. Random thought fragments about the project flashed through his mind. He felt intoxicated.

Two men dressed in dark blue business suits met them at the exit. The two showed them their shields and identified themselves as FBI agents.

"We are members of the presidential staff. We are to take you to FBI headquarters. You will meet with the head of the FBI and then you are to begin interviewing to select your personal bodyguards." Bill the older of the two explained.

"Well, the President warned us about this. Is it really necessary?" Zack asked.

"Evidently it is. Whatever you are into has already made the internet. You guys have already gotten some threats, and no one even knows what you are doing. All we know is it is about national security. Sorry guys if you haven't had security coverage before you may find us to be pests. I hope you are up to this since it will last for as long as we can foresee," the older of the two continued as they walked out to a black limousine.

The trip to the FBI headquarters took them through the nation's mall. Here all the symbols of power and American history seemed to reflect the importance of the moment. Zack and Craig sat quietly as they were driven toward the FBI offices.

"The bureau has done the initial selection of the candidates. The best of the best, all the brainy types or the best bodyguards with a chance of understanding what the two of you are doing were selected. All have undergone psychological checks and have had their security backgrounds rechecked. They will be with you twenty-our seven. I would guess they are all young, bright, single, and truly the best. Every one of them is probably dying to get picked. Take your time and make sure you get along with them before finalizing your selection. Sleep on it overnight." the oldest of the agents advised.

Chapter 3: Janet

Neither Zack nor Craig had considered selecting bodyguards with whom they would spend twenty-four hours a day. Craig's long and loving marriage at least prepared him with some understanding of the compatibility requirements.

"I have no idea how select a bodyguard. I don't even have a roommate. I will have to go on gut feel and intuition," Zack said to Craig as they walked into the interview room.

"I am in the same boat. Let's get started and see what happens," Craig replied.

He had mentioned to Emily about them getting a bodyguard and had given her the line about national security. She had looked at him in a bemused fashion but had not pressed the issue.

They were supported by an interview facilitator. The job of the facilitator was to escort in, introduce, keep time, and escort out the interviewees. Each interview was to run between thirty and forty-five minutes. They were to select a total of six bodyguards. Two would be back-ups.

Craig and Zack spent the morning interviewing. They did six interviews by lunch.

They stopped for a sandwich and soft drink.

They found interviewing a rather challenging process. Most of the agents proved to be humorless and too intense for their liking.

"I guess the people going into this line of work have a totally different attitude, background and thought process from ours." Zack commented to Craig.

"Yes, I suppose so. We tend not to worry about the motives of those around us but focus on pursuit of the solution to a problem. They tend to look at people as potential problems." Craig mused.

He was finding it hard to determine whom to select. He agreed with Zack about the attitude of some of the interviewees.

Janet sat outside of the interview room in a waiting area. Her thoughts drifted. It seemed ironic for her to be waiting for an interview to be a bodyguard to some highly placed professors. The irony for her was she had a PhD and yet she hoped she would get this job protecting one. She had no idea who the two professors were or why they needed protection.

The rumor mill put this as a once in a lifetime opportunity. None of her other current opportunities attracted her. Her boss and mentor told her this was one opportunity she did not want to miss. She had taken his advice and was now cooling her heels in the waiting room.

The memory of cowering and hiding from her drunken father in the corner of the locked bathroom unexpectedly surfaced. It had been a long time since she thought of that scene. She did not know why it would surface now but suddenly she was reviewing the memories of her life. She remembered making a pledge to herself to get away from her dysfunctional family.

She promised herself she would get away and be a success.

Her father was an alcoholic. The evenings were filled with his constant drinking. The weekends were a challenge. Every time he got drunk; he would act like he was going to attack her. Her mother ignored each of those incidents and never provided any support or advice. In fact, her mother told Janet she should be thankful her father was such a good provider. Several times he beat her mother, but he never hit her.

Each time her father got drunk Janet renewed her pledge to get away and succeed. She came to fear him, though she had wanted to love him.

It was paradoxical.

Her success was founded on the fear and dysfunctional behavior of her father and the uncaring or helpless nature of her mother.

Both of her parent's behaviors had influenced her future actions.

She always envied the acquaintances that had grown up in a stable home life. She wondered what it was like to feel the warmth of caring loving parents.

She focused her energy and emotions on school, her grades and being active in various school clubs. She became the editor of her high school paper. She learned to lead others and get them to work together to get results. During her editorship, the school paper won an award for its innovative content.

Her grades, her leadership at school and her parent's near poverty level served her well. She got into the University of Pennsylvania and received the need-based financing the school promised to all accepted applicants. This provided her the ability to make her own way through college.

The campus and Philadelphia became her world.

She put her family behind her. She did not return home.

The UP environment let her blossom. This was where her personal ideals and principles took root, found fertile ground, and grew. She was not sure what her major should be, but she slowly drifted into Law and Law enforcement.

The next few years melted away. She was active in the University clubs and events. She had a group of friends and went to many of their parties. She was not seeking and did not find any serious romance. She valued her newly found freedom too much to allow someone else to put any restraints on her.

After four years, she earned her Bachelor of Art in Criminal Justice.

She enjoyed her time at UP so much she decided to continue her education. Again, she was accepted at UP and went after a master's degree in criminal psychology. She got a grant but needed to work part time to cover all her expenses.

The year went by quickly and once again she felt unprepared to go out to a working life. The campus environment suited her.

She also admitted to herself it was a safe environment.

The freedom of thought, the give and take of ideas, and the energy of those involved all came together to form an invigorating environment.

She was not sure about life on the "outside."

One of her professors showed her a recruitment poster circulated by the FBI. It offered to pay for her doctorate's degree in Psychological Analysis and Law Enforcement. In return she promised to work for them for a period of three years. She would co-op with them for three months each year and she would also receive training at the FBI training academy.

Over three summers, while pursuing her PhD, she attended the FBI training academy. At the end of her third year, she received her PhD and went straight to work for the FBI.

Her FBI academy experience tested her physical and mental reserves. She enjoyed the martial arts and the weapons training. She ranked second in her class. She became a serious martial arts student on her own time and had since continued her belt progression in Tae Kwon Do.

She was still active in Tae Kwon Do and was now a third-degree black belt.

Janet's final weeks at UP were full and hectic. Her Black belt certification, her PhD commencement and her swearing into the FBI all happened during the same week. The whirlwind swept her into her new role on a tide of excitement and anticipation. She was motivated and eager.

As a PhD she was hired at a relatively high position. She began by reviewing and evaluating field case studies. She expected more action then what reading and evaluating someone else's work provided. She quickly became bored by her role at work.

She looked around to find something to better engage her energy and interests and found the special support division.

The division provided bodyguard support for the President and visiting dignitaries. Her black belt in Tae Kwon Do and her high ranking in her FBI class served to get her accepted. She eagerly and enthusiastically joined a group of very professional and able-bodied personnel.

When she arrived for this current interview and saw Andrew Pennington she was not surprised. Andrew had bettered her in the martial arts and weapons classes. His reflexes, speed and accuracy were phenomenal. He was bright and always agreeable. She really did not know him well but was comfortable around him.

He never made any advances and was always very professional. She was not attracted to him in a romantic way but admired his capability.

She always preferred to compete upward, and he had been the one she always challenged. This helped her develop to a new level. This meant she had repeatedly practiced and competed with Andrew and though he almost always out did her she knew she was a challenge for him. On the one hand she cringed but on the other she felt a sense of relief to know someone with so much skill was also interviewing for the same job.

She became nervous as she thought about her interviewers. Would the persons interviewing, feel comfortable with a woman bodyguard? If they knew Andrew graduated first and she graduated second, wouldn't they pick the better person? And who was the better person? In her heart she knew she was.

"To hell with it, I will be me. If they want someone else so-be-it," Janet thought to herself as she put down the unread magazine in her hand as her name was called.

She knew instantly she didn't mean what she had just thought. She wanted this job. She sensed it would be the most important opportunity to present itself in her lifetime.

She called up her reserve self-confidence, stood up straight and promised herself to let the interviewers know she was the best candidate.

Zack and Craig had been at it all afternoon. Zack had interviewed many well qualified people but his hopes of finding someone really compatible was fading.

"I think I have two suitable candidates. One is Mary Ringhold and the other is Jeff Malory," Craig indicated.

They were also on Zack's list. This made Zack realize he really had no candidates at all. He felt his energy ebb slowly out of him. It was now four o'clock and there were only a few candidates left.

They opted to push on and signaled the attending facilitator to bring in the next candidate.

Zack took in the young dark haired, rather petite woman dressed in a conservative dark blue pant suit. He was immediately drawn in by her grey blue eyes. There was no escaping her, she looked at you seemly deep into the soul.

The moderator introduced Janet.

"Hello Dr. Romero, I am Zack, and this is Dr. Garrity. We are each interviewing for two suitable bodyguards. Please tell me something about yourself and explain why you, a person who has earned a PhD. would want to put your life on the line as a bodyguard for me," Zack said.

He immediately sensed a connection. Her dossier was impressive. He hoped she would interview well.

"Hello, I'm Janet Romero, and yes I earned a PhD in the Psychology of Criminals from the University of Pennsylvania. I have a third-degree black belt in Tae Kwon Do. I am applying for this position because, guarding you has been described to be of extreme importance and a once in a lifetime opportunity. A once in a lifetime opportunity is exactly what I am looking for," Janet replied smoothly as she studied the two men sitting on the opposite side of the table.

She was not sure who she was to guard. The younger one seemed to be more to her liking. Neither one seemed to be the type needing protection.

"Keep your mind on the interview," Janet told herself. She felt an immediate link to the interviewer named Zack.

"I see you ranked number two in your academy class. Where is number one and why do you think you are the better candidate," Craig followed?

A mental groan went through Janet. Here was the question she had dreaded. She decided to be bold.

"The year I finished the academy, was my first year in Tae Kwon Do. I have continued my development and I am now a third-degree black belt. I am better now than I was then. Number one will probably still be number one. He is extremely good and has unusual speed. He is out in the lobby, and you will be interviewing him soon. You will be able to draw your own conclusions.

However, you should choose me for my overall capability, intelligence, my attention to detail, teamwork, compatibility, and desire. I will be second to none when it comes to my role and responsibilities. I have developed myself and I have become both a leader and team player," Janet replied smoothly though she was feeling a cold sweat building and her hands were clammy.

"Perhaps I should not have mentioned number one was out in the lobby, damn," she thought to herself.

She wanted to blurt out more, but she held herself in check. She did not want to come across as too talkative or to appear too needy.

Zack liked her honesty, directness, and coolness. Having been around Craig all these years, he knew how it felt to be considered number two.

She would be one of those he would choose. She was at the moment at the head of his list. Of course, she was the only one on the list.

"What if this job would require you leave the US and your family for good or at least a good part of the foreseeable future," Zack asked?

"Well, then I would hope the two of you and I get along very well, and we are partners in whatever it is we are up to. I do not have any ties to hold me back," Janet replied.

"Thank you, we will finish the remaining interviews and then let you know our decision tomorrow," Craig said in closing as he saw Zack give him the nod indicating he had all he needed.

Janet was caught a little flat footed. She stood and walked out feeling she had missed on the interview. The entire interview had taken just over ten minutes. She had waited for more than an hour and most of the interviews before her had gone thirty to forty minutes. She had expected to spend a similar amount of time and to experience a more rigorous interviewing process.

What had gone wrong?

Had she been too candid?

Had they already found the bodyguards they wanted?

She felt like going back in and telling the two how much she wanted to be chosen.

Why had there not been more questions?

"Well, she made my list," Zack said after Janet closed the door to the interview room.

He had studied her records and liked the history of her school progress. Her independence and self-confidence were apparent in how she presented herself and did not fear mentioning number one.

Zack and Craig got through the next couple of interviews and then informed the FBI about their decision to wait until the next day to finalize their choices. They tidied up and walked out of the building under the watchful guardianship of their temporary bodyguards.

"Well, did you find any good candidates?" the agent they knew as Bill asked.

"Well, they were all very qualified like you said they would be. This is probably worse than getting married. When you get married, you are intoxicated by love and compatibility is not a question in your mind," Craig replied as they walked to the car.

At Craig's home they sat at the kitchen table enjoying a hot cup of coffee and discussed their choices. Craig was impressed with the qualifications of all the applicants but commented on their consistent serious nature. He felt comfortable with several of them.

Zack, share he had selected the young woman, Janet but he was hesitant on the second one.

He joked with Craig, "If I am going to be shadowed, I might as well pick a good-looking shadow. Besides, she has a PhD and the best chance at understanding what we are doing."

Zack personally hoped this was his only reason and made a deal with himself to keep the relationship on strictly business terms.

Emily came in to say good night. She now knew of the project and about the bodyguards. She still was not sure what the two were up to but knew it was something to do with national security. She was very curious but was not going to bug Craig about it. She knew if he could, he would tell her the details. However, it was clear to her these two had in some way become very important to the US government.

"You two can talk as long as you like. I do hope I get along with the bodyguards you are selecting," Emily said as she bid them good night.

She was nervous about the situation she found herself in. How would this affect Craig and her lifestyle. Their relationship was at the center of her life. She did not want to lose the closeness the two shared.

"Well Zack, I am beat. I think I will hit the sack and get a good night's sleep. Tomorrow we will have to make our final decisions. I think you can get a ride home from one of the many agents surrounding the house," Craig said as he patted Zack on the back and left the kitchen.

Zack gathered his things and quietly walked out the front door. He was immediately greeted by several agents, one who had been assigned to guard him and who drove him to his apartment. On the way he was informed two agents would stay at his apartment with him.

"You will always have several of us around. Tomorrow you will select your personal bodyguards. They will become your room mates. However, they will always have backup outside or close by," the agent informed him.

The night was a long one for Janet. She waited until Andrew finished his interview and invited him out to dinner. The two of them went to a small local diner and chatted late into the night. They both experienced short interviews and felt they had missed on being selected. They consoled each other and after dinner they each got into separate cabs and went to their apartments.

Janet made herself a cup of tea, worked out, took a long hot shower, and then snuggled up in her favorite chair with a book. She kept going over the interview wondering if she could have done anything differently. She knew in her heart she badly wanted this opportunity. She was also wondering who the two men were and what was so important or dangerous that it required the use of bodyguards. No one seemed to know exactly what the two scientists were up to.

She went on the internet and Googled, "Zack Milton" and was surprised to find he was in the field of astronomy and had written several articles about Earth's astronomical history. And Dr. Craig Garrity had tons of published material in the field of physics and astronomy. He was a globally know leader in his field. Janet wondered why these two men required twenty-four-hour protection.

She went to bed to do some reading but fell asleep with the unread book in her lap. In her dreams, she kept losing the person she was supposed guard. She awoke in a cold sweat when in her dream she found her client with a bullet hole in the forehead.

"What will this day bring?" Janet thought as she ate a light breakfast before departing for work.

Zack and Craig met back at FBI headquarters. Craig had discussed the two bodyguards he planned on selecting with Emily. He let her know these two would guard them around the clock. He like Zack decided on one female guard and one male one. Hopefully, this would give Emily someone who she could better relate to.

Zack selected agents Dr. Janet Romero and Andrew Pennington.

Craig selected Mary Ringhold and Jeff Malory.

At the request of the FBI, they also selected two additional agents as backups. He and Craig agreed on Susan Sanderson and Mitch Kennedy. These two had interviewed well but were out done by the other four.

All six were called back for a final confirmation meeting.

Janet was ecstatic when she was called back into the interview room in the morning. She was more surprised when she saw Andrew walk into the meeting room. She knew a small miracle had happened. They had both been selected by Dr. Zack Milton to be his bodyguards.

She immediately began to analyze Zack. She knew it was important for her to become familiar with all of his good and bad habits. She was going to do everything in her power to make this assignment a pivotal success.

It was hard for her to listen to the general discussion around her. Over and over, she kept hearing, "you are one of the two people I have selected to be my bodyguard."

Andrew was surprised as well. This he felt was one of the most important events to happen to him so far in his life.

After letting the six know of their selection whom they were to guard, and who were the backups, Zack suggested they all discuss the project as a group, and they do several "get to know each other" events. Craig volunteered a cookout at his place, Janet suggested a boat ride, and Jeff suggested a walking tour through the Capital's Mall.

"Well, it all sounds good. Why don't we plan to have the briefing, about our project start tomorrow morning, at our new office? Today, Dr. Garrity and I will pull together our material," Zack ended as he got up ready to leave.

To his surprise Janet and Andrew stood up as well.

"Oh, right, you two will now be my shadows," Zack said as he realized he would now be followed everywhere by these two.

"I guess we will all learn about this project together as we prepare the materials for all the other people we will need to brief. Let's all work together on the project materials." he continued as they walked out to a waiting car. He asked Susan and Mitch if they could join the rest of them.

Chapter 4: Nano-Bots

Dr. Samuel Trimble, his eyes glued to the screen with its 1000x magnification of his nano army's fixing the damaged red blood cells was thrilled. He was watching his fighters at work doing exactly what he had been striving for years to get them to do. It had been years of close but not quite the right experiences.

His army could be deployed against a host of problems faced by the human body. He had worked for over fifteen years on this project. These had been years of toil, much tedious work, and a few rare stimulating moments.

This was the big moment. He had succeeded. The nano-bots were doing the job he had designed them to do. It seemed almost as if they were individuals with a mind.

Now after years of dreaming of this day, instead of elation, he had mixed troubling feelings.

The nano-technology robots programmed to find and fix damaged red blood cells were mindlessly going about their jobs fixing damaged cells. They were small enough to enter the cell and operate internally to fix the damage. These specific nano bots were designed to fix sickle cell damage in the red blood cell, and they mindlessly did so with amazing efficiency.

Dr. Trimble was watching just a few of his tiny inventions as they worked on a sample of human blood taken from a sickle cell patient. The nano bots were relentless in attacking the damaged cells and in fixing the less damaged ones. They ignored healthy cells.

He knew his breakthrough would revolutionize the field of medicine. This capability would allow many ailments to be attacked at the cellular level. This ability to focus on the cellular level would change the balance of mankind's battle against many diseases.

There would be no chemical side effects. There would be precise cellular focused correction. Cancers, tumors, tuberculosis, and many other ailments would be attacked at the fundamental cell level.

The nano bots were based on a genetically engineered virus. They had been altered enough to almost be considered man made. Normal viruses would be in danger of having to meet a counter agent produced by the body. The nano-bots were invisible to normal human defenses. They had a limited life span and flushed out of the body by the kidneys when they died.

It was also significant that the nano bots did not trigger a white cell response. Dr. Trimble envisioned a day when most medicines would not be needed. Or at least they would be used in a much more limited way and in conjunction with his nano-bots. The uses of this technology would revolutionize the entire field of medicine.

However, there was trouble brewing among his research team. He had kept this last break through secret and his team was not aware of it. He had a small team. They were split down the middle.

Some members of his team saw huge riches ahead.

A few of the team thought any breakthrough should be shared broadly with the world.

The two sides openly argued with each other as success loomed close at hand. The air was polluted with the tension of this disagreement. The stress was beginning to show on everyone.

Samuel was somewhere in between the two alternatives. He needed to recover financially from the enormous debt burden he was personally shouldering. He was not interested in using his nano bots to gain worldly riches. He did need the money to keep from being homeless and to recover from several lawsuits.

More than anything he wanted to be remembered for having given mankind the next big step in a better and longer life. In the future, he hoped his name would be mentioned with Pasteur, Edison, Watt, and the other great names.

First, he knew he had to get past this moment in time.

Samuel had used the money he inherited from his parents and the monies he got from a developmental advance from a venture capitalist group. He had borrowed money on his home and sold his car. All these financial resources were gone.

Over the past year as he came ever closer to success, he discussed how to handle a breakthrough with his business manager, and confidant, Melanie Baker.

Melanie had been with him since he set out on his own. He hired her to help set up the lab and to manage the four technicians on the team. She managed the budget and the business paperwork. The two had worked well for the last ten years. Melanie was happily married and had two kids. She was the practical one and helped him stretch the finances.

When it came to the handling of a breakthrough, Melanie thought the best course of action was to find the highest bidder and get a contract including royalties on the use of the technology.

This was a very practical action and one even Samuel felt would work. However, he was hesitant on the choice of companies. He did not want this breakthrough to be kept from the majority of the people just to make some company profitable.

Even Melanie did not know of this final breakthrough. Samuel felt uneasy about the current atmosphere in his office. He had everyone working hard on tasks he had farmed out to them.

As he listened to the discussions on how to handle success, he knew the moment he announced the success, the team would go separate directions on what action to take. So, he continued to keep each part of his team working on important work but work to support an outcome already in hand.

His financial situation was the monkey on his back. He was almost completely broke. If he did not make a financial deal soon, he would have to let his team go. On the verge of success, he was about to lose everything. This was a maddening situation for him.

He needed to take action.

His arguments with Melanie reached a serious stage. She knew of his precarious financial state and continued to argue for him to select a buyer. Several organizations had expressed interest in her general offering. He asked her to wait for another week.

The morning news and the Presidential address about the black hole in space provided Samuel with an inspiring vision. He immediately realized Project Savitar would need his nano technology. The repair of radiation damage had been one of the studies successfully carried out with the nano-bots. The nano-bots could be used to counteract the radiation assault and mend the damage.

The Savitar project needed his breakthrough. Dr. Trimble immediately sent faxes offering up this technology to both Dr. Milton and Dr. Garrity. In the fax he outlined the basics of his breakthrough and asked them to reply back as soon as possible.

Now he was sure he had been right to wait. Project Savitar would be where he would perfect his nano-bots.

He returned to his work with a focus on how his army of nano-bots could tackle the problems and side effects of radiation damage. There were still many unknown aspects and potential pitfalls associated with turning these efficient seekers of micro problems loose in the body.

Once the nano bots fixed the problem they had been sent in for, they continued their search. He was not sure what would happen if they were left in and could not find the defects they were looking for. He had designed them with a short life expectancy, and they always died and were filtered out.

This was one way for him to maintain control over his almost invisible army. He would need more work on his miniature army before using them in human subjects.

During the time he waited for a reply back from Dr. Zachary Milton, he efficiently organized all of his materials.

He used the last of his money to send his entire team on a vacation. He told Melanie he was in the process of securing funds for the future and by the time the two weeks of vacation was over he would be able to tell his team good news.

Melanie was not surprised at her boss's generosity in paying for the team's vacation. Unaware of Samuel's communication to the Savitar, she did not believe he had a new source of financing. She had been the one doing all the external communications and she had only heard from a few companies. None had yet made an offer.

In reality Samuel was now totally broke. He would need help and a small miracle.

He hoped the Savitar needed his breakthrough.

He had expected and immediate call back that had not materialized. He was beginning to doubt the message had gotten through.

He was sitting dejectedly with his hands on his forehead when the phone rang.

He picked up the phone when the ringing almost caused him to have a heart attack. He heard, "Dr. Trimble, this is Zack Milton. I am sorry about the delay in my reply to your fax. The folks handling my messages had no idea how important your breakthrough is to the success of the Savitar mission.

Can we get together and review the status of your work?"

Sudden hope coursed through Samuel's body. He felt light-headed and took a moment to recover. He tried to remember the last time he had eaten.

"That would be great, where shall we meet?" Samuel replied.

He desperately hoped Dr. Milton planned to come to Boston. He did not have the money to go anywhere, and he hoped he would not have to ask for a favor.

"Well, I suppose the best place would be your lab," Zack said to Samuel's relief.

"I will come up with my team to review your work and see how your capability can be utilized on our mission," Zack added.

"I am looking forward to sharing my work with you," Samuel replied with an internal sigh of relief.

The world around him gained color and stabilized beneath his feet.

"Dr. Garrity and I will arrive tomorrow. Shall we meet at your facility in Belmont around 11:00 am," Zack inquired?

"That would be fine. I will be expecting you then," Samuel replied.

He was surprised Dr. Milton knew the location of his lab.

Dr. Trimble would have been even more surprised and perhaps disturbed had he known Zack and Craig were aware of almost every detail of Dr. Trimble's research. They also knew the condition of his personal and corporate finances and the current struggle going on within his team of scientists.

They were even aware that Dr. Trimble had sent his team on vacation with the last of his personal funds. They had both commented for their admiration for his generosity.

As Zack hung up, he thought about the timing of this critical break-through and the overwhelming forces soon to roll over Dr. Trimble's research.

The fax from Dr. Trimble had lifted the lid of the coffin the Savitar journey represented. Radiation poisoning or damage was a topic no one was willing to discuss. Zack and Craig had only discussed the issue with the President.

The best radiation shielding possible was designed into the Savitar living quarters. However, the required external work would cause everyone to get high doses of radiation.

Everyone on the voyage would be at risk. There would be no safe location. No one talked about a return trip. No one would survive. Zack knew that up to this point the journey was a one-way trip. Without this breakthrough the crew would move the black hole and they would slowly die.

Samuel sat quietly for some time after getting off the phone. A sense of unease and a feeling of doom came over him. The fact Dr. Milton knew so much bothered him. He realized he had not been very cautious about his research. He had been very open. He had shared it quite broadly. In fact, to raise money for his work, he regularly published articles about his work in the science journals.

Who else knew about it? Had anyone on his team shared critical information with others? Where was Melanie? Her vacation tickets were still on his desk. She was to have picked up her tickets this morning.

The realization that the tickets for her and her family were still on his desk immediately set off alarm bells jangling in his mind.

Suddenly he felt the cold finger of doom send a shiver up his back. Frantically he turned on his computer and copied his critical notes onto four thumb drives. He turned on all the other computers and sent the critical files from those computers to his brother's email address.

The fire station alarm in his brain kept getting louder.

He changed the combination of his large office safe and put all the computers and any other notes he could find into it. He had never used all the space of the old safe until now. It had six computers and a pile of notebooks and all the external hard drives. He threw in anything else that looked important and then closed and locked the door.

As the morning went on, he became increasingly paranoid.

This was to be Melanie's last day before she went on her vacation. She was supposed to work with him to button up his research and prepare for a request for more funding.

He had been planning to share his communication with the Savitar team with her. She had not come in and had not called. Her cell phone was off. Samuel left a message inquiring if anything was wrong.

He went once more around the lab and destroyed all trace of the nano-bots. He kept several test tubes with him to share with Dr. Milton.

He walked out of the lab building with all the evidence of his research neatly organized in his brief case and a small box with his samples. He went to the post office to mail his thumb drives to his brother, sister, and mother. He then went to a pay phone and called each and told them to peel off the label on the envelope and immediately send the envelope on and not to take the mail home. He asked his brother to forward the emails to him in two days.

He next went to Dick's barbershop. He had cut his hair in the same shop for over twenty years. Dick, his barber was as much one of his counselors and confidant as he was his barber. He didn't even bat an eye at the strange request Samuel made. Dick took the brief case and put it on the floor next to the cabinet holding his old-fashioned cash register. Samuel asked if he could leave his box in the small refrigerator.

Dick asked, "what's up?"

Samuel looked at him speechlessly. He did not want to explain his current situation to Dick.

"You don't have to explain. Everything will be here when you get back." Dick said sensing the hesitation.

A sense of relief came over Samuel. He knew his treasure would be safe under Dick's watchful eye.

He then left and got on the subway and went to his home.

Melanie Baker was convinced the breakthrough would result in extremely long-life spans and a fortune could be made selling it to some large drug company. She had been adamant Samuel should commercialize his findings and cash in on the riches. She prepared a list of potential companies to be approached. She sent out initial inquiries. Several large companies responded with interest. She organized discussion and demonstration dates with these companies. She was planning to share this with Samuel before leaving on vacation.

A group not on her list called and immediately made a very substantial offer and a request to meet. She was suspicious of the immediate offer but agreed to meet with them. Melanie was convinced she had solved the financial problems they faced. The bidding was beginning.

Once the companies understood the potential of the Nano-bots, they would pay hundreds of millions. She had acted to help Samuel but felt guilty because she had not yet gotten his permission to negotiate these deals. She knew she was a better business manager then he and felt confident Samuel would respond positively to her efforts.

She would get the offers organized and he would have the final say.

As Samuel reached the post office, Melanie was letting the group that had shown interest and had requested a meeting, into the lab. Melanie expected to find Samuel working as usual and hoped the offer from the group would sway him in selling the information. What she found surprised her. The lab and the office areas had been cleaned out. There were no computers anywhere and Samuel was not to be found.

A leak in Craig's and Zack's security had allowed one of the many anti-Savitar factions to learn about the Nano-bot beak through. This anti-Savitar faction immediately acted and contacted Melanie.

Their offer to her was substantial but was just a ploy to meet with her and Samuel. They did not care if a breakthrough had been made. Their only interest was to destroy and eliminate any breakthrough useful to the Savitar project. Their plan included the destruction of all notes, test materials and the elimination of the people most closely associated with the effort. There was no substance behind their offer. They were only using the financial discussion as a way to quickly gain access to the most critical people and materials.

Samuel took the subway to his neighborhood. The morning ride, the slightly stale smell of the subway, the clickity clack of the wheels on the tracks and the flickering of light and dark through the windows of the car provided a surreal atmosphere as he pondered his next move.

He had a bad feeling, and he was acting immediately on it.

The clarity and certainty of some doom awaiting him caused him to go home, pack some clothes, eliminate all trace of his notes, and get out of the house as quickly as possible. He left his house before 10:00 am. He returned to the subway and planned to randomly get off and stay in hiding until his meeting with Dr. Milton the next day.

His paranoia was now complete. He was sure sanity had left him. He still felt the cold finger sending shivers up his back.

Shortly after noon, two men entered and ransacked Dr. Milton's home. They were looking for him and the information he had so effectively destroyed or hidden.

In following his instincts, Samuel was just a few hours ahead of the people seeking his secrets and his demise.

He randomly selected a motel after getting off at a stop he had never before used. He took an afternoon nap or at least he tried. He felt rather silly as he finished his sandwich and soda and watched the evening news on the television.

"I have gone crazy. The pressure was finally enough that I've snapped," he thought to himself.

The next morning, he checked out and after a casual breakfast he put his last $1.25 into the subway ticket vending machine and boarded the subway. He took a different way back to his lab. He timed his arrival a little after 11:00 am.

The morning air was cool. He could hear the birds chirping up in the old Oaks that lined the street leading to his lab building.

He saw what he took to be official government automobiles parked in the street outside of his laboratory. Two men in dark suits and sunglasses, stood by the cars.

"Dr. Trimble?" one of them inquired.

"Yes, that's me," he replied.

"Dr. Garrity and Dr. Milton are waiting inside.

Samuel walked between the two men into his laboratory facility.

"Hello, Dr. Trimble, I am Zack Milton, and this is Dr. Craig Garrity. This is Janet and Andrew. They are FBI agents. When we entered and found the place in shambles, we took the liberty to examine your facility. I am relieved to see you are safe. I have already started an internal investigation and the local police have been notified. Do you have any idea what happened here?

"No, after our conversation yesterday morning, I had a strange premonition something was very wrong. I secured my notes and some key samples and then destroyed all traces of my work.

Then I went into hiding. I felt a little silly and thought I was paranoid, until now," Samuel replied as he looked at the ruins of his very expensive and still unpaid for electron microscope.

He had a bitter taste in his mouth and felt tears coming to his eyes. His emotions were at the brink. He had worked so dam hard. He had kept his research team together and made sure they got paid. He was at the end of his finances and at the end of his mental stamina. He sat down on the edge of his desk tears of anger welling in his eyes.

As you can see, I have nothing left at all. Without the electron microscope I have nothing to show you. I guess, if you wanted to see evidence, it was a waste of time," he said through his tears.

His hands would not stop shaking as he talked.

"Why don't we collect the sample you mentioned, and the notes or disc you have stashed away and go back together to our offices. We will set you up in a new lab with new equipment. If you have made the break-through you say you have made, you will be amply rewarded," Zack offered as he put his arm around Dr. Trimble's shoulder.

"You must have the break-through you described for someone to go to this trouble. However, the folks who were here were not looking to support you." Dr. Garrity spoke up as they were leaving the building.

"Is there anyone on your staff that might be involved in this?" he inquired.

"It is hard for me to believe any of my team would be involved in this. We have been having a running discussion on how we should share this breakthrough, but I cannot believe any of them would have done this. Besides all of them but Melanie have already left on vacation," Samuel replied.

However, Melanie's face flashed in his mind. Had she pursued finding a buyer? Where was she, and was she safe?

"Please let the police know Melanie Barker may be in trouble," Samuel said to Janet.

She was supposed to pick up her vacation ticket yesterday, but I did not see her.

He had already concluded Janet was the one in charge of security.

The five of them walked out to the waiting cars and got into the one in the middle. Janet and Andrew signaled the rest to begin their journey back to the airport. The waiting agents were nervous and eager to get moving and away from the scene of a crime over which they had no control. One agent was left behind to await and work with the police.

The three cars drove to Dick's barbershop where Samuel picked up his brief case with his notes and his sample of nano-bots.

Dick looked out at the cars. "Are you alright and are these the good guys?" he asked as he retrieved the brief case and box.

"Thanks Dick. These are the good guys. They have come to the rescue. I will tell you the story at my next haircut appointment," Samuel replied.

Dick just patted Samuel on the back and said, "I can't wait."

The caravan then proceeded to a small local airport where a helicopter waited ready to take them back to the Capital.

They were scheduled to see the President in the morning.

The three of them stayed at Craig's home for the night. Emily prepared prime rib, broccoli, and sweet potatoes. Then she and the four bodyguards stayed in the background as Zack and Craig chatted and discussed Samuel's break-through. The three sat up late into the night in intense discussions.

Emily quietly said good night as she brought the trio a pot of coffee and some cookies. She knew it was hopeless to expect them to go to sleep at a reasonable hour. They had some treasure of knowledge needing discussion.

She would happily leave them and get lost in one of her books.

Zack was impressed with the progress and technique Dr. Trimble had used to create his nano-bots. The technique though successful still needed months of development before it could be tried on humans. This development would need to be accelerated to meet the needs of Savitar's departure. Even then they needed to have more basic tests done before they could possibly inject the nano-bots into a person.

Zack went to sleep with new hope for the crew of the Savitar. Perhaps this journey would be one of great challenge but not of great grieving.

"Well, you men certainly stayed up late. If you didn't have an early morning meeting with the President, I would have let you all sleep in. I hope the coffee and omelets hit the spot for you this morning," Emily said as Craig and Zack came in and sat at the kitchen table.

Samuel came in soon after. All the bodyguards had eaten earlier and were sharing the one newspaper.

"I wonder if the Boston police have found out anything about the break in at Dr. Trimble's lab," Craig asked of no-one in particular.

Janet spoke up and shared that the Boston police had found Melanie Baker strangled and dumped in the Mt. Feake Cemetery on the bank of the Charles River.

Samuel let out an Oh, No. Why would anyone harm her?

The news of Melanie's death felt like a knife being driven through Samuel's stomach. He knew it was his fault. She had only been trying to help him succeed.

How would her family take this? He dreaded having to face them at the funeral. He would make sure her family received the benefits of his success. It was the least he could do. Her good but impulsive intentions had taken her life and almost his as well.

There seemed to be no clues as who had perpetrated this act. The investigation was continuing.

Little did anyone know how close to all of them the catalyst for that action resided.

Chapter 5: Designing the Holder

It was obvious the President had cleared the way for them. Zack and Craig met with a very supportive NASA director who described how NASA would do the initial screening of potential project personnel. Their oversight roles were reviewed and agreed to. NASA would do the initial screening and Zack and Dr. Garrity would get the final say on all personnel. This meeting went more smoothly then either Zack or Craig had expected. They would be spared the grueling details a project of this magnitude entailed but would essentially remain in control.

Their personal training activities were clearly defined. They and their bodyguards would start immediately in getting their flight and astronaut training.

Their training was modeled after the normal astronaut's training but took into account that they would not be operating the shuttle. However, the space simulation and flight simulation were all to be done. Additionally, they would need to participate and pass the physical portions of the training.

The astronaut training was modified to take only three months versus one year. The physical training schedule was adjusted to continue until the date of departure. This ensured both Zack and Craig would be physically capable and would qualify against the basics of the normal training.

Zack and Craig also spend quite a bit of time each day with the scientific and technical teams working on the details of project Savitar.

Only a month after the meeting with the world's dignitaries, Zack was in front of a group of people describing the basics of how the black hole would be captured and how the entire structure would be built and then moved to the black hole. He had developed the basic plan in an outline fashion. The final design and the required structural strengths and thicknesses of materials had yet to be determined.

"Ladies and Gentlemen, what we need to build is a giant spherical frame able to withstand the enormous forces exerted by the black hole's pull.

This can best be accomplished using a Bucky ball spherical structure. A heavy-duty version will form the inner sphere.

Long heavy steel cables radiating outward will provide the support and stability for the outer most sphere. This outer sphere will be of the same design as the inner sphere but have a much lighter structure.

The inner sphere will be at approximately nine G and the outer sphere will be at one G," Zack said as he talked to a group of scientists and engineers.

"My initial calculations puts the inner sphere or nine G level, diameter at forty miles and the one G level will be a sphere having a two-hundred-fifty mile diameter," Zack paused for a moment to let the dimensions sink home.

He answered several questions and then returned to explaining the basic design of the capture sphere.

"The inner sphere or nine G level will need to be the strongest man knows how to make. It will be totally constructed in Earth orbit with the exception of internal joint welding which will be completed during the journey. The one G platform will be only partially completed. If the project is successful the remainder of the sphere will be finished and Earth will have a giant space going vessel," Zack said as he scanned the faces of the leaders in the room.

Zack made it clear success was capturing and then moving the black hole. If they were unable to move the black hole their efforts, the monumental cost and the hardships would have been futile.

"We will assemble most of this sphere in orbit around Earth, but the finish work will be done as we race to arrive at the black hole about two years ahead of Earth. This means we will need to work as we move out ahead of the Earth's path," Zack continued.

"The crew living area will be built out at the one G level. The living and working areas for the crew will be constructed at the juncture point of the two halves. The sphere will rotate around at this juncture to create a one G environment for our trip. The living quarters will have their floors to the outer surface of the sphere. Once we capture the black hole, we will have a gravitational pull in toward the center and the living quarters will be flipped.

Supplies and materials for the remainder of the sphere will be stored in a balanced fashion around and inside of the sphere. If the assembly progresses as planned, all the radial extension cables will be installed during Earth orbit. This will more easily be done with the extra hands we will have during this period of construction.

Each person in the room was in charge of a specific aspect of the project and taking copious notes. Questions of clarity were asked and when answered, Zack would continue with the general description of the overall project.

The scope and magnitude of the project was overwhelming. Each team would need to work through and address the details in their area.

Zack's part of the meeting came an end and Benjamin Samuelson, NASA director took over and described how the group was going to work.

Zack and Craig took the opportunity to step out of the meeting.

Zack arranged to get a tour of the aircraft carrier USS George Washington. He wanted to understand how the Navy managed such a large number of personnel in a rather small space. He spent several weeks to understand the function and staffing of each department. He found the learning invaluable.

He made sure the designers of aircraft carriers were added to the design team for the Savitar.

What he learned from his tour of the carriers made him decide on having eleven organizational departments. Once he was clear on the purpose and function of each department, he was able to estimate the number of people for each department.

He listed his departments, their purpose and then determined the staffing.

His leadership team would be made up of the leaders of each of his departments.

The functions of each department determined the number of people assigned.

Station management with a minimum staffing of one hundred twenty would handle police work, internal communications, training and education and recreation.

Maintenance management would have five hundred personnel.

Construction would be staffed with two thousand personnel.

Food Production and Services would have three hundred personnel.

Health, Safety and Environment would have seventy-two personnel.

Religion would have six, religious, leaders.

Science and Engineering had a staff of thirty.

The Navigation, Supply and Logistics and Training departments would each have twelve personnel.

This brought the minimum staffing to three thousand, seventy-five personnel. Due to the radiation threat, he communicated a number three times greater than his estimate. Ten thousand was the number he communicated, and it was the number for which the facilities on the Savitar were to be designed.

A small city for ten thousand volunteers was about to be built in space.

This meant food, clothing, medical support, living facilities, water, place to live and sleep, a place to exercise were all needed elements of the design.

To keep the size of the crew from exploding, each crew member would have several roles. A person might be an assembler and welder but would also serve as a worker in the hydroponics farms and maybe be a cook.

This multiplicity of responsibility was to reduce the crew size but also to keep each person busy. The team would be going out ahead of the Earth and be in space for six years or longer. Many people felt this was beyond what the human body and mind could sustain.

Zack planned to make the trip so interesting that the people would thrive.

The Savitar would be equipped with the latest medical diagnostic and analysis equipment. Two doctors, one Canadian and the other American, were saddled with the job of keeping the crew healthy. They would have a full staff, a fifty-bed hospital and be in charge of crew's well-being.

Janet sat behind Zack listening and noting the reactions of the audience. Zack was intense. He devised one of the few possible solutions to the world's potential demise. She noticed no one else had any counter proposals. Instead, they seemed overwhelmed. Zack was very inclusive and quickly had those around him contributing their ideas and needed details to make the project a success.

She felt she had jumped into the center of a whirl wind, and she loved it. Her training did not lend itself directly to the building of the Savitar, but it blended in with all the rest of the work and the organizing of the crew itself.

The astronaut training appealed to her, and the project Zack described fascinated her. She knew this was what she had been looking for all her life. She had made a point of keeping her and Zack's relationship a purely business one, but she knew deep down this would be hard to manage and continue.

"Let's look at the overall drawing of the sphere and determine how this will be assembled. Each of you will need to fill in the details. This design is only an outline." Zack continued talking as he displayed a drawing he had sketched for the presentation.

He wanted the nine G spherical structure, the radiating cables and a good section of the one G frame assembled in Earth orbit. This would leave a few remaining cables and the completion of the outer sphere for the long trip out.

He was also working on getting enough sand, soil, water, and food, to ensure the Savitar crew could survive at least four years beyond the capture of the black hole. There had been initial resistance to do this, but he had pressed this point and finally got assurances for it from the President.

Zack anticipated a forgetful populace after the blackhole no longer posed a threat to the Earth. If he was to play the pied piper, then he would collect the minimum payment up front.

The assembled project managers for the different aspects of the project were from all countries and were among the best. They were soon off and running their portion of the projects independently except for the weekly reviews. Teams were scattered around the world and coordinated by a significant NASA staff.

Zack kept close watch on all the leaders. Many of them would go into space with him. He replaced or identified alternate persons for several positions as it became apparent the leaders were not compatible with him or the rest of the team. Zack's concern was the ability for these leaders to successfully complete their work and to collaborate with the others and even help them when possible. Once out in space, roles would likely change and evolve. His team needed skill, flexibility, and compatibility.

The other critical issue was the health of the crew. They would spend more time in space than had ever done before. He and the two ships doctors, Drs. Henry Twillinger and Ned McMillan spent a great deal of time discussing how they would keep the crew healthy and safe. The fact they would have one G gravity would have a very positive effect on the general health of the crew. However, as the crew went out to work, they would be blasted by the radiation of the Sun and later they would be traveling so fast even small particles of dust could prove fatal.

The health information and points of concern Henry, and Ned identified were passed on to the Savitar design team. These concerns were translated into the design of the walls, floors, and ceilings of the living facilities.

Zack made it a point to connect the doctors with Samuel so that the impact of the nano-bots and how to use them would be incorporated into their thinking.

The living quarters would have six inches of water surrounding them. This would provide radiation shielding while they were around the inner planets. It would also provide significant but not total shielding from space dust and other particles. The water in the shielding would also be the water used for the needs of the crew and recycled back to the walls.

Zack charged the two doctors to design a routine of activities to make the crew into well trained, healthy individuals. Henry and Ned designed a routine and diet to accomplish this goal. They would later help Zack get a rigorous training and workout schedule developed for all of the crew.

Zack recognized Janet as his secret weapon. She provided the name and personal information for the people Zack met each day. She carried a computer pad giving her access to all personnel records. She thoroughly checked out the people Zack dealt with. She reviewed all data the FBI or other agencies might have on all personnel working on the Savitar.

This was her way of screening the people and providing protection for Zack.

Zack regularly reviewed the progress of the entire project. The assigned teams were pouring over the design basis and initial outline of each of the project plans. The pace needed to be and was frantic, fast but also accurate.

Payloads into space needed to be planned and optimized. They had only three more months to finish their design and begin launching and staging materials in space.

During this time, the staffing team frantically worked with each of the project teams to identify the skills and number of personnel needed to do the work.

The team leader for the personnel team was Indira DeSouza.

There was an instant magnetism between Zack and Indira. The two seemed to be on the same wavelength and anticipated each other's questions. Working on the staffing became a fun part of the job for Zack. He set up a once-a-week review process to check the status of the personnel.

He really liked Indira and thought about seeing her personally.

The stress of getting the Savitar designed and constructed kept him so busy he did not pursue his personal interest in Indira. When he thought about it, he always ended up finding a reason for not contacting her. He was not sure why, but the time never seemed right.

Janet noticed this situation and made sure her feelings about it stayed within herself. She was not sure whether it was jealousy she felt or something else. She was careful not to let her emotions get in the way of her job. She did however do a thorough analysis and review of Indira's past but found nothing suspicious. It appeared Indira was squeaky clean.

This in itself bothered Janet. Her own records showed her dysfunctional family as a potential weak spot and just about every other person working on the Savitar had some blemish.

This perfect record stood out and she planned to continue to keep an eye on Indira.

The launch of the materials into space began in earnest. Zack was pleased and felt reassured when he found out that Craig was in charge of optimizing the launches. The launch payloads were always one hundred percent full. The order of materials going up was based on what was ready by the time the next launch was scheduled. Craig made sure every ounce that could be lifted was launched. No rocket launched without taking one hundred per cent of the load it was designed to lift.

Along with the materials, went a host of workers. Never before had so many people been out in space at the same time. Any person with previous space experience or training was called back to help.

New people were run through a three-month abbreviated astronaut training.

Previously trained and qualified astronauts of all ages became the leaders for the teams going out to space.

The launches of personnel went up from the US, China, and Russia.

The sky was a maze of materials. Workers frantically put together what at first seemed to be a random array of material. The latest smart chip technology was used so each object could be tracked electronically and its location in the maze of materials accumulating in space could be pin pointed.

Back on Earth each piece of material was being tracked and maneuvered into position by a crew responsible for getting it to the right place.

Each rocket went up filled with sections of Bucky balls. The Bucky balls would snap together and later they would be welded together. Most of the welding would be done after leaving Earth orbit.

Craig was utilizing every launch to get the official and unofficial material into orbit. The unofficial materials were the materials that Zack was continually adding to his need list.

Out in space, two circular rings, ten miles in diameter were created. These were joined but were designed to let the sphere open and then close around the black hole. On each side of the center rings, twenty-foot diameter piping was added to form a huge Bucky ball. This would be the nine G level.

The insides of the twenty-foot diameter piping was a maze of two-foot diameter Bucky balls as reinforcement. The design was a giant Bucky ball with multiple layers of Bucky balls internally. These sections were made on Earth and only the joints connecting one section to another section needed to be finalized in space.

The material continued into space by almost continuous launches from the US, France, Russia, China, and India and two new locations one in Australia and another in Brazil. The rockets were packed with an eye to one hundred percent loading for each launch.

The living quarters were built on Earth and made in long rocket shaped sections and then launched. Most rockets were one-way shots. Everything making it into space was processed to be used on the Savitar. Solid fuel rocket launches were the primary way payloads were lifted into orbit. The space shuttles were used almost exclusively as human transport busses.

Slowly the sphere took shape. It was visible to almost all the world. Its size made it appear a new moon had taken up orbit around the Earth.

The main crew worked on assembling the sphere. Other crews assembled the living quarters, and the hydroponics facility. These units had been assembled on Earth but needed to be attached and commissioned. They were in the shape of a cylinder and the diameter of the rocket launching it. Once in space the sections were joined to the required length.

Watching the progress of building the Savitar became an international hobby. The sale of five-inch observation telescopes exploded. Observation clubs were formed. These clubs would send in requests for information and improvement suggestions. Craig Garrity set up a team just to deal with the communication with and the handling of all the information requests.

Each day, Zack would spend a part of the day training for his role as captain of the Savitar. The organization of the crew of the Savitar would be semi-military in nature. All countries in the world were nominating crew members. This made for a very diverse and unaligned crew.

Zack began by arranging them into mixed, small teams. Each team had several roles and each member on the team was responsible for one of the roles. The majority of the teams would be assembly teams with secondary duties in the mess, and the upkeep of the living quarters. A few teams were specialized. These teams were responsible for piloting and maintaining the shuttles and their support systems, maintaining the hydroponics, navigating the Savitar, cooks, doctors, nurses, religious leaders, engineers, scientist, and storekeepers. The list of went on. After a while it all became mind numbing.

Zack finally hired several city planners to review the situation and to make organizational suggestions.

Savitar would have three station managers responsible for managing the day-to-day activities. They would be like city managers during their on-shift hours. They would be part of the leadership team and work directly for Zack. There was a police force to look after security and personnel problems. There would be a medical department to manage the health of the crew.

The direct leadership team Zack established was,

Zack Milton	Command and Station Master # 1
Enrico Hidalgo	2nd in command - Mexican
Janet Romero	Station Master #2 - American - BG
Andrew Pennington	Station Master # 3 American - BG
Lisa Hemming	Food Production & Services, English
Chiang Lee	Navigation -Chinese
Gregor Menkowski	Supply and Logistics -Russian
Victor Marquis	Construction -French
Conrad Zepf	Science and Engineering -German

Paulo Souza   Maintenance Management -Brazilian
Indira DeSouza   Chief of Personnel -Indian
Dr. Henry Twillinger Health, Safety, Environment -English
Rotating Religious Leader

As the time for departure got nearer, Zack in concert with his leadership team trimmed the crew size down to the minimum possible.

The first to be cut were the special projects crew members. Projects unclear as to their purpose were trimmed. These projects had originally been used to gain the support of certain groups or countries. It would be difficult to deal with the politics of trimming them.

Zack talked these cuts through with President Lansing.

The President guided the cuts from a political perspective. He knew some of the projects were fronts for various organizations. He took the opportunity to cut those with potentially posed negative impacts on the mission. President Lansing took responsibility for dealing with the politics.

"Zack, the military of various countries are upset the mission will be led by you and not a military leader. The US chief-of-staff is upset with me. There may come a time when I can no longer control them. I would like to give you a code word as signal to you when I am no longer in control of the situation, or I want to let you know to make your own decisions. The signal word is *valor*.

If I use it with you in conversation in the future after you have left Earth orbit, you will know whatever I am saying I no longer support or you should do whatever is necessary in your own judgment," President Lansing said with a grave look on his face.

"I want you to work with your leadership team to vet the crew very thoroughly before you leave. I know there are plants of various insurgent organizations.

The FBI will give you the details about the ones for which we know are out to cause you trouble once you leave Earth's orbit. Each of our partners has similar information. Please use all this information as you see fit. I have made sure the crazies never made it onto the team or out in space. However, there may be some deep moles you will need to vet as you travel out to the black hole," President Lansing concluded.

"I want to thank you for selecting me to lead the mission, for your support, for your guidance and for the very good advice you have given me. I hope you remain in control, and you don't ever need to use the code word you have given me," Zack said as he stood up at the end of their meeting.

This was the last of their every two-week planning meetings. Time was drawing close to the departure. As Zack left the oval office, Craig got up from the chair outside.

"That was a bit unusual. Why did he ask me to leave?" Craig asked

"I'm not sure," Zack lied knowing the President wanted to deliver his code word in secret. He did not want to hurt Craig's feelings, but he would honor the President's desire for secrecy.

"Maybe he didn't want you to see his emotional side," Zack continued flippantly.

"OK, kid, I'm a big boy and will leave you alone about it," Craig said casually.

By this time, the two of them were very close. He was curious but not concerned. He knew later he would find out if he needed to.

He went on to say that he figured Dan wanted Zack to have a way of knowing when he had to lie.

Zack's smile confirmed the statement.

Craig was staying behind with a ground crew who would track and communicate with Savitar. He thought about going but Emily could not think about leaving Earth at this time. She told him to go without her. Though he wanted very badly to go, he could not leave Emily behind. He knew the way out would be dangerous and likely hood of ever getting back to the Earth was slim.

He would stay. He would continue meeting with President Lansing on a quarterly basis and manage the affairs of the Savitar from Earth.

That afternoon, both of them rocketed up to the now almost assembled sphere. To Zack it was beginning to look like the spherical trap he envisioned to be used to capture the black hole. The shuttle they were riding made a tour around the structure. The size and magnitude of the Savitar became apparent as the shuttle flew around the one hundred twenty-five-mile circumference.

There were people everywhere. Last minute spot welds were being put on each joint. Full seam welds would be made during their voyage. On a six-hour shift rotation about three thousand workers were out on the structure at a time. The work went on twenty-four-seven with four crews rotating and being flown down and back up. There was not a day when a dozen personnel launches were not being made.

Several accidents ending in serious injury and two fatalities occurred. Though sad, this was no worse than when giant skyscrapers, were built on Earth. The work went on at top speed.

Zack and Craig got out in the main living area. The living area was designed in such a fashion it could be reoriented when gravity was provided by the black hole. Until then the rotation of the sphere would provide the equivalent of one G. The main rotation power and propulsion power would come from fifteen large ion engines. Ten would provide propulsion and five would provide rotation. The ten space shuttles would be hooked equal distances apart, along the circumference and would provide the initial launch propulsion in conjunction to the Ion engines and later they would provide maneuvering propulsion. Currently the shuttles were in constant use going to and from the Savitar and carrying the human payload around the structure. There was equipment, parts, and supplies anchored around the structure.

There was the official launch list and then there was the "unofficial" Milton launch list. On the Milton launch list were the materials Zack was having sent up unofficially. Only he and Craig knew the exact list. The President knew about the Milton list in a general nature. He had essentially given his blessing but did not want to know the details.

Zack thought through what the Savitar would need beyond the capture. It would need the equipment and materials to become a self-supporting system. With this in mind, he made up a significant list of equipment, materials, seeds, weapons, and other items needed to make the Savitar self-supporting. He had also secretly sent up dirt.

The main core Bucky, ten miles in diameter and the initial forty-mile diameter ring with cables between them were all temporarily joined. The two hundred forty-five-mile diameter sphere was all tack welded and had the cables to the core sphere attached. Each of the twelve-inch diameter cables were woven stainless steel wire manufactured in one long continuous run. The front and rear pentagons were decked and complete.

The back pentagon was the platform for the main drive engines. The fuel tanks for the engines were mounted on the underside of the decking. The Savitar was a gigantic skeleton of what it would become.

The housing for the welding crews had been the first to be commissioned. These would later be remodeled to hold a smaller permanent crew. These were all located out at the two hundred forty-mile diameter area.

The rotation provided one G gravity and provided better living conditions for all the personnel in space. Once rotation was established, all personnel stayed on the Savitar longer since workers could sleep and exercise. The living areas also provided the crew with a break from the radiation bombardment suffered while out on the structure.

The rotation would be maintained by five huge, modified Ion engines. These engines provided the rotation, and they were also generating the electricity for the sphere. Originally, they thought of using the shuttles to provide this rotation, but Zack had made a recent decision to save the shuttles for the final maneuvering once they reached their destination. This reduced the required amount of shuttle fuel that needed to be launched.

He came to realize that his focus on minimizing the crew size would provide a bigger safety margin for air and other critical supplies. He was secretly pleased the crew would be smaller.

On this inspection trip there would be a walk through the hydroponics area. The gardens had been activated in the past few weeks.

The Savitar's rotation had been started to allow the hydroponics gardens to get established.

Lisa Hemming met them at the entrance to the hydroponics.

"Ladies and Gentlemen, welcome to my paradise. About eighty percent of this unit is up and running. We will have six such units. The other five are in various states of commissioning. This unit is the one farthest along.

The hydroponics garden was designed to contribute a large portion of fresh food. Zack had great ambitions for the gardens. He would continue expanding it until the food raised would feed the entire crew. The materials to do so were on his list of extras being sent up.

Today you will be served a dinner salad with the first crop of lettuce and mint. The tomatoes are not yet ready. Eden will be growing a variety of fresh fruits and vegetables; tomatoes, potatoes both regular and sweet, cucumbers, squash, pumpkin, and grapes," Lisa rattled off.

Janet immediately liked Lisa. She had reviewed Lisa's personal files and was surprised at how much they had in common. She especially liked the fact Lisa, unlike many people did not act like she and Andrew were invisible. When she talked to Zack, she made a point of talking to the three of them.

Zack presented Lisa with several small-rooted stems.

"Instead of roses, I brought you the plants so you can grow your own. Here are six varieties of roses." Zack said as he presented them to Lisa.

"Oh, you are a dear. They have not let me bring up anything not directly related to feeding the crew. Thank you," Lisa said as she took the plants and put them in a special container she hid away.

Zack walked through the cylinders and knew Lisa would see a lot of him. He also realized this would be a great rest and relaxation work assignment for those who were getting burned out. He mentally put this on his list of things to talk through with Drs Twillinger and McMillan. Zack saw an opportunity to cycle everyone on the crew through this assignment as both a mental and physical recovery from the rigors of working out in space.

"Lisa, how many people do you have on your team?" Zack asked as they stood in front of a row of tomato plants.

"There is one person per cylinder per shift plus one maintenance support per shift. Additionally, there are four experts for a total of thirty people," Lisa replied.

"I would like to use this assignment as a place people can recover from their isolation in their other work. I also have a surprise for you once we are under way," Zack said mysteriously.

The whole crew assembled around them, and Zack took the opportunity to thank them for their hard work in getting the gardens up and running.

"This is the center of our life and well-being. There will be no other work affecting us so directly as what is done here in the hydroponics area." Zack told them in closing.

In the next month, the team would rotate once more down to Earth before departure.

Of the ten thousand welders and other workers only about three thousand would return. This had not been communicated to any of the crew. Zack would be meeting with his leadership team at the end of the week to make the final crew selection. This would be communicated to the crew in a few weeks.

After three days inspecting the various activities and the condition of the structure, Zack was satisfied everything was ready for departure.

The structure was hard to imagine. The shuttle taking Zack around could fly among its various parts. The inner forty-five-mile diameter Bucky ball was completely assembled, and the joints were being welded. The inner fill of Bucky balls had not been connected at the joints but the internal ones filling each of the twenty-foot diameter sections had been totally welded before launch. This construction provided the strongest frame that he, Craig, and several other structural engineers were able to come up with and it could be assembled in this manner and at this speed.

All materials were commercially available, and the sections could be assembled in all the launch countries and then immediately launched. Assembly speed was one of the main concerns during the design.

The propulsion ion engines were mounted on the aft pentagon. The engines had been tested but would not come into use until launch. If they failed, then the mission would fail.

The fuel for these engines was being brought up on a daily basis and would continue until the last minute. One of the twenty-four containment magnets had been mounted and secured. This would serve as the model for construction of the rest of the magnets. The two hundred forty-mile diameter sphere was tack welded and looked complete. All the cables between it and the center forty-mile diameter sphere were connected and tack welded. The crew housing was at the point where the two halves of the forty-diameter sphere came together.

"Well Craig, are you sure you don't want to come along?" Zack asked as they came around the Savitar on their way back to Earth.

"Well, my dear friend sometimes I am tempted but someone has to stay here and watch your back and keep the home fires burning. And I am married to a woman who does not want to go and whom I won't leave. So, it goes without saying, though I support this mission one thousand percent, I will not be going.

I do wish you luck. You seem to have assembled a good crew and you have mastered the art of leading them. I hope we have found all the troublemakers and weeded them out. Once we announce the final crew you will need to make haste in your departure, I am sure each slighted group or organization will try to change your selection," Craig said as they were coming back down.

"I will call for a final meeting at the end of the month. This will be the departure meeting where we announce the final crew membership and begin final preparations for departure. Between now and then I have arranged for the crew to get their final furloughs. Only the selected members will make the journey back out." Zack shared as the shuttle touched down.

He followed Janet as she led the way to their waiting car.

Chapter 6: Indira

ℋer sensual beauty, keen intellect, and a fierce desire to control events boosted Indira up the ladder of success. Her God father, friend and supporter, General Walker, used his connection to get her into a position that allowed her to be selected as the personnel director for Project Savitar and was certain she would soon run the entire operation. She would be able to place her people where she wanted.

Born in India to two ambitious doctors, Indira grew up in Chicago along Lake Michigan. The only daughter of two plastic surgeons, she always had the best of everything. Her parents were very loving but also very strict.

Devout Catholics, the couple brought their daughter up in a strict Catholic home. Indira grew up in this loving but strict environment and flourished.

With an IQ off the scale, Indira was intellectually smarter than her two parents. She excelled in everything she attempted. Every summer she attended Northwestern University's program for gifted children.

This was her summer "camp." She loved being with kids of similar capability. At the summer camp she was not a freak. She was one of the group and she was a leader within this group. She was recognized and ranked number three among gifted children throughout the United States.

One summer, when they were both about twelve, Indira and Zach attended the same class.

Neither remembered the other.

Indira graduated at the top of her High School class and was accepted to Stanford University. There she pursued a degree in business. This was a huge disappointment to her parents who continued to try to influence her to become a doctor.

However, Indira did not want to be like her parents. She thought of them as too focused on their careers, a little stale and very boring. She wanted to run a business, rise to be a CEO, or develop and lead some organization.

While going to Stanford, she frequently stayed at her God parent's home along the beach. The Walkers were friends to the DeSouza family since college. Childless, they became like Aunt and Uncle to Indira. They had been honored to be Indira's God parents.

Mr. Walker was a three-star General in the Army. General Raymond Walker was a career officer and had excelled in serving his country. He was now out and enjoying a comfortable life.

He and Indira were especially close.

Through this relationship, Indira was influenced greatly by General Walker's ultra-conservative thinking. The two would spend hours discussing politics and the situations around the world. It was not unusual for them to stay up late at night discussing one problem or another. This relationship greatly influenced Indira.

Indira was innately judgmental and looked down upon many of the common problems facing people in everyday life. She had no reference by which to evaluate problems she herself had never faced. Erroneously, she extrapolated her thinking and abilities and applied them to the rest of the population. She had a naive and shallow wisdom.

Upon graduation, Indira took a personnel management job with a large industrial company. The interview was arranged by General Walker through a retired Army colleague.

Once in the door, Indira's capability and her beauty were the fuel to her quick rise. She played a hard game and put all her energy to getting ahead. She was excellent at making the organization do what she wanted and getting the results the business needed.

When Indira entered a room heads would turn to follow her. She was by any measure exotically beautiful. This was a fact she understood quite well, and she dressed to make a statement.

Throughout her university career, she had used her charm to get what she wanted from her male competitors. Now, she used her beauty to disarm her competition. She was always proper about her relationships at work. However, she would get all she could from her male colleagues as they tried to get on her favored list. Her intellect was all she needed to accelerate and rise above her distracted competition.

In only five years she climbed five levels up the ladder and became one of the youngest directors in the company. Everyone knew she was headed farther up. Indira's drive and capability were at its peak.

Then the President addressed the nation to share the fact a black hole was in the path of the Earth. He announced a plan to move this object out of the way.

Indira did not like President Lancing just for the fact that she saw him as too liberal and giving too much to the common person.

Her reaction to the announcement was immediate and illogical. She came to the conclusion it would be impossible to move a black hole and the time and money should be spent preparing the Earth to survive the encounter. She also doubted it would affect the Earth the way it had been described.

One evening over dinner she discussed this with General Walker.

"Well, I am not sure I have anything against trying to move this black hole, but I do have an objection to having some civilian professor in charge of the effort," General Walker replied.

In fact, he was outraged and had contacted his colleagues to determine what could be done about the getting that person replaced.

His concern about the ability to move a black hole was secondary.

"We should be thinking about how to make this a military advantage for the US," he continued.

He was happy to see Indira so against the venture. He knew that a selection process to staff the effort was underway. He desperately wanted someone on the inside to feed him information. Indira was the perfect candidate to be an inside contact on the mission.

"Would you be interested in getting on the crew of the Savitar?" General Walker asked.

"Why would I want to help the effort?" Indira asked in reply.

Her intellect was indeed being teased by the curiosity of how something on this scale would be carried out. She knew she would excel in such an environment. Her belief in her superiority influenced many of her decisions.

"Well, if you were in charge of personnel selection, you would be able to place key people on the roster. At some later stage in the journey, you would be in the position to take over the vessel and turn it over to the US military. We could then either, carry out the mission or end it," General Walker replied.

"Are you asking me to volunteer to be a spy?" Indira asked somewhat surprised.

She thought of herself as open and forthright not as someone who would purposely hide in the background.

To be a spy never crossed her mind, but she found it curiously appealing. It would be a challenge. She knew she would never get caught.

"Well, I guess I am but only if it interests you and if you want to. There is no pressure from me. I was just reacting to your strong negative feeling about this venture," General Walker replied.

He personally hoped Indira's curiosity and rather strong negative reaction would lead her to accept the role. With her totally clean background, she would make the perfect mole. There was no way to trace her to any of the active military.

He did not think anyone knew he was her God father.

The more Indira thought about it the more she wanted to go on the Savitar. She was sure she could use her superior intellect, and her looks to control the situation once she was on the Savitar staff. She would be able to set up the organization the way it pleased her. She would have control soon after getting into the role.

She let General Walker know she was indeed interested.

General Walker made the calls to his active military buddies to arrange for an interview the following Monday. He spent the next few weeks talking with various generals to position Indira in her role as a deep operative for the US Army! He felt a little guilty, but he figured Indira was her own woman.

Indira took to her role with relish. The intrigue and risk energized her.

Her interview with NASA went without a hitch. She dazzled the young interviewers with her looks and brilliant smile. She wore conservative clothing, but it was form fit and complimented her looks.

She received technical coaching on the various aspects of the Savitar project in preparation for the interviews. This put her in a great position.

Her command and understanding of the project impressed her interviewers.

"This is too easy. They are just as stupid as I thought they would be," Indira thought to herself.

Her interview with Zackary Milton was a surprise. She liked him immediately and seemed to sense he was interested in her. She planned to make sure the two of them would become close.

Her selection as the chief of personnel thrilled her.

She saw total control of the Savitar venture within her grasp. She was now looking forward to her role.

Indira took an immediate dislike for Zack's female bodyguard. She recognized her as competition for the attention she hoped Zack would expend on her. She wanted to establish a close personal relationship with Zack as soon as all possible.

She made a mental note to replace this bodyguard as soon as possible.

This relationship seemed to be in the works as she and Zack worked on the personnel lists and discussed staffing. She knew it was only a matter of time before he asked her out. She was certain he would succumb to her charms, just like all the other men in her past.

She knew control was only a matter of time. She felt she was slowly making progress in gaining control of the Savitar.

To her surprise Zack never took the next step. Indira was furious and blamed this on his bodyguard, Janet. She erroneously conjectured more than body guarding was going on.

She began her efforts to see if she could displace this female bodyguard.

To Indira's surprise Janet's personnel files were not accessible to her. She also discovered she had no access to the records of any of the bodyguards and she had no access to Zack's files as well.

She made a list of the people she had no access to. It turned out to be the entire leadership team.

This situation infuriated her. Why was she denied access to the people closest to Zachary? She was furious. Never before had she faced such a situation.

Indira kept her outer appearance neutral. If she ever displayed her consternation or anger, no one noticed. Indira figured it would be a long voyage and she could still work her magic when the opportunity arose. She would put her the people that were to be her leadership team into roles she wanted them to be in.

She had little doubt she would eventually win out.

Indira almost lost her position. She hated the physical training and tried to cut corners. She was put on probation by an old Air Force sergeant who actually disliked her because he saw through her use of her beauty to get what she wanted. He told her to step up or get out.

Indira appealed to Zack to get her out of the training. He looked at her and simply told her that a successful completion of the training was required to stay on the crew of the Savitar.

She began to realize that Zack was not a person she could charm to do her bidding.

Indira was furious and wanted to get even with the old sergeant, she would have taken revenge if she could have figured out how to do so quickly and not get caught. However, she needed to focus on the Savitar staffing.

She grudgingly stepped up.

She pushed herself to pass the three-month training ordeal.

Indira's interaction with Zack highlighted his top-level control of every aspect of the program. This included the control he had over her. She was not pleased about this.

Indira gained additional respect of Zack when she found out he met with the President every two weeks. She began to realize that she had stepped into a situation tougher than she had ever faced before.

Chapter 7: Final Goodbyes

Zack closed his eyes and took in the breeze, blowing in across eastern Florida's inter-coastal waterway and wafting the smell of salt mixed with decaying vegetation gently passed him. The slightly fishy pickle odor was a welcome relief from the tensions of the day. He opened his eyes, took in the stars on the horizon and then looked down to where the crab lights cast their bluish green glow up from below the water. He was out crabbing and sitting on retaining wall tending one of the crab nets on a long pole.

Conversation was muted and minimal. The quiet was interrupted only by the arrival of a crab into the lamp illuminated area. He then positioned the long-handled net, and he took in the whispers of encouragement and direction. He snared the crab and carried it in the net to the tub holding the other crab catch of the evening.

The inner coastal water way appeared as a smooth black surface. He could see the reflection of the bright moon and there was a faint trace of the sparkling rings of the Savitar. The air was warm, and the breeze carried the faint music of some night spot on the other side over the waterway to where he and a contingent of family and military guards were all participating in the crabbing that he had chosen as the venue of where to say goodbye to his family.

He took a sip of his beer in silent celebration.

This was his bridge. Only a short distance from the Cape, the bridge spanned the inter-coastal water way. This was where he and his dad had come to crabbed several times before times. This was where he and his father celebrated his acceptance into MIT.

This was where more recently he had come to relax.

The enjoyment came from the preparation, the quiet conversation, the smells, and the visual beauty of the night. Catching crabs was secondary but he and his father usually caught enough for a family dinner.

Quiet conversation occurred between the excitement of some lonesome crab sidling its way slowly into the light on its way to drag away the chicken wing or leg tied out as bait.

Dolphins leaping and gliding through the moonlit waters rewarded those sitting on the waterway retaining wall. Zack interpreted the leaps as jumps of joy. These were smooth gliding leaps that highlighted the dolphins grace as well as their strength. Zack had always been fond of dolphins.

On occasion a gentle manatee's huge body suddenly outlined by the crab lights would result in a ripple of fear. Everyone would jump back. His heart would always be in his throat. For him it was the image of a great white shark coming up out of the water with its jaws open ready to swallow him that always cause this reaction. He really came to hate the fact that his very visual mind had unconsciously imprinted that scene from the movie.

Laughter and teasing always followed such an episode.

He loved to watch the graceful bodies of sting rays gliding effortlessly through the water like swallows swooping after insects on a cool summer night. Their agility to fly in the water mesmerized him.

This was the end of the crabbing season and not the best time to crab, but it was the setting Zack had wanted. He did not want to be trapped inside his childhood home for this last visit.

This evening was like the countless other ones he had enjoyed in the past. However, this evening there was a sense of finality, and he felt a quiet tension.

Also, this time there was a noticeable group of additional participants. He was now never alone.

His mother and sister were present. The two of them had seldom gone crabbing because they thought the flies and mosquitoes too challenging. They had come this time because they understood that this would most likely be the last time the family would share this experience or to be together.

Almost unnoticed but surrounding the entire area was a perimeter of Marines.

These days Zack often felt like a prisoner. In reality he knew the government was providing for his safety.

High in the sky toward the southwest shimmering like a twinkling star but the size of the moon was a new bright light in the evening sky. To the naked eye it was the size and looked like a large silver white pearl almost the size of the moon. The twinkling was caused by the rotation of the Savitar and the light reflecting from the surfaces of the cables and tubing.

The Savitar was the largest object mankind had ever built. It was a testament to the capability, ingenuity, and determination of the collective people on Earth.

Zack was where he wanted to be. He was in the environment he wanted as he sat with his family as they spent their last evening together. He was sure he would hold this memory for a lifetime.

He was totally relaxed and enjoying himself. Crabbing had always been relaxing to him.

He sensed that it was especially hard for his mother, but she was holding up well.

Zack knew in his heart he would never return to Earth. He had not mentioned this to his family. He thought his parents knew and probably talked about it. Neither mentioned anything to him.

Janet and Andrew were also in attendance. Over the last year, Zack's mother adopted both of them as family and spent a great deal of time talking to them.

Janet Romero came from a broken family and fell in love with Zack's family and the good feelings she always experienced around them.

She enjoyed the family chatter and got along well with Zack's sister and mother.

Andrew Pennington was very quiet and only gave general hints of his own family.

The evening of crabbing ended with a lot of hugs and kisses.

Zack left the inter-coastal waterway in a limo with Andrew and Janet. His mother gave all three of them a hug and wished them well in their journeys. She invited both Andrew and Janet to visit the next time they had a chance.

"Take good care of Zack for me," Zack's mother whispered as she hugged Janet goodbye. "I know I may not see either of you again. So, take care of each other." She continued.

"I will," was Janet's quiet reply. She was somewhat surprised but had a warm feeling about the implication that she sensed Zack's mother was communicating.

"You have a great family. I wish mine was as functional and warm," Janet said to Zack as they sat in the car on their return back to their quarters.

"I am going home tomorrow for my family's get together. I know it will be the last time I will see them all, but I dread the occasion. There is bound to be some sort of fight or disagreement accompanied with screaming. There is always some silly argument," Andrew confessed.

"When are you going home?" Zack asked turning to Janet.

"I won't be doing the family thing. I come from a really dysfunctional family. I have talked to both my mother and father by phone. They live apart and neither invited me to visit. They wished me well and asked, "where would my paycheck go?" They both asked the same question. It made me a little sick.

"I'm sorry, Janet, you make a great shadow and I want you to know I have really grown to rely and depend on you," Zack said as he held back a tear.

He was always amazed at how his immediate family functioned smoothly and supported him. He could not imagine his life without the support and confidence his family gave him.

He knew he was a softy when it came to people's personal happiness.

"Life is short. Each of us deserves some happiness," he thought. His mode of operation and decision making, though as hard and as tough as it needed to be, was always to treat others the way he wanted to be treated and to walk in their shoes as he was making the hard choices.

"Hey, thanks but don't let my family life interfere with our working relationship," Janet said with false energy.

"Well let's get a good night's sleep. I will see you two early in the morning for our jog. It's going to be a long hard day," Zack said as they all walked up the steps to their quarters.

They lived in a compound outside of the Cape where the three of them were housed in the same quarters. Zack had a room in the center with an attached bath. Janet's and Andrew's rooms were L shaped and went totally around his. Their three doors were in a common entry foyer with a single common door. Zack opened the door and walked down the hall to his bedroom.

Once he closed the door at the end of the hall, he could hear the hall close. Now there was no way into his room other than through the two outer rooms occupied by his two bodyguards.

Zack always thought this design was a little over done but it had been duplicated for his quarters on the ship on a smaller scale.

"After tomorrow, I will probably need this level of protection," Zack thought as he got into bed and fell asleep.

Sleep came easily for Zack. His approach to his work and in dealing with people was one of honesty and directness. This left him unaffected by the pressure of the work he did and the tough decisions he made.

The next day was the big announcement meeting where Zack would deliver some bad news to a large number of people. Only about a third of those that had made the selection list would be going on the mission.

For the past two weeks he had scrutinized the records of the people selected by his leadership team. The President sent a message identifying Heinrich Muller one of his key leaders as a mole. All the people on Muller's team were identified as subversive. When confronted, Heinrich's reaction was bizarre and unexpected.

"You are tampering with the will of God. You will not be successful," Heinrich screamed at Zack as he was escorted from the project offices.

"Well, that was disappointing. I thought Heinrich was a very interesting fellow. He was good with his people and seemed to be doing an excellent job managing the welding teams in sector four," Zack commented

He then instructed Paulo, ships welding manager, to take a crew out and inspect the work done in Heinrich's sector. He wanted to make sure the welds were to specification. If not, then an immediate fix was to be put in place. He wanted a report by the end the day.

He then focused the review on the people on the various teams.

He had come to the conclusion that his original estimate of the number of people would be the goal for the staffing of the Savitar. He had hope and was putting a great deal of confidence in having the nano-bot technology to alleviate the Savitar from serving as a space hearse.

He personally went through the ten thousand individual records. He easily reduced this number in half.

Then the selection process became more difficult.

He asked for input from his leadership team. The list had was brought down to four thousand. After hours of discussion, they had stopped at this number.

It was more than the three thousand Zack had initially estimated but it was significantly less than the ten thousand utilized during the assembly.

The stores and materials sent up had been for ten thousand. Zack wanted to have three times the supplies needed. He knew once they captured the black hole and moved it out of Earth's path, the price of getting more supplies would come with many conditions he would not be happy about.

He planned to have the Savitar be self-sustaining once they had captured and gained control of the blackhole.

The original higher number for the crew had also been based on the expected fatality rate due to radiation exposure. The promise of the nano-bot technology Dr. Trimble was perfecting would dramatically reduce this number.

"Well, Zack you almost got the crew size to the point that you have a safety factor of three," Janet commented after everyone had left.

"What are you talking about," Zack said surprised by her uncharacteristic vocalization of exactly what was on his mind.

She usually remained just a shadow.

"I know you have been loading up the Savitar with a bunch of extra supplies and equipment. Now you try to cut the crew to a third. You are figuring we will get abandoned once we are successful," Janet replied.

"Please keep this quiet," Zack requested as he looked intensely at her. He was surprised about the sense of confidence that he saw.

"Boss, I am your shadow, I am going where you go. I will suffer what you suffer. I am on your side, and I like you're thinking, I talk only to you." Janet replied with a salute.

"Ditto," Andrew added.

Zack looked at Janet and realized how close the two of them had grown. Her daily presence and support had made him complacent. He had almost forgotten this beauty at his side. He realized for the first time how much she meant to him.

He would prepare for the future. It would be whatever the future might be, but he was pleased that she was part of that future.

He had no idea just how important Janet would be to his survival.

Chapter 8: Andrew

Since childhood Andrew hid the major fault forming a gigantic chasm in his soul. His Father indoctrinated him in the ways of the Clan. Andrew took to the Clan's philosophy with a zeal and energy which surprised and pleased his dedicated and ardent father. By the time he was six Andrew had attended hundreds of Clan meetings and dozens of rallies.

Andrew was brilliant. But his brilliance had a warped hateful formative guidance. Neither of his parents were religious therefore there was no "Sunday school" where Andrew might have picked up the life guiding principles taught by the church.

His mother was a follower of the Clan's ideology and did not teach him anything but to go along with the view that being white was superior and that the superior race should have absolute control..

His father was a very smart but very racially biased, self-centered bigot.

The Clan provided Andrew a warped set of principles around which he formed his life.

He was a leader and took an early lead in clan activities.

The school environment allowed Andrew to test his social maneuvering skills. He became the classic good guy. He was good looking. He had good grades. He was good in sports. He enjoyed mixing with the good people. The good "white" people.

His closest friends all continued to attend the same Clan rallies as they had in their younger years. He however publicly kept his participation with the Clan at a very low profile. He sensed such a connection would work against him in general society.

He planned to put himself in control of some organization or company and knew that his background would be scrutinized.

He and his three closest friends had formed the Purity organization when they were 13 years old. They recruited and managed a group of young KKK Clan members. Through this group he was able to execute many actions which would have landed him in trouble.

Mock lynching, harassment of people of color, ruining people's reputation with rumor and occasionally physical force were all things Andrew planned and saw executed through the Purity membership.

However, he operated remotely. He never got his hands "dirty."

Through the years Purity continued to meet and discuss politics, racial issues, and the government. They continued to develop their antigovernment, anti-Jewish, anti-other race views. Andrew was always the brainy, quiet one who remained invisible but who guided the action.

His buddies were constantly getting into trouble for openly vocalizing or acting on their beliefs. His involvement was never connected with the vile actions of the organization he nurtured.

His scholastic and athletic ability got him accepted by Princeton. His interest in the affairs of government and in the control it had over people led him to pursue a degree in Criminal Justice.

He continued his quiet participation as a key leader of Purity. He was careful to never be connected to it in public or in any written record.

An FBI recruitment program caught his attention. He applied and was accepted. He went full throttle into the program. He loved the inside view this gave him of what he considered the opposing side. His skills opened many doors for him and soon he was in the heart of the FBI Security operations.

On his trips home he would discreetly meet with his buddies. They had reduced their visibility as the leaders of Purity but all of them were very much in the center of the activities the group carried out via its newest recruits. Secretly they provided guidance and funding for the various Purity activities.

The meeting that Andrew arranged with his friends was always outdoors in some park or countryside local. These were places that had few people, no cameras, and no records of credit cards.

He was surprised how easy it was for him to remain undetected.

The selection to guard Dr. Zachary Milton was an opportunity he felt was pre-ordained.

He was able to position the Purity organization as one of the most sought-after underground groups. Purity was able to sell his governmental access to the likes of Al-Qaeda and Osama bin Laden. This was a strange alignment since Purity stood against not only the US government, but all other people not considered "white." However, Purity was anti-government. and it now had a way to gain a tremendous amount of funding.

A closer association with Al-Qaeda came about because of Purity's continuing desire to blacken the eye of the US government. Al-Qaeda was willing to pay a great deal of money. This helped convince Purity this was in their best interest. They did not have to like or agree with the Moslem radicals. The money would fund Purity's anti-government effort.

Money was more important than being pure in following their beliefs.

Andrew's successes and inside information allowed Purity to enjoy information others could never get. When he was selected to guard Zachary Milton the stock of Purity went through the ceiling. They had an inside track to what all the other resistance groups desired and that these groups were willing to pay for.

Andrew had orchestrated the leak when Dr. Trimble contacted Zack about the nano-bots. He discretely misplaced the fax, so it was a couple of days before it was noticed to be missing.

Andrew had been furious when he learned Dr. Milton had escaped.

He had to stand silently by and watch as Zack brought Dr. Milton into the safety of the Savitar project.

He had failed to get others to impede the success of the Savitar project and now the moment for him to act had come. This was an action he would need to take himself.

He was going to assassinate Zack. He actually fell a sense of guilt because he had come to understand that Zack was a fair and generous person.

But he also saw the need to stop the Savitar mission as his destiny.

It would be one clean shot and then he would hasten to establish himself at his parents' home. He had made his plans to visit his parents widely known and figured he would be there quickly enough that the time element would most likely not connect him with the assassination.

It was risky but he felt in the confusion he would be able to get the blame of Zack's death placed on Janet. She was the one currently guarding him and responsible for Zack's safety.

He really had nothing personal against Zack, who he considered a square guy, but this was business. He had accepted the assassination contract for one hundred million dollars. He was not sure who was behind the money, but it did not matter. The money had been wired to his offshore account as agreed.

He figured that it gave the means to move any exotic place and enjoy a very comfortable life.

He lay and waited for Zack and Janet to come out to go jogging.

He had arranged for his replacement, Henry, to be delayed at the compound entrance by a group of demonstrators.

Henry was another front Andrew had developed. Henry was black. Andrew had selected him as a roommate when he joined the FBI to ensure his racist attitude would not be uncovered. He and Henry appeared to be the best of friends. He had recently been invited by Henry to his upcoming wedding. What a laugh.

He wanted to go to the wedding and shout out what an idiot he thought Henry was.

He would drop Henry immediately after this all cleared up.

If Henry got involved during the assassination, Andrew figured he would also take him out. Then later he would "console" his grieving wife to be. He smiled as he thought how that would put the icing on the cake.

Andrew knew he was having one of his adrenaline highs. He recalled similar feelings when he had faced Janet in their Tae Kwon Do bouts. He had come to hate her more than anyone else.

As he waited, he absently stripped the bark from a twig. The really irritating person was Janet. She was constantly pushing him and making him act in ways he did not like. He decided to shoot her as well. That would suit the bitch. She always pushed him to his limit, and it always seemed like a miracle when he came out first in their competition.

He never felt like number one around her. Her confidence always made her seem the winner. People seemed to naturally like Janet and these same people never seemed to get close to him. He always seemed doubly invisible when he and Janet were together.

His hate had slowly been getting stronger as Janet ensured Zack's safety and made it harder for him to carry out the mission he was now having to do personally.

He saw the limo Henry was driving approaching from the side street. Henry drove it into the driveway and stopped. He was talking to someone on the phone and did not get out.

He was conscious that something was different. Usually, Zack and Janet would have gone jogging first. Something slightly different was happening.

Andrew had hoped that Henry would go in and then come back out with Janet and Zack. It would have been a cinch to do all three. He knew he was fast and accurate enough to get all of them.

The timing was not the same this morning as on most mornings.

This did not concern Andrew very much.

He just wondered, "What changed the routine?"

He was calmly scanning the quarters. He saw the door opening and Zack coming out. Janet was immediately behind him. This was unusual since she always went out first.

He like the order. It would give him a clean shot.

This was it. His opportunity was at hand.

"She looks pretty good in a blue suit," Andrew thought as he looked at her through the scope.

He then moved his aim to Zack. He would first shoot him twice in the chest and then as he fell, he would shoot him in the head.

He was just squeezing the trigger when Janet took a flying leap from the porch and knocked Zack down. She was firing in Andrew's direction as she made the leap.

The sting of the bullet hitting his ear caused him to shoot high totally missing Zack and her.

He cursed as he reacted and chose to immediately leave the area. He picked up his spent cartridge and retreated through the brush. He could see Janet running toward him, zeroing in on the spot he was now hastily leaving.

He was amazed at how really good she was. He had not realized she was this good. He knew he was better, but she had won this round.

He would execute plan B.

He was in his car and out of sight and on the way to the announcement area before Janet made it to the spot of the shooting.

He would win in the next round. It was a round that he had planned as the contingent if this scenario failed. He had not planned to use it since it was personally riskier. But he figured that he could escape when the audience reacted. He would mix in with them and take off his disguise and effectively disappear.

He would walk away and make it to his parent's home and establish his alibi.

Chapter 9: Assassin

Zack opened his eyes and took in the room. His clock registered 7:00 am. He was almost an hour late. Then he realized that this was the day he would announce the final crew membership. He knew his decision to minimize the number of crew would surprise everyone and make many good people very unhappy.

He felt that he was making the right choice for the project's success. He knew he was making the right decisions and this morning he felt a sense of relief.

He hurried through his morning ritual and then pushed the button opening the hallway. Each time he did this he wondered if he ever rolled Janet or Andrew out of their beds. It never seemed the case, since by the time he got out to the outer rooms both of them would already be there making or drinking coffee. It seemed he was always the last one up.

"You're later than usual. Andrew already left for home. He said his buddy, Henry would take his place today," Janet said looking up from her cup of coffee.

She was already dressed in her blue business suit she would wear for this occasion. She would be standing next to Zack on one side acting as his aid while Andrew's replacement would be standing to his right.

"Well today is the big day. I think the two of you will really be earning your keep trying to keep me from getting shot after this meeting. Tomorrow most of the leaders of the Savitar will blast off into space. I have tried to be fair to all players. I think all of the countries and organizations involved have ended up with some representation. We have totally excluded only a few organizations, subversive in nature, as far I can figure out.

However, the President has warned me there may be some well, hidden moles. The big news for all of them will be their numbers have been greatly reduced. Additionally, I have re-organized the remaining teams to mix the players up. I am hoping to change their allegiance to the Savitar's crew and new culture," Zack rambled over his coffee.

This morning Janet was making breakfast. They each took turns doing this. This morning it was really Zack's turn, but he was totally distracted.

Janet set the eggs and toast in front of him and replied, "Well, I have watched you study the personnel files and the recommendations made by the various leaders. I am sure you have done your best to be fair and to select the best of the best.

Janet watched Zack and could tell he was really nervous. It was unusual for him to say so much about anything. Even though he would never admit it, he must be feeling the pressure of the situation.

"Well, I am trying to limit the number of us at risk and also trying to give us the best chance of surviving in the long run. I am worried that when we are successful, our mission will be abandoned," Zack admitted.

There was little he did not share with Janet and Andrew. They not only acted as his shadow but often filled in as his conscience.

This morning he was feeling a little light-headed.

"Have you considered if you are successful some group or organization will try to take over the Savitar," Janet asked.

"This point hasn't escaped me, but I haven't had the time to think it through. Would you be willing to study the possibility and get back to me on how I should prepare for such an event?

It's time we get going.

Is Henry here yet? He should have been here already," Zack said as he put his coffee cup in the sink and cleaned up his breakfast bowl and put it into the dishwasher.

Zack headed toward the front door. He was rehearsing his speech as he went out.

Janet was on the phone talking to someone on the other end.

"OK, we are on the way out," Janet said as she hung up and hurried after Zack.

"Henry is waiting out in the car. He got caught up by a demonstration going on outside the gates. Somebody leaked the fact you would be announcing a reduced crew size," Janet informed Zack as she came out behind him.

"Well, I'm surprised it didn't leak out sooner. I have never been firm on what the crew size would be. My initial estimate was between three and ten thousand," Zack replied.

"Let's get to the center and get this over with," Zack continued as he walked across the porch.

Janet came out behind Zack and was looking around uneasily. Suddenly she realized a red spot was traveling down her body

She instantly ran and leaped feet first toward Zack.

As she flew through the air, she drew and fired her gun in the direction she sensed the laser beam had originated.

She caught Zack square in the back and sent him hurdling into the side of the car with enough force to cave in the side panel. She hoped she had not broken any of his bones.

She fired two more times on the run. She was running in the direction she sensed to be the location of the laser beam. She hoped to survive her charge by firing. She ran out of ammo as she got to the spot she figured had been used by the shooter. She reloaded.

As Zack was walking down the porch stairs, he was suddenly hit by something from behind knocking the breath out of him and hurling him toward the side of the car. He was able to spin around so that he hit the car with his shoulder first and felt the panel caving in. Then he was on the ground by the side of the car. He realized almost immediately Janet had pushed him down with a foot to his back and started firing as she did so.

Henry was immediately out of the car and pulled Zack closer to the car and told him to stay put. Henry ran around the car and went into the woods to the right of where Janet had entered.

Zack looked cautiously around the end of the car. He caught a glimpse of Janet going through the brush. There was no sight of Henry. He heard the brush and snap of twigs as the two made their way into the empty lot across from their quarters.

The morning air was fresh, cool and the sky overhead was a deep clear blue. He hoped the shooter would not show up as he lay helplessly in the shadow of the limo.

At the moment, he really thought would like to have a weapon. Even in this situation he found a glimmer of humor in what he was thinking. If they let him have a gun, he would probably be more of a danger to himself then to his assailant.

The moment etched itself in his mind and he chuckled as he envisioned himself ineptly trying to fend off an attacker in a shootout.

He suddenly had a greater appreciation of how much Janet meant to him. He checked himself over and decided he was alright. He would probably have a bruise in the shape of Janet's shoe in the middle of his back.

Janet thought she knew the location of the sniper. She went slightly to the left of where she thought the sniper would be. She didn't expect to find anyone, but she needed to make certain. She heard someone to her right where she thought Henry would be.

The cool clear air of the morning helped her regain her composure. Her adrenaline was putting energy, quickness, and an elevated sharpness into her actions. Her movement was calculated as she cautiously made her way to the location where she thought the shot originated.

She and Henry came together on the spot at the same time.

"I'll check this out. You get back to Zack. Get him down in the back seat and keep him safe until I return," Janet said with a voice of authority.

Without a word Henry turned in the direction of the car. He had not expected any action. So far, the morning was going totally wrong. He was still recovering from a verbal disagreement with his fiancée the night before.

Andrew had informed him in the middle of an ongoing argument of needing to be on duty this morning. This had been effective in ending the argument but not in settling it.

Then this morning, demonstrators at the gate had stopped and surrounded his car. It had caused him to be late. He had hoped the rest of the day would be better.

Now he knew it would be hell. He knew that he was about to be put on desk duty as the investigation into this assassination attempt went into full swing.

Janet cautiously approached the site where she thought the shot had been fired. All her senses were heightened. She smelled the air. Slowly and methodically, she scanned the ground. She stayed outside of the actual spot of where she though the shot had been fired.

There was a clear view of the car, the porch and she could see Henry getting Zack into the car.

The morning was now quiet and still.

She heard the chirping of a bird off to her left. This had been a professional job. Nothing had been left behind.

Janet was turning to leave when she noticed a small, discarded twig. The bark was peeled in a familiar pattern. The person made to waited here had been nervous and had been made to wait longer than expected. He had broken a twig and pulled off strips of bark from it. He had created a pattern; one off, the next section left on, the next off and so forth.

A chill went through her as she realized who the shooter was. She looked quickly around and over her shoulder. She pulled out her phone and placed a call as she hurried back to the house. She went inside and got a picture she knew she would need.

Janet went out and got into the car. She apologized for having kicked Zack in the back. She then told him that she wanted him to sit on the floor and stay out of sight.

"Zack, I want you to sit on the floor and keep your head down," Janet instructed.

"Stay down until we get you to the Auditorium. If you see Andrew, get away immediately. I think he was waiting out in the bush. I have called this in, and they are checking to determine where he is," Janet quietly informed Zack.

Henry muttered, "You have got to be kidding!"

"I can't believe he would do such a thing," Zack said looking up at Janet's grim face.

He could not picture Andrew in the role of an assassin. They were all friends. They had been inseparable for more than a year.

"I can't either. But who ever sat out there waiting for you stripped the bark off of a twig in the same pattern that Andrew does when he is nervous or when he waits. It's a small signature but we can't take a chance until he is cleared," Janet said with dread in her voice.

She was almost certain Andrew had been in the woods. It was just too much of a coincidence that he would be visiting his family when this attack occurred.

"How could he have been so obvious," she thought to herself.

Chapter 10: Stage Assassin

Janet got into the car and looked back where Zack was sitting on the floor.

"Once we get to the auditorium you stay in the car," she said looking at him.

She then instructed Henry to drive at a normal pace to the auditorium.

The car made it to the auditorium without incident.

Janet was in the role of protector and was in full control of all those around her.

She got out and got four marines positioned around the car. She asked Henry to get out of the car and tasked two other marines to escort Henry away to be turned over to the FBI. She did not think Henry had anything to do with the shooting, but she knew Henry had been Andrew's roommate and friend.

"Henry, I will apologize to you later when you are cleared but right now, I will not take any chances," Janet quietly informed him.

"Hey, I understand. If you think Andrew is the shooter, then I will be the first to be suspected along with him. It fits how the day started out. Good Luck." Henry replied as he was led away.

"Zack, please stay put until I get things arranged," Janet quietly instructed him as she opened the back door to talk to him as he remained seated on the floor.

Zack knew better than to argue with her when she took on the presence she now exuded.

This was a side of her that he had not experienced before.

"I picked this one well," he thought.

Janet was talking to a Marine Colonel. She took out a photograph and handed it to him. After about fifteen minutes of discussion and what Zack took as instructions, Janet approached with four more marines. These were big, tall marines. They were all at least four to six inches taller than Zack.

They took up tight positions immediately around him. The other four led the way with weapons drawn and at the ready. They were looking in the rafters and any elevated position giving a shooter the ability to target them.

High in the auditorium on one of the lighting walkways, Andrew was looking down realizing his plan for a shot from his vantage point was going to be impossible. He would wait until Zack was on stage to make his speech.

He was now moving on to plan C.

He realized that Janet had taken the exact precautions he would have had he been trying to protect Zack.

She was good. He wished that she was just not so good.

"Zack, I have alerted everyone about this situation. A bulletproof shield will be put around the podium. The back of the stage is being combed to make sure no one is back there.

The FBI will soon be here in mass. Until then, I have a contingent of Marines spreading out around the auditorium.

Let's get the program started. I think you are not on for another forty-five minutes. Originally you were to be on stage but now I would like you to wait with me in a secure area," Janet said as she opened the door to a lounge area behind the stage.

The leading four Marines entered rifles at the ready as if there might be someone dangerous inside. After receiving an all clear the four marines immediately around Zack pushed him into the room and entered behind him.

Janet closed the door behind her as she took one last look around outside.

Zack sat down and reviewed his speech and the message he was going to deliver to the world and more specifically to the people who had been working so hard on the Savitar.

Periodically he would look up and watch Janet as she paced back and forth as she spoke into her cell phone.

He had not seen Henry since their arrival and wondered where he had gone.

A few minutes later there was a knock on the door. Zack cringed as all the marines turned and brought their weapons to bear on the door.

"Please enter with your hands in the air. Come into the center of the room and remain there until you are instructed otherwise," Janet said in a voice of authority.

Four men in black suits entered as instructed. Janet searched each one and took their weapons and gave them to a one of the marines.

She then examined each of their badges.

"Jesus, Janet, it's us," one of the agents said.

"Yes, and Andrew is one of us. Have you found out where he is?" Janet replied as she told them to put their hands down but not to reach for anything.

She had made the impression she had wanted to make.

"I'm sorry, Janet but he did not go home to his family. He is the current top suspect. I agree with you about your security. He was one of best," the oldest of the four spoke.

"The arrangements you made with the Marines are more than adequate and well thought out. We will take up positions outside the auditorium as you have requested. Our internal control unit is in full swing. This will be hell for all of us until they check each of our records and clear us.

You sure have stirred the pot and poked the hornet's nest at the same time. Do you think this situation is that serious?" he continued.

"Fred, Zack is the key to the success of this mission. If it fails, Earth is doomed. You tell me if this is serious," Janet snapped back.

She could feel the beads of sweat on the back of her neck. She was upset at herself for not having paid more attention to Andrew and for not learning more about him. How could she have missed such a threat?

She would not let it happen again.

Zack had never seen Janet in this mode of operation. He realized he had chosen well as far as she was concerned. There was no give in her at the moment. He was surprised at her total command of the situation and her ultimate concern for his safety.

"I guess I missed with Andrew. I hope fifty per cent selection hit record will be good enough for me to win," he thought as he returned his thoughts to what he would say.

"Fred, you stay with us and keep us in contact with what the agency is doing. The rest of you join the group outside the auditorium. Carefully pick up your weapons and holster them. You can reload once you are outside. Please no sudden moves. Those Marines have orders to shoot." Janet instructed her peers quietly as she handed them back their weapons with one hand and their bullet cartridges with the other.

"Fred, I am holding onto your weapon until later. I will return it to you if anything breaks out. I hope this doesn't affect my raise," Janet said with a chuckle as she handed the lone gun and ammo to one of the marines.

"Yea, it probably will. You're in the right place, at the right time and you have taken the right action. I figure you will be bumped up to be my boss," Fred replied with a chuckle as he walked casually over to the coffee pot and poured himself a cup.

His actions helped release some of the tension in the room.

I recruited this young lady. Told the agency she was one of the best I had ever seen. She showed great potential. Then she volunteered for this job. I told her it would sidetrack her career. Little did I know," Fred said as he sipped his coffee and looked around the room.

The phone rang and Janet listened quietly.

"Zack it's time to get you out to the stage. I want you to immediately get behind the bulletproof screen. If I say "down," I want you to immediately drop down flat on your stomach. Do you understand," Janet said as she took hold of Zack's arm and looked at him with her troubled, now almost steel gray eyes.

"Janet, right now I am more afraid of getting you upset with me then of Andrew out there with a rifle. He doesn't have a clue what he is up against. Thanks, and I will do whatever you tell me. " Zack replied giving her a hug.

"Thanks for the vote of confidence but Andrew outperformed me in every drill we did at the academy," Janet confided.

She searched her mind for what more she could do to protect Zack before they went out on stage.

"Fred, are you wearing a bullet proof vest?" Janet said as she turned to look at him.

"Yes, its standard procedure," Fred replied.

"Please take it off and give it to Zack. If you want, you can stay off stage in the wings. But I need the extra insurance for Zack," Janet commanded.

"OK, kid. I will stay in the wings. It will give me a better view of the crowd any way," Fred said as he peeled off his suit jacket and then removed the bulletproof Kevlar vest.

Once Zack had the bulletproof vest on, they marched out to the stage and Zack immediately got behind the bulletproof screen. He didn't think Andrew would dare attack while he was on stage.

It would be suicide.

Andrew meanwhile was in place. No one suspected or guessed at his current disguise. His hair now black with grey edges and his beard provided the perfect disguise. He had recognized this opportunity several weeks ago when the attendees on stage had been identified. He was currently dressed in traditional Indian garb effectively hiding his revolver and silencer. The real Indian representative was incapacitated and hidden in a supply closet nearby.

Andrew was somewhat surprised at the change in the proceedings. Janet was indeed wise in trying to limit the window of opportunity. He had thought through this situation and felt he was one step ahead of her. He was ready. He was calm and had the same feeling he always had just before a critical contest or challenge. He watched as Zack finally approached the podium to stand behind the bulletproof glass.

Chapter 11: The Shot that Mattered

"Ladies and gentlemen, the world has risen to face the daunting challenge affecting our very survival. Our resources have been pooled and we have co-operated on a scale never before achieved in the history of mankind. In the next two years the means of our salvation…"

Suddenly, for the second time that day Zack was hit from behind and knocked to the floor. This time however it felt different than when Janet had knocked him down.

"Dam, I didn't hear Janet tell me to drop," Zack thought as he fell to the floor and was immediately jumped on. His face was pinned sideways, and he could not determine who was on top of him.

Andrew quickly drew his pistol equipped with a silencer and shot Zack twice in the middle of the back. He was about to shoot him in the head when Janet knocked Zack down the rest of the way to the floor and sat on his back.

She aimed her weapon at the shooter at the other side of the podium.

"Finally, I am going to get you bitch," Andrew thought as he shot her several times in the chest.

To his surprise she did not go down. He raised his aim to her forehead and pulled the trigger.

A single marine launched himself in front of Janet and the bullet meant for her struck him instead.

Everything was progressing around Janet in what she knew was her adrenaline high, slow motion world. She saw Andrew stand up and fire. At the same time, she pulled Zack down and jumped on his back to protect his head. She felt each bullet hit her in the chest and one rip through her arm. She knew she was about to die but was determined to get her replying shot in.

She had her gun sight on Andrew's forehead.

She saw the marine jump in front of her.

Janet squeezed the trigger and Andrew's world came to an end as her bullet found his forehead and went through, taking his life with it as it exited cleanly out the back of his head.

Andrew's last thought was one of surprise. She had out done him! Then the world went black.

There was an oohing from the crowd, and they heard gunfire and one of the guests on stage went down in a shower of bullets. The guests around the target all fell to the floor and covered themselves.

Someone was straddling his back and Zack couldn't get up. There was blood dripping on his face. Zack rolled and Janet collapsed on the floor besides him. He got up slowly feeling as if someone had kicked him in the back. However, seeing Janet bleeding seemed to kick in the adrenaline he needed.

He quickly applied pressure to the spot where blood was pulsing from her arm. There was a big hole in her blouse, and she was having trouble breathing. In a moment of fright, he tore open her blouse and then realized she had been hit three times in the chest, but her bulletproof vest had stopped the bullets. She was having trouble breathing but she would be all right. She had been hit at total of four times!

One of the Marine guards was down as well and was being attended to by another Marine. The downed Marine seemed to be wounded in the arm.

Janet opened her eyes.

"You are going to be OK," Zack said quietly to her and gave her a peck on the cheek.

"Andrew?" Janet managed to whisper her question.

Zack looked across the stage to where Fred was examining a person Zack assumed must be Andrew. Fred just shook his head and pointed to his own forehead with a cocked finger to indicate where Andrew had been hit.

"I think he is dead," Zack told Janet.

The ambulance and the medics arrived and one of them moved Zack aside.

"We will take over now," one of them politely told Zack.

Zack moved aside but did not want to let go of Janet's hand.

Zack was still in a state of confusion and was not sure of everything that was happening. He knew but yet he could not make any sense of what had just happened. It was like being in a dream taking a bad uncontrolled turn.

He kept telling himself, "It will be alright when I wake up."

"Zack, I'm afraid I will have to move you back into the lounge until we get this reorganized. I have given instructions to reschedule this event to 1:00 this afternoon," Fred said as he watched Janet getting wheeled off. They watched as she was taken by one group of medics to an ambulance and the Marine was taken to another one.

Fred walked quickly over and said a few words to her and then came back.

"I don't know what you did to make her so loyal to you, but that young lady saved your life. The four shots she took in the chest were meant for the back of your head. I don't know how she managed to get her shot off, but Andrew took her one shot in the forehead," Fred said as he led Zack and seven of the eight Marines back to the lounge.

The missing marine had been wounded when he had jumped in front of Janet to protect her.

Much later in conversation with Janet, she would credit the young Marine with giving her a chance to get her one shot off. If it hadn't been for his help, they both would probably have been killed.

Andrew had been that good. Too bad he had been on the other side, whatever side that was. Zack was not sure what or who Andrew represented and at the moment, and neither did the FBI

"Well, I would like to get my bullet proof vest back. We will arrange for you to have your own for this afternoon," Fred said as they got into the lounge.

Zack began to take off his jacket when Fred muttered, "Jesus."

And took Zack's sports jacket and put his finger through a two-inch hole in the middle of the back. Zack peeled off his bulletproof vest and there stuck to the fabric were two flattened .215-millimeter bullets. They were each the size of a nickel.

"My god, if Janet hadn't made you put on my bulletproof jacket, you would be a dead man at this moment," Fred whistled as he examined Zack's back.

"As it is you are going have one heck of a bruise. Lay down. Tomorrow you are going to feel like a mule kicked you. He turned to the group of Marines and asked that one of them get me some ice and get a doctor to come back here and examine Dr. Milton," Fred instructed the Marines.

Zack followed instruction and lay down on the couch. It was not long before he was asleep. These days, anytime his body got in a horizontal position and lay still, it fell asleep.

Zack awoke a little later as he felt someone feeling the bruise on his back. He could feel the stiffness already setting in. When Zack looked at the clock, he saw about forty-five minutes had gone by.

"Well, other than being a little stiff, I don't believe you will have any ill effects. This looks bigger than bullet marks. Did you get kicked as well?" the doctor asked. "It was a good idea to put on the ice. Now put some heat on it. I have a patch to heat up your back for the next several hours. Then I recommend a hot bath, an aspirin if you feel any discomfort and a good night's sleep," the doctor gave his prognosis looking at Fred as if Fred were Zack's father.

"Thanks, doc," Zack said as he sat up.

"How is Janet?" he asked looking at Fred.

"She is going to be alright. She lost some blood because the bullet hit an artery in her arm. You did the right thing putting pressure on the wound. She just underwent surgery to fix the artery and should be up and about by tomorrow," Fred replied.

"Will she heal soon enough to get out in space with me?" Zack thought selfishly to himself, but he did not say anything to anyone.

He felt a sudden fear. He could no longer imagine a day without Janet somewhere nearby.

Lunch consisted of sandwiches and a diet coke brought in by one of the Marines.

Zack figured that a sandwich and a coke was just what he needed.

The Marines were all animated and excited about having been in on the action. It was obvious why they were Marines. They had reacted immediately and aided Janet in cutting Andrew down. Their barrage of gunfire, though after the fact, would have taken Andrew down if Janet had missed.

At one o'clock Zack once again was back on stage. As promised, he had his own bullet proof vest. He stood on the stage with four Marines behind him. Fred was backstage directing events.

"If I can get that young lady healed fast enough, I may end up with a promotion yet," Fred chuckled to himself as he organized the security for the rest of the day.

"Ladies and gentlemen, I began this speech earlier in the day and I was praising the people on Earth for working together. As we all now know, a few radical elements do not approve of what we, the people of Earth have decided to undertake.

The Savitar crew promises to move the obstacle threatening Earth and our solar system. To do this we have undertaken the greatest concerted effort the human race has ever cooperated on and achieved.

We have assembled a cage with which to capture a black hole. Luckily for us, it is a very small black hole. Even so it will take all our skill and ingenuity to put this genie into the bottle. The Savitar team will capture this black hole and move it, so it poses no harm to the Earth or any other planet of our solar system.

I have had the privilege to work with thousands of dedicated and extremely capable people who have directly been out in space assembling the Savitar. There are untold thousands more all around the globe, who have labored in building the elements making up this glorious spaceship. The world on the whole has contributed the resources making this voyage possible. To everyone, let me personally give you a sincere thank you for a job well done.

Today, I am announcing the final crew, member list. The crew will be smaller than originally estimated. Determining the size of this crew has been difficult. Its final size is just slightly larger than my initial estimate but less than has been talked about publicly.

My immediate leadership team and I have struggled with this, and we have opted for the smaller crew in hopes this gives us the necessary leeway in the resources required to protect the lives of the crew and the success of the mission.

I know for many, who have volunteered to go out into space with the Savitar, not being selected will be a disappointment. To all of you, I am deeply thankful. What you have already contributed will be noted. A monument, with all your names, has been approved and will be erected on the commons of the Capital of the United States and similar commemorations will be erected in each of the participant countries. Your names will go down in history. You will not be forgotten.

This same monument will have on it the names of the crew of Savitar. These names are being posted on the internet as I speak. There are three thousand, nine hundred, ninety-nine names on this list.

For a reason I do not yet know the four thousandth person was the one shot and killed here on stage this morning.

He was, I thought, a friend. God rest his soul.

The Savitar will get underway in the next two months. The selected crew will have one last opportunity to meet with friends and family and then they will be sent up to the Savitar. The leadership team and a few of the crew already had this opportunity. They are awaiting their crewmates up on the Savitar and getting everything ready for departure.

What more can I say? A prayer would be best, I believe. In the names of all of our religions, I ask our one God to guide us, to give us the strength, to give us the wisdom and to make the outcome a success. I have the confidence the selected Savitar team is blessed and will successfully carry out this mission.

Thank you and good day.

Indira was a little surprised. She had been in on the reviews of the crew staffing cuts. However, every time a cut came, another one of the people on her personal list of take over accomplices was removed. She was now down to just a few people.

After listening to each of the leaders, Zack always made the selection by himself. His choices were final. She tried a couple of times to change his mind and had quickly realized she could not do so.

After the presentation, Zack had to endure another hour of questions and discussion from the press. The focus not so surprisingly was on the shooting. This was a silver lining to an otherwise sad day for Zack. He was glad the distraction had occurred because so many questions about pay load and specific resources, all of public record did not get asked.

"Fred, this evening, I am to be at a dinner at the White House. How is Janet and will she be able to make it?" Zack asked almost sure the answer would be no.

"Well, I am not sure whether she feels well enough for an evening at the White House, but she insisted on being released from the hospital and is at your quarters. I guess you can ask her when you get there. By the way I really liked your speech," Fred said with a tone of respect.

He had not thought much about the effort being mounted but the events of the day had crystallized his position.

He was now an ardent supporter.

Zack was riding in a Marine hum-vee with the seven Marines who had refused to leave him. They said Janet had given them strict orders to keep him safe and they would protect him until she relieved them. By this time, they had heard the eighth Marine, who had been shot, was doing well. The bullet hit him on his bullet proof vest but had deflected and lodged in his arm muscle. He would no doubt be recognized for his unselfish bravery.

As they arrived at Zack's living quarters, Fred spoke up once again, "Well you have gotten the attention of the brass. I am not sure who is at your place, but they are all high up. It is probably the Director of the FBI.

I probably won't be speaking to you again so let me wish you luck," Fred said giving Zack a handshake.

The Marines jumped out first and took up their positions around Zack. They were met by the General of the Marine Corps.

"Well done, Marines," he said with a salute. "I understand you are working under the direct orders of a certain young lady named Janet Romero and that you promised to guard Mr. Milton with your lives.

She is inside and thanks you and releases you of this duty. You will notice your comrades have a perimeter set up around this place. I will escort Mr. Milton into his home. You will remain here and relax until I return. At ease," the general boomed as he led Zack up the stairs into the building.

Fred followed quietly behind.

The first thing Zack saw as he entered was Janet sitting in the easy chair having a cup of tea chatting with the director of the FBI.

A feeling of relief swept over him. The calm sweeping through him was the feeling he had experienced long ago while out in the Idaho wilderness. He remembered sitting on a fallen tree trunk peering down into the valley as the clouds parted and the sun's rays cut through and illuminated the valley below him. A large bull elk had walked into the clearing and stopped and looked him in the eyes. Zack could almost hear the voice of God. It was the last day Zack hunted with a gun. He knew he was destined to protect not harm the creatures of the Earth.

Now he saw Janet through a new light coming from his heart.

Zack walked over and gave her a gentle hug.

"Thanks for saving my life," he said to a hushed audience.

"She has made the FBI proud. She just turned down a job being my assistant. She says she has the job she wants already. What is your secret Zack?" the director joked with him.

The Director and Zack were actually on first name basis. They had spent many hours working together going over the security risks that various personnel might pose.

"Well Bill, it must be the attention because you control her pay, and as this day has shown I certainly seem to be drawing the attention," Zack jokingly replied.

"By the way, Fred over there is looking for a better job. He has said something about needing to feed his family. Maybe you can consider the old man to be your assistant. Oh, and by the way, I owe him for a new bulletproof vest. He loaned me his and he got it back with a bullet hole in the back. Can you do something in this area," Zack continued as he put his hand through the hole in the back of his jacket. Zack looked over to where Fred was looking totally aghast and gave him a wink.

"Thanks for all the attention. Are you all going to be at the White House dinner? I need to get ready for this event.

How do you feel, Janet, can you make it as my date?

I am sure Bill will spring for some other bodyguards," Zack said as he looked at his watch.

"Are you asking me out on a date in front of my boss?" Janet said in mock horror.

Zack was glad to see she was at least in good spirits. His back was feeling sore from the two bullets and her kick in the back. He could only image how she felt after being hit by three bullets in the chest and one in her arm.

"Yes, I guess, I am. What's your answer?" Zack replied.

"How many girls get an invitation for a night out at the White House? I would go if I had to crawl. I will see what I have suitable to wear," Janet replied.

Chapter 12: White House Party

About thirty minutes later, after a hot shower and a couple of aspirin, Zack walked back out in his tuxedo. He was greeted by two, blond, blue-eyed men in black. Bill was still there and made the introductions. This is Larry and Samuel. They are part of the President's security and will serve as bodyguards for both of you until you go up to the Savitar.

"By the way, what happened to Henry?" Zack asked.

"He is getting checked out. He was Andrew's roommate until Andrew became your bodyguard." Fred spoke up.

"Well, if he clears the check, and if Janet agrees, you can offer him a job with me," Zack said.

After making a call he let Zack know that he had done some quick checking and said that Henry thanked Zack for the offer but was married in about a month. So, he sends you, his regrets.

He reminded Zack that Janet and Andrew each had a backup incase anything happened. They are space ready and eager to go. I am having both of them extensively checked and will let you know when you can re-interview them. Is this OK with you?" Bill asked as if Zack had another choice.

Janet and Andrew had been training to be the security leaders for the trip. Andrew would certainly need to be replaced. Zack had interviewed the two backups and was familiar with them and felt comfortable with their capabilities.

"I stayed behind to escort you and Janet to the White House. My wife will meet me there. Orders of the big boss and I don't mean my wife," Bill continued.

Just then Janet walked in, and the room became quiet.

"Wow, I didn't realize my bodyguard dressed up so beautifully," Zack said as he jumped up to greet Janet. She was wearing a long black dress with a high neckline. Long black gloves covered her arms. The long glove for her right arm had been made large enough to go over her bandages. The sling for her arm was made of the same fabric as the dress. Janet wore earrings with a large diamond dangling from a gold chain and a similar necklace with a very large diamond dangling from a gold collar around her neck. Stunning was a good description for her appearance.

"Whoever picked this out has great taste and knew exactly what I would need in my condition," Janet said as she slowly turned around.

"The outfit comes from Danti's and was arranged by my wife. The outfit is compliments of the company. The earrings and diamond necklace are on loan from Danti's. I figured Janet would be able to put in an appearance. If you hadn't asked her, I would have had to. Orders from the boss," Bill said with a chuckle.

For the first time Zack was speechless and just put out his right arm for Janet to hold on to as they proceeded to the door.

When they arrived at the White House, they were escorted into the Roosevelt room. There a crowd of dignitaries from around the world greeted them. They gathered around Janet, offered her a chair, and politely demanded a firsthand account of the events of the day.

Zack quietly moved away from the group and fetched a glass of wine for Janet. After giving her a glass, he again faded out of the group. He was intercepted by one of the President's men.

"Pardon me sir, the President would like to talk to you in private," he said politely.

His two guards were at his side by this time. They nodded to each other, and Zack took this to mean it was safe to follow.

The President was sitting behind his desk going over some papers when Zack was escorted in.

"Well, from what I understand, you are a very lucky person," the President said as he walked around and shook hands.

"I don't think luck has anything to do with it. Janet Romero deserves all the credit. She saved me twice today. Her thoroughness and intuition are why I am alive," Zack replied as they shook hands.

"Did she take the promotion Bill offered her?" the President asked.

"No, she chose to stay on the mission as my bodyguard. I don't know how to repay her," Zack replied.

"Well, the arrangements she requested for her family have been made. She figured she wouldn't need her pay out in space, so she set up a trust fund. Several generous people have contributed significant amounts to it. When you return, she will never need to work again." President Lansing shared.

"I am glad to hear this. I know her family was not close, but she always felt she should somehow help them out. This will help her conscience about leaving them. She knows the likelihood of returning is very slim," Zack responded.

"I understand you spent some time with your family in the last couple of days. Are you set to go?" the President asked politely.

"Yes, I have created a trust as well. This will provide support for emergencies, and education for family members. I think the trust has enough to last so my great grand something or other will benefit," Zack replied.

"You will be under very tight security; as tight as my own, maybe tighter. I just wanted to give you, my sympathy. You won't be able to go to the bathroom without someone checking it out first. You will have someone in your room sitting up at night. I am sorry but we can't take any more chances.

Janet will remain with you, but she too will be under her own security. She will probably find this harder than you will since she will not be in control. You will need to help her get through the next couple of weeks," the President continued.

"I know you have culled the list of crew members and selected the ones you think are the best. I wanted you to know I am having a final look at each member you selected. If my team finds even a few unaccounted moments in their past, we will pull them. We will not replace them. The first priority is to determine if there are any other potential moles. I wanted you to know this firsthand. There is no room to negotiate. These are my orders. Now let's go and be politely bored," the President said as he escorted Zack back to the party.

Zack went out to the reception. He was approached by several dignitaries and made small talk.

A little later Janet approached him, "Zack, I hate to be a poor date, but my arm and chest is killing me. I feel like one big throbbing bruise. I need to go home," Janet confided quietly as she leaned on his arm.

"Good, I have a great pain in the back where someone kicked me. It is just calling for me to lie down," Zack said as he chuckled and escorted her over to where the President and his wife stood.

They explained the situation and said good night, thanked both of them and then followed their guards out of the White House.

"There go two people meant for each other. I hope they figure that out very soon," the President's wife observed as Zack and Janet walked out.

Chapter 13: Susan and Mitch

£ike a tidal wave hitting the shore, the upheaval at the agency immediately swept over Susan and Mitch. They were caught off guard and unprepared for the onslaught.

Andrew's actions shocked them.

The fact one of their own had had tried to kill the person they were to protect was unprecedented.

The entire organization was under scrutiny. The internal security division was in full swing. They were putting everyone through new background checks. A massive security evaluation of every individual was underway. No one was going to escape the scrutiny and the after the fact thoroughness check.

It was the old "the cow's out of the barn, run, hurry close the barn door," drill.

Susan and Mitch had experienced a constant see-saw in their feelings about being the backups for Janet and Andrew. They had discussed the fact they would fill these back up roles only if the worst happened to two people, they both admired. The situation they found themselves in was beyond what they could ever have imagined. It was the worst possible way for this opportunity to present itself.

They were the first to undergo the scrutiny of the internal security team.

They were treated as if they had conspired to get the opportunity and had somehow contributed to the assassination attempt. They underwent a week of psychological exams and interviews. Their friends, family and acquaintances were questioned as well. They were interviewed separately and together. They were accused of wanting the situation to happen. They were turned inside out and were not sure how they fared.

At the end of the week, they were told they had been cleared for their roles.

Susan was happy for Mitch since she saw him as Andrew's natural replacement. However, they were both to be interviewed for the replacement position. She held little hope for herself. It had been a surprise two women had been picked by Drs. Milton and Garrity in their first selection of bodyguards.

The selection of Andrew's replacement was different. It was now common knowledge Janet had turned down a promotion to director to stay on the mission. They both knew that Zack and Janet got along great. It only made sense to Susan that the replacement would be Mitch.

She would be a long shot to be selected.

Mitch was not sure about the opportunity now presenting itself. He certainly wanted to be on the mission and yet the situation was different than a few months ago. His personal feelings for Susan had grown and he was not sure he wanted to leave her. He felt he was the natural replacement for Andrew, and he was eager to be picked but was totally conflicted.

"So why the doubt," he wondered to himself.

"Well, he thought, let's see how the interview goes. The situation may be the other way around. Susan may get picked and I will be left behind by myself," Mitch thought to himself.

Susan and Mitch had known each other since Burlington High School in Iowa. They had not dated each other but had been on the student council at the same time. They had the same councilor, and both ended up going to the University of Iowa. They were constantly surprised to be in many of the same classes. They attended many parties where they saw each other while at U of I but never dated each other.

They were hometown, high school friends. They began kidding each other when they found out they were both seeking the same degree. Later they both went to work for the FBI. They became very good friends. Each of them dated other people but no lasting relationships ever came about. Neither had thought of the other in romantic terms. They were just friends.

When Dr's Milton and Garrity were interviewing for bodyguards, both of them volunteered and were interviewed. When they saw Janet and Andrew come in to be interviewed both had moaned and given consolation to each other. They knew competition had reached the highest level. They had experienced the intensity Janet put into her physical training. She was a very likable person but when you competed against her you competed against one of the best. And Andrew, though quiet had always beaten what seemed an unbeatable Janet.

Susan and Mitch were not surprised at the final selection, nor were they upset.

They were surprised when they were called in and informed that they would both be in shadow training to replace anyone that dropped out for any reason. Both would have loved to have been selected to the primary positions but at least they had been selected as backup. It helped that they both felt they were backups to the best and it kept them close to the game.

The selection meant they participated in all training and took part in many of the project reviews. They would stay current on what was happening with the project. They were like the extras on a jury. They were glad to remain so close to this once in a lifetime event.

They approached their new assignment with purpose and keen intensity.

They especially got to know Janet well. They admired Janet for her thoroughness, determination, and energy level.

They became friends with her because Janet treated them as equals and kept them informed of many of the details they would otherwise have missed. Janet took the time to get to personally know them by going out to dinner and once to the state fair. They had also periodically shared lunch together with her and Zack at Janet's invitation.

There had been little time for any of them to socialize.

Andrew's absence in these outings now seemed to be so obvious but at the time he always found a good excuse of why he could not join them.

During the months of their shadowing activities both Susan and Mitch began to see each other in a more personal way. Since they were work partners, they were each hesitant about changing this relationship and decided to wait until the Savitar was underway and their roles as backup over.

As they reviewed the events of the assassination attempt, they realized just how good at shooting Andrew had been. He had fired seven times before being shot in the temple by Janet's one and only shot.

Thoroughness, ultimate tenacity, and teamwork had been what Janet used to overcome Andrew's personal advantage. Janet organized the Marines, alerted the bureau, erected bullet proof glass, and put Zack in a bullet proof vest. The speed of her reaction had saved Zack. Her bullet proof vest and the heroic action of one of the Marines allowed her to get her one winning shot, even as she was hit four times. This was an example of planning, instant response and teamwork and pure courage at its very best.

Susan and Mitch spent most of the next few days gathering all the data about the assassination attempt and analyzing the actions Janet had taken.

They asked each other, "Would we have done as well? Would we have spotted the one clue identifying Andrew as the assassin?"

Probably not, Janet was the only one who knew Andrew so well.

Wow, to have out done Andrew on two separate assassination attempts. How had she been warned about the first attempt? How had she reacted so quickly to protect Zack?

On the second attempt she had literally placed her body over Zack as a shield.

Susan commented that Janet had shown them a standard of protection duty that would be hard to measure up to. How would they have compared?

They commented to each other about their own probable failure to save Zack.

They gave all the credit to Janet.

Now, after a grueling week, they were walking down what seemed to be an extra-long corridor to the interview room. They were both mentally exhausted from the intensive interrogations and the detailed analysis of the assassination event during the week. They were both nervous about the upcoming interview with Zack. They had wished each other good luck.

Unspoken, they both had reached a common conclusion. Neither would accept the job unless the other was also accepted. However, neither had expressed this to the other because both recognized if they did, they would change their relationship of being very good friends to something more important. In the business they were in they were not sure they could afford to do so and still be effective. Also, they did not want to influence the choice one of them must make.

Zack had been uncharacteristically quiet throughout the morning. For the last week, both he and Janet had been guarded by some of the Presidents security personnel. Janet found this situation a little frustrating. She was not in control and yet she felt it was her job to protect Zack.

For the last few days Zack had become quiet. She knew from her close association with him for the last year this meant he was trying to reach a decision he thought was important. She wondered what the decision might be and why Zack was not sharing it with her.

She wished he would discuss whatever it was with her, but she kept quiet. Since the assassination he had treated her in a soft and concerned manner.

She wished he would stop this behavior.

Zack meanwhile had been contemplating asking both Susan and Mitch, but he was not sure how Janet would react to having him select another woman.

He decided to wait until the interview of the two backups before bringing up his idea.

If Janet had a negative reaction to this idea, he would not make the offer.

Zack and Janet sat in the interview room waiting.

Craig was not part of the interview process. He felt making the backup selection was none of his business. He wanted to give Zack his own space.

Janet had a strong opinion and would have shared it if Zack would have given her a chance, but she kept quiet.

It was his decision, and she did not want to put pressure on him.

This was the first day Janet felt halfway normal.

After the party at the White House, she had returned to their quarters. Once the adrenaline from the day's excitement wore off, the pain in her arm and chest kept her awake for the rest of the night. The next few days were painful. She did not take her pain pills but did take many aspirin. Her bruises were now going yellow and black.

Her arm wound was healing so well she could barely see the scar. Her surgeons had been the best and had done a marvelous job in the repair. She smiled as she thought of her doctors. They had been like doting fathers worried about the beauty of their daughter.

Thanks to the care she was receiving, she would be able to go into space in the next few weeks.

"I would like your opinion on this interview," Zack said as they got to the interview room.

"Well, what would you like an opinion on?" Janet replied casually as her heart raced.

She was not sure why, but she was really nervous. She sat down immediately because she felt a little faint.

She had hoped to be asked about the interview.

"Well, we have lost Andrew and the President sent me a note yesterday there were several hundred people he and the intelligence agencies are planning to cut. I'm not sure of the exact number but this gives us quite a bit of latitude.

Why don't we recruit both Susan and Mitch?" Zack said as he watched Janet's face.

He wanted to read her reaction. If it was negative, he would quickly back up.

"I think we have been together too long. I wanted to propose this exact idea. They have trained with us and have demonstrated high capabilities. We all seem to get along well. I also know they are close friends maybe even more," Janet replied as an instant warm feeling went through her.

At this moment, her respect and feelings for Zack went up to a new level. She felt more connected to him than ever before. Tears were welling in her eyes.

Zack smiled and replied that he would ask both to be the replacements.

After a light knock at the door, Mitch and Susan walked in. There was a moment of silence as the two parties looked at each other.

As she looked at Janet, Susan immediately sensed something important had just been shared between her and Zack.

Susan looked at Mitch and gave a brief smile.

Susan was feeling a little faint and could hardly stand to shake hands. She was more nervous at this moment then at any other time in her life. She realized she did not want to lose Mitch. She felt a little stunned and a picture of a soldier in shock flashed through her mind.

"Well, I am only going to ask one question. Do you want the job?" Zack said as they all sat down.

"Who are you asking," Susan inquired in a tremulous voice.

"I am asking both of you. If you want the job, we will be happy to have both of you," Zack continued.

Immediately Susan's eyes were brimming with tears. She had brought a tissue in case she cried. She took it out and wiped her eyes. It was like when as a kid you got the one gift you had dreamed of but dared not ask for and dared not think about because you knew if you did it would not happen.

"You are not joking with us, are you?" she said looking at both Zack and Janet.

"No this is serious and real. There is enough work. It makes sense to have three of us guarding Zack and to lead the security force for the Savitar." Janet replied in one of the rare occasions she spoke when guarding Zack.

"Of course, I am not guarding him at the moment," she thought as she looked at the two.

"Well, yes, we want the job," they both said in unison as they each hugged the other. Then they got up and gave Janet and Zack hugs as well.

Great let's all go to lunch and celebrate. The interview is over," Zack said as he stood up and shook hands with both Susan and Mitch.

The two Presidential guards looked at each other. They had totally missed the intensity in the room and had no clue to the bonds that had just formed. All they knew was they would soon return to their normal assignments.

"There will be jokes about Zack in the middle when the press finds out that I have chosen another woman to protect me," Zack kidded with Janet as they walked out ahead of the other two.

"Well, maybe they will recognize us as the fiercest sex," Janet replied as she uncharacteristically took Zack's arm as they walked out of the building.

That same day, Susan and Mitch moved their things into the quarters with Janet and Zack. Zack wanted to find out immediately if they were going to get along.

He knew the journey on the Savitar would be long and cramped and that compatibility would be a key trait that was required.

The atmosphere in the living quarters improved immediately. The four seemed to share camaraderie and enjoyed constant light joking. They took turns cooking their evening meals and even played card games.

Susan and Mitch would spend the rest of the time before the Savitar left on its journey refreshing themselves on all the aspects of the program and the people selected to be its crew. They had to catch up on many of the details they had taken lightly or ignored before.

Their work was increased when Janet was called in by the Director of the FBI and told she was to go on vacation for two weeks. This was an arrangement Zack and Bill the FBI director had agreed to. Zack wanted Janet to get a chance to totally recover. Zack also did not want Janet to know he had anything to do with the arrangement and had expressed this to Bill and the director.

Janet at first refused. She was told it was not a request. It was the condition she would have to accept if she was to stay on the mission.

Once she accepted, she decided she would walk the beaches of Hawaii as she had often dreamed of doing.
She wished she could walk holding hands with her soul mate.

Chapter 14: Departure

Janet reluctantly left her protection duties for her recovery vacation. She thought that she had challenged the director by selecting Hawaii. The director did not even blink when he had picked up the phone and instructed his secretary to make the arrangements.

Janet had always dreamed of going there on her honeymoon. She was going to Maui alone and she knew that once she went up to the Savitar she would never have her Hawaiian honeymoon.

On the way, she enjoyed her first-class status flyer. Sitting in first class had been a first for her. She was being shadowed by two bodyguards who felt they had for once gotten a great assignment. After a five-hour flight from LA, she looked out of the window as the plane was making its approach. She could make out the figure eight shape of the Island. Maui was made up of two volcanoes peaks whose bases had merged. She mused as to its meaning of the shape made from two destructive forces.

After deplaning, she walked along quietly talking with the two guards. When they came out past the security area they were greeted and given leis by two young women. After collecting their luggage, the same two led them to a minivan. From the airport, they were driven across the Island of Wailea to a house directly on the beach. This was someone's multimillion-dollar vacation home. Her bedroom and a huge glass fronted porch below the bedroom both faced the beach. Tall palm trees were spaced around the house and a soft spongy grass covered the yard.

She was shown to her room and informed dinner would be ready whenever she would like it. A fish dinner was planned for the evening, but she would have her choice of menu on all other days.

Janet wanted a walk on the beach before dinner. After coordinating with her two guards, she went for her walk. She asked her guards for some space. One guard went several hundred paces ahead and the other followed the same distance behind her. They had been instructed to give Janet the room she asked for.

The two hostesses were to cook, chauffeur, plan, and schedule activities for Janet. After dinner they spent about an hour describing the planned activities. Snorkeling, a sunset catamaran ride, tuna fishing, a trip to Hanna and the seven sister pools, a hike in the Io valley and seeing the sunrise from the top of Mount Haleakala were all planned.

Janet asked to go to a traditional Hawaiian Luau on one of the evenings. They made the adjustments Janet requested. This exclusive treatment was unexpected to Janet. She decided she would relax and enjoy it.

Her two guards were ecstatic. They both knew they would have the vacation of a lifetime.

Each morning she took a several mile walk along the beach. The rhythm of the waves washing onto the shore and surging around her feet soothed Janet's mind.

"This I will miss," she thought as she looked out to where Molokini's small crescent was shadowed by the bigger island of Kahoolawe in the background.

She stopped to look into the pools of water among the black lava sticking out into the sea. Each pool presented a miniature world with life going on in ignorance of its larger surrounding. Small crabs scuttled quickly into hiding as she bent over to examine their miniature world. The various small fish either buried themselves in the sand or swam as far away as the pool allowed.

To her their miniature world was so much like the world as a whole.

She was preparing to go out into the solar system in an attempt to counter act an unknown threat. Most of the people on Earth were going on ignoring the impending doom and burying themselves in the world around them.

She was the bodyguard to the one-person key to the whole effort and who she believed would carry the day. Zack was a great guy, and he was the only one to come up with a unique idea to save the Earth. His solution was at the limits of what she thought humans were capable of doing technologically or physically.

How he had come to be in charge of the whole endeavor puzzled Janet. She was sure he was the right person. However, how he had managed to get past the military establishment and the rest of the political machine puzzled her, but she was thankful that he had been put in charge.

In selecting Zack, President Lancing must have recognized what she herself saw. The President made a very courageous political decision. It was clear Zack enjoyed the President's total confidence.

She had watched as Zack developed his leadership skills and ability to pull the Savitar's contingent into a unified team.

She knew she would do everything possible to keep him safe and also to make him successful.

As she resumed her walk, she concentrated on the waves rolling up the beach and washing across her feet. There was a comfort in the rhythm and the pull of the water.

She took in the people on the beach. There was a lady throwing a ball to her dog and rewarding him on the retrieval.

A young man ran past her just above the wave breaks in order to keep his shoes dry. An apparently newlywed couple walked toward her with their arms around each other.

What were each of them thinking?

Were they aware of the potential devastation of the Earth?

Were they taking this in for the last time?

Would project Savitar really be able to save the world?

She could have used the shower in her private residence to rinse off, but she liked the open shower provided at the public exit.

There early each morning she chatted with an older Hawaiian service department employee who every morning hosed the sand dutifully back to the beach from where it had been tracked by all the beach walking tourists.

In her conversation with him she learned that he was aware and informed about the danger the Earth faced and he was at peace. He expressed the fact that man might or might not survive. This had always been the case as far as he knew and was not really new. It was just that now it was known in advance.

Janet liked him and his simple perspective. He gave her hope.

Janet made the round of the entire Island. She took the obligatory sunset cruise and the snorkeling trip out to Molokini. She spent one day out deep-sea fishing. She and her bodyguards were the only ones on the charter.

She was glad to see that her bodyguards were really into her vacation.

She was entertained by the porpoises whose seemingly effortless swimming kept pace with the boat she was on.

No one on the boat caught tuna. She had hoped that one would be caught. She caught several smaller fish and between the three of them they had enough for a fish dinner.

Janet's thoughts were constantly coming back to the Savitar and Zack. By the end of the second week she was healed, rested and in high spirits and more than ready to return to action.

She knew she would return to a whirlwind of frantic last-minute activities as the day of the Savitar departure neared. She felt she was ready.

Launches to the Savitar were continuous and fully loaded. Susan and Mitch were now in full swing in guarding Zack. Janet's absence allowed them to get to know Zack more quickly.

They greeted Janet on her return and then were immediately off trying to keep up with him.

Janet felt a moment of jealousy, but she managed to let it pass. She decided she would reintegrate and reinsert herself in the lead in the next few days. She realized everyone would need to get readjusted to her return.

Zack surprised everyone by letting them know they would be having a special welcome home dinner at Craig's home. Emily, Craig's wife had made the invitation to all of them. Emily had taken a liking to Janet on their first meeting.

She told Craig, that Janet was a perfect match for Zack. Craig's reply was she should quit her match making as it would muddy up the water. Emily gave no reply, but she did not change her mind and decided to get Janet back into the groove by holding a dinner upon her coming back from Hawaii.

The five bodyguards and Zack, Craig and Emily sat around the dining room table. Everyone was surprised when a well-known local Chef came out to greet them and to explain the meal, he would serve them. He would serve them a lobster, and steak dinner. He was a friend of Emily's and had volunteered his services in exchange for getting pictures with them and having them comment on his meal afterwards.

He smiled and said that he hoped for gushing comments on the wonderful tasting food that they had been served.

The meal was exquisite. Each course was specially prepared and brought out by one server for each of the diners. Everyone kept commenting on the wonderful flavors and tastes. A light Rhine wine complemented the shrimp, and a Cabernet Sauvignon was served with the steak. Compliments flowed freely to the chef and Emily. She was elated to have pulled off such a great event.

Zack was happy to have Janet back. She had a healthy tan look and appeared refreshed. He had missed her but had not realized how much until her return.

He was very pleased Emily thought of this way to greet Janet and to have the whole team get together.

He made a toast to Janet, "to my protector and shield, she took several bullets for me."

Janet once again felt the camaraderie of the four of them. She felt she was home.

She made a toast to Emily and to the friends sitting around the table.

Zack was totally consumed in trying to get all the things he wanted sent up to the Savitar. Janet was surprised after dinner when Zack inquired how Craig was doing in getting all the things that he had asked for. The two rarely talked shop outside of work hours. They usually left work out of their personal interactions.

Janet knew immediately that Zack had needed a vacation as much as she. She wished he could have come with her.

Zack had sent Lisa Hemming, the head of the hydroponics, several plants of grapes and smuggled up as many other plants as he possibly could take himself. What he took up openly was only a small portion compared to what he was sending up in secret. He was determined to have all the possible types of plants he could.

Lisa sent back a warning for him to quit testing the balance of nature on the ship but always thanked him for each of the contributions. She stopped complaining about the limited selection she had been allowed to bring up. She was not sure how Zack was bypassing the group trying to control what went up to the Savitar, but she was pleased to be on his list of beneficiaries.

Zack did not tell her of the wide variety of seeds from around the world sent up in a container of spare parts. He, Craig, and President Manning were the only ones aware of this private material. He had a long-term vision of the Savitar as an independent self-sufficient entity. He was filling every nook and cranny of every container with items he thought might be useful.

A message from the President let Zack know he would be losing about one hundred more people from his crew. When he looked at the list, he was surprised by some, but he knew at this stage it was out of his hands. He worked immediately with Indira and his leadership team to adjust to the changes.

He was surprised at Indira's look of disapproval when she looked at the list of names being taken off the roster. He wondered about her reaction.

Little did he know that Indira's plans had taken a big hit with the last set of cuts and would affect her behavior later in the journey.

Dr. Trimble had been whisked through space training and continued his work on a lab provided for him on the base. Meanwhile, Zack arranged for a lab to be built for him on the Savitar. This lab was the best equipped lab anywhere in the world and as large as one of the gardens. The nano technology was a technology Zack desperately needed and wanted urgently. He did not want to face the deterioration of his crew due to radiation sickness.

Each day he would check in with Samuel and they would review the progress being made. The two agreed speed was crucial. Samuel promised he would have his nano-bots ready to do radiation repair when the time came. He was working about twenty hours a day and was determined to keep his promise. He drove his new team to the limits of their capability.

The President, Craig, and Zack all agreed Dr. Trimble would be better off and safer as a member of the Savitar. The services of the nano-bots would be crucial on the way out to Mars. Once the technology had been proved out, it could be shared with Earth

Only one of Dr. Trimble's original team from his office in Boston qualified to go on the Savitar. However, several top scientists in this and related fields were selected to join the team on the Savitar. The infusion of new minds provided some additional ideas to advance the effort.

Dr. Trimble and his new team were the second group to be moved to the Savitar permanently. When they entered their new lab on the Savitar they were amazed by the size of the facility and the equipment provided. It was newer and more advanced then what was in their lab on the ground. They all walked around and were glad that they had qualified to make the journey.

Their lab was next to the primary hydroponics garden unit housing Lisa's quarters.

The crew staffing the hydroponics were the first team to move up and considered themselves as plank owners. They cheerfully greeted the newest members and treated them to the fresh vegetables now growing on the various plants.

Fried green tomatoes was one of the offerings.

It was clear to the scientists that they would enjoy the benefit of having their lab next to one of the gardens.

Craig and Zack met every day to review the route the Savitar would take. The navigation crew and the pilots of the shuttles, forty people in all met daily during the last week. This group would be the last to leave Earth. They were making last minute adjustments in the course the Savitar would take on its journey. Their Earth counterparts also took part in these meetings. Most of it was routine but Zack wanted each passage around a planet or moon to be reviewed in detail.

The shuttles that would launch in the coming week would not be returning to Earth. The fuel for the long journey had been going up for the last few weeks.

Three years of fuel, even with the possibility of using the Moon, Mars, Jupiter, and Saturn to slingshot the Savitar outward toward its objective took up a massive amount of space. Every possible container was being used to store, fuel, air, and water. These final loads being sent up almost continuously were the margin of safety Craig and Zack were trying to achieve.

Craig was working furiously to get everything sent up. He was only getting a few hours of sleep each night during these final days.

Emily warned Zack, Craig was near the end of his stamina. She had never seen him so exhausted.

"He has not been home for a week. He is sleeping in a cot at the launch site. I have been taking him supper and making him eat to make sure he keeps up his strength," Emily said with concern.

"I am not sure everything we talked about is going to make it," Craig said on one of the last days.

I am sending the stuff up as fast as I can get the next rocket to launch. Your crew is fastening the loads along the main axis of rotation and keeping everything in balance. All they are getting is the size and weight of what is arriving.

Most of this last-minute stuff is the stuff you requested for the long haul. I will give you an inventory sheet personally before you depart. This will be the only record. Even I won't have a copy.

Don't lose your list," Craig warned Zack.

"Thanks for accepting my paranoia and doing this for me.

You and President Lansing have been great about it," Zack responded.

At times he felt they humored his paranoia about the future.

"It's not your paranoia. It's a very real scenario that the President agrees with. He feels the situation should be handled in advance. He has used all of his current political clout to get the requested materials. He has been pulling all the strings he can to help me get this stuff out to space. I think he has called in every favor ever owed him and he probably has promised the kitchen sink in return. I hope he survives the next election," Craig responded.

He had his doubts about President Lansing's chances.

The President had alienated almost all his constituents, the military, the right, the left and he had spent more money than any president since Roosevelt and the great depression and he still did not get any praise from the left.

The final week was a blur to Zack. Finally, he, Janet, Susan, and Mitch, were suiting up to go out to the Savitar. The launch was just another launch as far as the public was concerned. No announcement of their leaving had been made.

Zack was scheduled to give a final departure speech from the same stage where he had been shot in the back and Janet had been hit four time.

The media was of the impression this speech would be live from the Cape. The normal media coverage and full interviews were planned along with a departure dinner. It had been planned this way to throw off the possibility of any last-minute attacks. The events would be held but Zack was to be represented by Craig. Zack would do the interview from the Savitar.

"Well, my friend, I know we will be in constant communication for the next few years, but this may be the last we see of each other. Emily sends her best wishes and God speed," Craig said as he gave Zack a hug.

Zack had spent the previous night at Craig's and Emily's place. They all had a wonderful dinner and a quiet evening of conversation. Emily had wished him well and said she hoped to see him in the near future.

Craig had become as close as a brother to Zack. It was all Zack could do to keep tears from his eyes.

"If you change your mind, plan to join us after we capture the black hole and have no doubt we will move it out of Earth's path, afterwards we will ask for some more resources before we sail out in search of new adventure," Zack said quietly to Craig so no one else could hear.

Janet and the rest chatted quietly with each other. They all knew of the close friendship between Zack and Craig. They then helped Zack get the remainder of his suit sealed up.

Together the four moved out of the room to the walkway leading to the shuttle. This shuttle would not be returning. It would be the first connected to the perimeter of the Savitar.

The launch went smoothly and after the multiple G forces of launch subsided, Zack, Janet, Susan, and Mitch watched the Earth recede as they approached the Savitar. Each was in their own world of thought as they looked back upon the Earth. This was probably the last time to see it this closely.

The shuttle docked on the Savitar at the command center. This area housed Zack's quarters and the navigation system. One of the Main cafeterias was located next to the command center. The shuttle docked directly above the command center. This would be its permanent location until after the capture of the black hole.

Zack moved his meager belongings into his quarters. The space was about a fourth the size of the room he had enjoyed on Earth. Even so, he had more space than anyone else on the Savitar. Janet, Susan, and Mitch shared about the same amount of sleeping space. They each had a private work area, and all shared a common lounge.

Zack made sure the living quarters for the rest of the Savitar crew was comparable. He might enjoy a few more amenities due to his position but had he insisted this be kept at a minimum.

Now the remaining loads could be counted. All final structural inspections were being done. Many of the personnel were already on board. The remaining would come up on the one way shuttles.

Finally, Zack watched as the last shuttle blasted off from Earth. The crew of the Savitar continued to work on the structure even as they prepared to leave Earth's orbit. The work was planned to continue throughout the two-year voyage.

Zack had worked with the crew leaders to plan the work week and the relaxation events. There would not be many off hours. The work at hand would in fact have everyone putting in double shifts. He quietly accelerated the pace of the welding. He hoped to increase the structural strength of the Savitar at a record pace.

Monthly entertainment was planned, and current movies would be sent from Earth.

Lack of space would be the biggest problem for the crew. The Savitar structure was unbelievably huge, but the available living space was minimal. Zack sent up enough materials to dramatically change this after the capture of the black hole.

Zack sent up enough materials to dramatically change this after the capture of the black hole.

The day of departure finally arrived. Zack got on the intercom and instructed each unit leader to verify their space was ready for launch.

The launch itself would barely be noticeable.

The acceleration would be a constant one tenth of a G and would build the speed to slightly more than twenty-five thousand miles an hour. This would allow them to leave synchronous orbit. They would sling shot around the moon and double their speed.

They would then race out toward Mar's for yet another sling to send them on toward Jupiter at almost three times their entry speed for a final sling sending them toward the blackhole at almost a quarter the speed of light, which was a phenomenal 250,000 MPH.

The crew would be working on the Savitar as they sped through space. It would have been nice to have a safety net dragging along behind but there was no drag to space and the structure of the Savitar was prohibitively large.

The work Dr. Trimble's nano-bots would be needed on the way to Mars if the external structural work was to proceed at the pace Zack planned.

This need put the nano-bot work at the top of Zack's priority list.

After the shuttle rockets fired, Zack addressed the Earth.

"Gentle people of Earth; Savitar has begun its departure and is slowly accelerating toward the Moon. We will be racing out ahead of you, and we will reach the blackhole ahead of the Earth.

Our mission is to capture and move this blackhole, so it poses no threat to you.

The crew of the Savitar will achieve this. We have a solid plan. You have given us the resources and we have the skill. We have the passion and the will to succeed.

Keep us in your prayers and wish us well in this long and historic journey.

The Savitar is your shield. She will be your sword. We will capture the prize and harness it to our will. This will be a point in history, where mankind will take control of the solar space environment.

Zack ended his speech.

Immediately the communication system was full of incoming messages. He had organized his leadership team to deal with and answer the incoming messages.

Zack left the command center and sat in the observation room watching Earth recede ever so slowly. At this moment, everything came rushing over him. He felt light-headed and sat down. He was really off on this unbelievable adventure. He hoped he could deliver on his promises. He was leaving behind his beloved family, and an Earth he cherished. He did not think a return in his lifetime was truly possible.

He felt a gentle hand on his shoulder.

"We will succeed," Janet said quietly.

She too felt the intensity of the moment. She sat down beside him and looked out the small window to the blue green jewel they called Earth.

Neither of them had any idea to the trials and personal dangers they each would face.

Chapter 15: To the Moon

And so, began a long and relatively slow journey out away from Earth. After a few moments of contemplation, Zack decided to act on a nagging premonition.

He called his leadership team together and announced, "For the next few days as we take this relatively slow journey toward the moon, I want all of the major nine G and one G joints welded. Pull all non-essential support personnel and augment the welding teams. Put everyone on double duty from now until we get to the moon.

There was silence in the room as everyone took in the magnitude of Zack's request. He was asking for everyone to support around the clock welding. It was a huge undertaking.

"Why the rush, I thought we would have years to complete this structure." Enrico Hidalgo asked as he looked at Zack and wondered what information he was not sharing. Enrico wondered whether to support or challenge the request.

"That is a fair question. The first stress this structure will experience will be the moon's pull as we sling shot around it. We cannot risk a failure this early. The entire Savitar structure is held together with a few tack welds. This leaves us in a very fragile state. If I wanted to cause this mission to fail, I would make sure the Savitar would experience forces beyond what it is capable of withstanding. Our only choice would be to abandon our current effort or risk total destruction.

That is why I am giving you the mission to complete the welds before we get to the moon.

To protect those doing the work, plan on doing most of the welding from the inside of the structure. I also want a team to set up robot welders to be used to do at least one pass on the main outside joints. We can greatly increase our welding production if the human welder can sit in the comfort of one of our facilities shielded from the radiation and let a robot welder do the welding. This will not only be safer, but I think it will speed up the process.

Double the number of tack welds on every cable on each end. Put additional tack welds on every joint at the forty-mile structure if total passes are not possible.

Have each team leader create a plan to get this welding done. The fourth shift team will be split and will give one hundred fifty people to each of the other three shifts. The one hundred fifty people left over will assemble and test out the robot welders. Please get the three teams immediately out to work and have a plan ready to review with me in two hours," Zack instructed the leadership team.

For a moment everyone just stared.

"Ok, let's get to work and see what we can come up with." Enrico spoke up as he decided to support Zack.

The leadership team broke into a loud animated discussion on how best to carry out this request. The most technical one hundred fifty people from all the teams were identified and were put on the robot building teams. The structure was mapped out and the Savitar was divided into three areas, one for each team. One team would focus on the central sphere and the other teams two would focus on the outer one.

Zack left the room with his three bodyguards and went up to what served as the ships command and navigation center. Here he reviewed the journey out to the Moon and the sling planned for the Savitar. This first part of their journey was being controlled from Earth.

A nagging feeling continued to bother him.

He instructed the navigator to review the current plans for their journey around the moon and the margins of error for the trajectory. He wanted to know the forces the Savitar would experience. He instructed the navigation team to prepare a plan where navigation was controlled solely from the Savitar.

"Please do a physical star check of our course and compare it to what the computer is telling you. Please have a full evaluation ready for me by tomorrow morning," Zack requested.

Chiang Lee the senior navigator was surprised but he immediately organized his team to take the necessary readings and determine their trajectory.

The Cape control center was doing all the navigation control via computer control.

He had not anticipated the need for what Zack was asking but he immediately put his team to work.

Zack stopped for some coffee in the canteen before returning to the leadership team room.

"Do you know something we don't," Janet asked quietly as the four drank some coffee and had a roll or some other snack item.

She was aware that this was very different from Zack's normal, calm planned approach at getting things done.

"No, these nagging feelings have been building for the last few days. I learned a long time ago to trust my feelings and act on them. Suddenly after you commented about us making it, the feeling solidified into a certainty that I had to take action. At worst I will make folks do a lot of extra work before it was needed," Zack replied as he finished his coffee and rose to go back to the leadership room.

"Well folks, your time is up. Tell me about your plans, any problems and issues and what resources you need to pull this off," Zack said as he sat down.

"Well, you certainly ask for small miracles. The leadership team has an action plan. We have mapped out the Savitar. All the module and team leaders have already been alerted and are suiting up now to begin their work. They are setting up the welding materials and resources. We selected the best and most talented to put into the group of one hundred fifty to produce the remote robot welding units. We assigned ten of the best people to produce the first model. They will then deploy the model and validate its capability.

Then each welding unit will be staffed with an operation group of four people and be immediately deployed. This will allow us to quickly produce and deploy the maximum number of units. We should be able to produce fifty welding units a day.

As we get these units online, we will assign a two-person team per shift team to each welder and begin the full welds of the external joints. For internal welding we will have each team do a half a weld of each joint they are assigned. Then they will go back and complete the weld at each joint. This insures, a significant increase will happen rapidly, even if some welds do not get totally done.

We plan to be ahead of your goal. In fact, we think we will have full welds on most of the joints of the Savitar by the time we reach the Moon," Enrico shared as he pointed out the different zones where the welding was to be done.

Zack was pleased with the immediate and positive response of his leadership team. He knew he was stressing their loyalty. He hoped he would not be losing their trust.

"Please let the folks know once we get around the Moon, we will take a break and we will reorganize for the long haul out to Mars. However, let them know I think it will be critical to our safety to dramatically increase the stresses the Savitar can handle," Zack told the leadership team.

"I believe the sling around the moon will be the first likely time to sabotage this journey. The Savitar is currently structurally anemic. I want us to take the countermeasure you have planned in hopes this makes any attempted structural sabotage fail," Zack said looking around at his team.

Zack asked the engineering leader, Conrad Zepf to have his team evaluate the stresses the Savitar would experience during its sling around the Moon and asked him to determine what the maximum stresses the vessel could survive given its current condition.

By the end of the day, Zack had a much clearer understanding of the risk and the lack of safety margin with the current condition of the Savitar. It was clear in its' current structural condition, any deviation that took the Savitar closer to the moon would doom its existence. The Savitar would come around the moon in pieces.

"The only factor in our control is to enhance the structural capability and the integrity of the Savitar. I have acted to have this happen. The Navigation team is determining if we are on our planned trajectory. By now I am sure you three are wondering about the guy you are guarding. Are you still with me," Zack said as they sat in the common sitting room they all shared, and he sipped slowly on his tea?

"I am with you. As you said the worst thing that can happen is we get a lot of work done ahead of time. The only other thing hanging out is your credibility." Janet replied.

At the moment there was no evidence of any sabotage, and she was wondering if Zack was overreacting.

"Well, its bedtime for me. Let's turn in." Zack said putting his cup down as he stood up.

Sometime during the night Zack was awakened by his intercom.

It was Enrico.

"Zack, you had better get up here fast. I am in the navigation room. The pot you stirred has come to a boil," Enrico said.

Zack, Janet, Susan, and Mitch all got quickly dressed and the four of them went through the module to the command center. The place was like a bee's nest.

"What's up," Zack asked as he entered the navigation center.

He was always surprised by the action of his bodyguards. They always checked the entire room before strategically situating themselves around the room. Every person in the room noticed the same thing. No one on board would ever dare attack Zack and live to get even a blow on him.

"Well, you asked us to check out the trajectory and the navigation around the moon. Given our current trajectory, we will barely clear the surface of the moon. We rechecked our celestial readings and calculations several times and can't find our mistake. We were about to contact the folks back on Earth, but Enrico instructed us to discuss it with you first," Chiang Lee, the senior navigator spoke up.

"If we are right, we need to make some corrective firings to move us to a higher orbit around the moon. Even then, we will be coming in closer than originally planned. We can't move the Savitar very much without using a great amount of the fuel. We will need this fuel later on our journey," Enrico spoke up.

Zack quickly understood the ploy. Save the Savitar and the mission is either delayed or totally stopped. Go in too close and the Savitar is destroyed. Either scenario was a win for their saboteurs. They didn't need to kill anyone only stop the mission. The discovery of the ploy this early gave the Savitar a chance.

"Determine the minimum corrective firing and factor in half of the structural strength Conrad calculates we will gain from the welding. Figure out and tell me what and when we must do something.

I will inform the President and have the security back on the ground try and capture the culprits.

Make sure Earth has no control over the Savitar's navigation systems but do not inform them or let them figure out they have no control. We will take control of our navigation from here on out," Zack commanded.

He took Enrico aside. He first thanked him for his clear decision making and making the right decision.

"I want you to set up a duplicate computer control system. This will be the system we use internally. The current system will remain connected to Earth but have no control on the Savitar. Earth is not to know of our second layer of computing. The command center on Earth must think everything is the same," Zack instructed.

"Well from now on I won't question your premonitions," Janet said in a conciliatory tone.

She was somewhat surprised at Zack's accurate read on the potential threat to the Savitar.

Surprise at of his vision and ability to take preemptive action would be a theme that would constantly surprise Janet.

Chapter 16: The Boss Saves the Day

Zack was still on Earth time, so he knew it was early in the morning back on the ground. He called on his secure line staffed by Craig and his people. He asked to speak to Craig and was surprised when a few moments later, Craig was on the line.

"Zack, what's up," Craig asked with concern in his voice.

"Are you still sleeping at the office?" Zack asked in surprise.

"Well, in fact yes, I have my people checking everything going on around here and we have been seeing if we missed anything of importance. Not everything made it up to the Savitar. I have three cases of Black Label now sitting here in my office. I will use them to toast your various accomplishments on this journey of yours," Craig responded.

"Well, I need your help. My folks project the current trajectory of the Savitar will put us very close to landing on the moon. We are taking action to correct this, but I need you to follow up to see who the culprits are back there. I leave this in your hands.

If you find out I am wrong or my navigators have made an error, contact me immediately because I am taking action now to protect the Savitar," Zack let Craig know.

"Dam, this is serious. I will get on it immediately. I will get back to you as soon as possible," Craig replied.

Immediately Craig dialed the President's personal line. This would require immediate action from the highest authority. The perpetrators had to be in high government circles or very well connected to the work on the Savitar.

"Well, can we correct our trajectory to make it around the moon?" Zack inquired as he looked around the room.

"We would need to burn a tremendous amount of fuel to get back to the original path. The closer we come to the surface of the Moon the less fuel we need to burn. A tighter trajectory will give us the benefit of building up more speed. However, the stresses would be above the current limit of our structure." Chiang Lee, the senior navigator replied.

"Let's use the minimum of our resources. Enrico, how do you feel about our welding program?" Zack asked.

"Well, we just got started but everyone is confident they can do what you asked and significantly more. I would say let's go for a faster, closer sling around the moon," Enrico replied.

"I will see if we can get more people assigned to do welding," Enrico continued as he turned to walk back to the leadership team room.

"Well, let's get busy making sure the rest of the facilities are ready for this event. Plan to have all compartment structural integrity checked and the interiors prepared for the additional stresses. Let's use all personnel not assigned to welding. Put everyone on eighteen-hour shifts and short breaks for meals. Put together several inspection teams to go around and make the integrity checks. Let's make sure we make it around the Moon," Zack instructed.

"How about some breakfast," Janet asked quietly.

"I could really use a cup of Coffee. How long will we have coffee?" Zack wondered out loud as the four walked back toward the cafeteria. He knew Lisa had plans to grow tea, but coffee trees were not in the cards at this stage.

Zack ordered eggs over easy with ham. He chuckled as he thought about the fact, he had smuggled rabbits, chickens, ducks, shrimp, frogs, some clams, salmon, and a variety of other fish including catfish, some crabs and lobster up to the Savitar.

He had selected "farmers" from several of the crew who had grown up on farms in Iowa, Vietnam, and the Philippines. He told no one and had instructed his farmers to be very tight mouthed. Sam, Quang, and Angela made a very unlikely set, but they had quickly become friends as they took care of their fish and animals.

Lisa had agreed to guide the team in integrating the farmers in with the gardeners.

"What's so funny?" Susan asked.

"I was just thinking about the future when eggs and ham will be difficult to order. Perhaps we will have to order eggs and shrimp or salmon," Zack replied.

"Oh, that's right. You managed to get part of your farm up here. "I wish you would have brought a pig along," Mitch said poking a little fun.

"Well, the fish, clams, and shrimp I brought up fit in a one-gallon container. The chickens and ducks came up as fertilized eggs and the rabbits fit in my pockets. My farmers are doing their best at getting this crop to be the seed for the future. I have connected Sam, Quang, and Angela with Lisa so she can combine her hydroponics farm with the fish, clam, and shrimp farming. The rabbits, chickens and ducks will have to be managed separately," Zack informed the group.

"Well Zack, we can come back to fish raising and farming after we make it around the moon in one piece. Are we going to make it?" Janet asked.

She was still surprised at Zack's accurate premonition, and she was worried.

"Yes, I think so. If we strengthen the structure by a third, we will make it with no problem. I just hope there is not another way to be sabotaged. We are going to have to be prepared for the worst. This structure is so expansive and there is so much to the Savitar we do not know. We will have to become system and structural experts.

In fact, the four of us will have to master all aspects of how the Savitar functions." Zack spoke quietly to the three.

Later during the day, Zack was called to one of the maintenance shops. He was shown the first automated welding machine. It had a body like a skateboard that had a giant snail shaped body with four universal magnetic wheels mounted on the edges. This allowed the welder to roll along the pipe but be magnetically attached. The main body could swivel, and the welding rod could go up and down. The welding wire was on a snail shaped spool on the back of the welder. The welding unit looked like a cross between an armadillo and a giant anteater. A camera was mounted on a swivel on what would have been the head of an ant eater. It enabled the welder to see.

Zack smiled as he though of the welder in the terms that ran through his mind.

"We want you to be the first to weld a joint using our new robot welder. We will be able to have fifty done by tomorrow morning and the rest done late in during the day. We figure these devices can weld six inches per minute on the large five G main frame.

We will have one hundred fifty machines out welding in the next few days. This will allow us to complete a single pass on each main joint of the inner Bucky ball frame and have every other joint with additional tacks by the end of the week.

We will want all the human welders we can muster out on the structure. Most will be following up on the auto welders and ensuring the job is complete. Another one hundred fifty people will work twenty-four seven remotely running these welders. We will completely join the interior joint at each major connecting point. Later after we get around the moon, we will connect the interior Bucky balls at these same joints." Lars, the big Swedish welding technician declared proudly.

"This was an extremely fast development. How did you do it," Zack asked in a surprised tone.

He had not expected this quick of a response.

"We already had the auto welders, but they were not set up to be controlled and monitored remotely. With the modifications we made we will be able to easily control them from anywhere on the Savitar. This allows the person guiding them to move them from weld-to-weld location. The only thing to be done manually is to reload the welders. We have set up several strategic reload stations. We will have an almost ninety-five per cent utilization of the welders," Lars continued proudly.

Zack sat down in front of a PC set up to show him the weld location. The program guided him to properly set up the welder. He followed the instruction and off it went welding. Only the start and the stop of the weld needed close attention. The rest of the time the welder proceeded on its own. He was surprised at how fast the weld went down. After about ten minutes Zack had welded about five feet along the joint. He stopped and looked around and gave his thumbs up.

"Well done, Lars and all of you who have contributed. This will be the safety margin the Savitar needs as we head around the Moon. Please continue and get these things all running as soon as possible. Each time you get one done, make sure it gets out there and it does not stop until I give the word. Thanks for giving me the honor of being the first to use one," Zack said as he shook hands all around before leaving the shop.

"Wow, those guys really have saved the day. Put them on the list to talk about and to recognize after we leave the Moon," Zack said to Janet.

The next morning at breakfast, Zack noticed a graph in the shape of a thermometer showing how many inches of weld needed to get done before arriving at the moon and a green bar inside the thermometer going up about ten per cent of the height.

"I really like seeing the team take this on as a challenge," Zack said to Enrico.

"Well, it's even better than the graph Several of the folks currently doing support work like meal preparation, and other support work have volunteered to make the welders environment less stark by bringing them coffee and refreshments or by giving them breaks. The response to this challenge has been very positive," Enrico told Zack.

He personally had heightened respect for the style of leadership being displayed by Zack.

Back on Earth, the investigation into the navigation of the Savitar indeed verified the course error the Savitar navigators found. The radar tracking system was projecting the correct course on screen. The error was traced back to a software problem, but no one knew who was responsible. The original programmer, who was from Russia, repeatedly denied making the error and was able to show his original programing.

The team doing the navigation when the problem was identified was removed. Someone on the team should have known or noticed the Savitar was off course. They were not checking the actual position from what was being shown on screen.

After a round of discussions with the Earth controllers and listening to the concern about the structural integrity, Zack prevailed in keeping the trajectory closer to the moon than originally planned. He did not share the fact he had a massive welding effort underway.

<u>Chapter 17: Special Message</u>

Zack sent a special message to Craig. "Listen to me closely. Please tell the President that because of my belief in the valor, bravery and the high skills of the men and women on my crew the Savitar will take the riskier closer path. We will prevail." Zack spoke his carefully selected words.

Craig, at first concerned, figured there was something Zack was not telling him. Craig was confident Zack was taking all the necessary precautions.

When he shared this message with the President, he heard a chuckle at the other end of the line.

"Well, he told you he was going to take the action that he had decided to do and basically told you to quit worrying," Dan said over the phone.

"His message told you that?" Craig asked curiously.

"Indeed, it does. Let's hope he has everything in his control as he thinks he does," the President finished.

The moon was now the main object in the sky for those on the Savitar.

Enrico was coordinating the inspection of the entire structure. He had five hundred people getting the Savitar ready for the sling around the moon. There were three thousand welders working everywhere on the structure. The Savitar's crew would have looked like the inside of a honeybee hive if one could have seen all the workers and their action at one time.

Zack was concerned with the level of radiation the crew out on the exterior of the Savitar was experiencing. He met with Dr. Trimble and asked about the progress on the nano-bots. He hoped the severe cases could be addressed. Progress had been made and the nano-bots were nearly ready for human trials.

"Let me know when you are completely sure you are ready for human trial. I want the first severe cases of radiation sickness to be treated with your nano-bots. You will try them if we have any severe cases no matter where you think you are in your testing," Zack informed Dr. Trimble.

Zack and his bodyguards were assigned to inspect several of the facilities. They inspected these looking for loose materials, lack of fasteners, structural weaknesses, and any other problem they might find.

Zack found traveling around the Savitar was very difficult. It required an individual to be in a pressurized space suit. There was a long distance to travel, and it was all on the exterior. This made the going slow and awkward.

The first day they made it around about a third of the way around the outer part of the Savitar and they were using specially designed wire scooters to pull them along.

"Rather than going back to our quarters tonight, let's stay out here. If we can find personnel quarters, it will reduce our exposure and will save us several hours tomorrow," Zack suggested.

Janet, Susan, and Mitch conferred for several minutes before they agreed to stay for the night. Zack's safety was their main concern. However, since this would be an impromptu sleep over, they felt it would be safe.

"Let's find some quarters where we all can put up for the night. We will follow the normal watch schedule," Susan said as she located the nearest living quarters.

There was no main mess in the area. There was only a facility used by some of the welding personnel. They decided that was where they would bunk.

The lone person in the facility looked up as Susan led the way in through the air lock.

"What are you folks doing out here? This is a temporary facility while we try to get the welding done," he said gruffly.

He did not recognize anyone in the group.

"Sampson, from Oklahoma, isn't it?" Janet said extending the hand she had just taken out of her glove.

Well miss, you certainly have me at a disadvantage," Sampson said as he shook her hand.

He was pleased someone as good looking as she would know his name.

Janet had looked up who would be out at this particular location before the group had come in. Sampson was the black welder of the group. This made it easy for Janet to make the connection on entering.

"Well, Sampson, I guard the ornery boss making you do all this welding," Janet said.

"You mean Lars has someone to guard him," Sampson said looking confused as he took in the remaining two figures entering the room.

He still did not understand the situation he found himself in.

"She and these other two guard me, Zack Milton. How are you doing?" Zack said extending his hand and looking up to the rather large and muscular Sampson.

He was appropriately named Zack concluded.

"Holy cow, I didn't know you would be out this way. No one told us anything about this. Here come on in and make yourself at home. It isn't much but it saves us about three hours a day by staying out here instead of going all the way back to the living quarters.

The entire Savitar had the appearance of a newly moved into house. Unopened boxes were to be found everywhere. Nothing was put away.

"Well, we hate to encroach on your space, but we had the same idea about saving time. We are out making a round of inspections to ensure everything is ship shape and fastened down. We plan to spend the night out here if we can," Susan piped in.

"Sure welcome, there are three of us out here. I just came in to get the food ready. The other two are out making their final rounds loading up those new welders for the night. Those are some gadgets. They are taking months off our welding time," Sampson said as he moved things around to make room for them. "They say Lars and his group developed them. They already have the name of Bead Daubers." Sampson continued.

"You're in luck we set this up for ten people when we planned to do the welding by hand. There are several makeshift huts like this around the structure. The bunks are in the back," Sampson pointed as he watched Susan, Janet and Mitch making their evaluation rounds.

"Don't, mind them, they are a little paranoid If I get killed, they lose their job and all the perks that go with it," Zack said as he sat down on a box across from Sampson.

"How do you get down to the central structure from the outer perimeter?" Zack asked curiously.

It was two-hundred forty miles down to the inner Bucky ball but is seemed that welders got there relatively fast.

"Well, we rigged a cable and pulley system and put in a cage. We travel up and down at about one-hundred miles an hour maybe a little faster. You should give it try in the morning. It's the best ride I have ever been on," Sampson said with a chuckle. "There are cable rigs set up at the eight locations where the electromagnets are located. There are another dozen strategically located around the structure."

Up to four big guys can ride at one time.

"So, Lars is your boss?" Zack continued.

"Well, no. Not directly. He is just the best dam welder and mechanic anyone has ever seen. He earned the nickname Boss because he gets everything done that he plans or promises and he sort of dominates the room if you get what I mean," Sampson went on.

"I didn't mean you any disrespect but when the lady said she guarded the boss, Lars popped into my mind. I wasn't thinking about the boss of the Savitar," Sampson said over his cup of coffee.

"No offense taken. I have seen what Lars can do and I would say Boss, is a good handle for him.

By the way, I see you like your coffee. How would you and your buddies like to do me a favor? I want to surprise our lady in charge of our gardens. I brought up some coffee beans. I need to get them sprouted and growing in the next month or so.

I don't want her knowing I have them. This is for her birthday. Once she has the coffee trees growing, we all will have a chance of having coffee when our current supply runs out.

"Can I get you three to take on the challenge of getting them growing?" Zack asked as he watched his three bodyguards moving the bunks and boxes around.

"Sure, love to. Give me something to do in the evenings. Those three sure seem worried about you. Are there bad guys up here with us?" Sampson continued as he watched them prepare their sleeping area.

"Well, the bad guys almost succeeded in getting me once. It turned out one of my bodyguards was the bad guy. Janet, the one greeting you first, saved my butt. She took four bullets saving me. Now she is super cautious about what goes on around her," Zack said as he watched the three come back to where he was.

Sampson looked at Janet with more respect and curiosity. She had just taken on a whole new aura for Sampson.

"She must be tougher than she looks," Sampson thought to himself.

"We have a secure area to spend the night. Who are the other two out here with you?" Janet asked.

"Well one of the fellows is from Australia, a Jarrod Michaels, and the other is from Italy, a Gabriele Tedoldi," Sampson replied.

Janet typed this into her computer pad and reviewed the information she had. Gabriele Tedoldi was clean. He was rough around the edges with a typical Italian macho reputation but had a respectable record of achievements. Jarrod was clear as well.

She looked at the other two guards and just nodded. Zack figured that everything was fine.

"You three have a cup of coffee and figure out what we are going to have for dinner. I am going to talk with Enrico and let him know what we are doing. I don't want him sending out a search party. He also needs to handle everything today and probably tomorrow," Zack said as he stood up to leave.

"Here are the seeds. You three come and visit me in my quarters in about a month. Remember this may mean coffee for years to come," Zack said solemnly as he walked back to the bunk area.

"What was that all about?" Janet asked curiously as the four of them went back to the far end of the structure.

"Well, I am playing Johnnie Apple Seed. I am passing out seeds for various crew members to cultivate. This will help them focus on something other than the tedious nature of our journey and it allows me to get plants growing I would not have time for," Zack replied.

The inspection took another two days. They found dozens of loose or poorly secured items. They resolved many of these immediately or planned or assigned it to someone. By the time the team returned to the main station, ninety percent of the fixes were already done.

There were only three days left until the rendezvous with Moon.

Zack went to see how Lars and his group were doing.

"Well, we have close to two hundred welders going full time. It turns out they weld about thirty per cent faster than we thought they would. One person can guide four welders. We will have every joint with one full weld complete by the time we get to the moon. Every cable will also get additional weld on each end. You understand this is only twenty-five per cent of the final weld each joint will get, don't you," Lars asked.

"No, tell me more," Zack replied.

"Well, we are doing the root past at each joint. Then we will come back and do another pass to the left and right of the first weld and then a third pass down the middle to connect the two outside welds. This is all that has been specified for each joint.

If it was up to me, we could come back and do still more passes and lay four more welds across the top of the three we are currently planning to do," Lars explained.

"Well, Lars, I like your idea of continuing to build the welds. Please develop a recommendation and bring it to the leadership team once we get around the moon. Specifically, please find out what additional strength this extra welding will give us," Zack said as he gave Lars a congratulatory pat on the back.

Lars felt ten feet tall as he watched Zack leave the room. He knew from his years at welding the beams of skyscrapers the extra welds would be worth the work. He set off immediately to find some engineer to calculate the increase in strength the additional layer of welds would provide.

For the next three days, the final preparations for the moon rendezvous continued at a blistering pace. The welding was almost complete.

The Navigation personnel now had a clear plot of their trajectory around the moon. They would come around the moon at a little less than half the distance from the Moon than originally planned.

Zack and had company made a complete inspection of all the material attached to the surface.

There was no time to inspect the enormous amount of material stored in the inside of the Savitar. His logistics officer assured him all the material in the center was interlocked and wrapped in a chain link fence material and would not come apart.

The journey around the moon would happen the next day. The moon looked huge and took up the entire sky ahead of them.

"Well, team, tell me about the Savitar. Please give me the status of your areas," Zack said looking around the table. He was nervous about the situation but put on a confident face.

"The hydroponics tanks are drained, the plants protected. All liquids in open containers have been transferred to closed containers. My areas are ready," Lisa announced. Her crew of thirty had put out a superhuman effort in getting their areas ready.

"The personnel facilities, including the swimming pools have been prepared. There will be no loose items in any of the living quarters. The defects the inspection teams found have all been corrected. In general, the facilities are ready," Victor Marquis continued.

"The personnel have all been instructed to be buckled into their seats or strapped into their beds upon notification. The Personnel organization is ready," Indira DeSouza filled in.

She had been surprised at Zack's immediate and thorough action upon recognizing the first threat to the Savitar. She realized she had underestimated him. She would have to move carefully when the time to take over presented itself.

"The welding will continue to the last moment. We have about ninety percent of all the main welds with a single weld pass complete. The remaining will be completed even as we begin the swing around the moon.

The idea of welding half at each location gives me high confidence in the Savitar's structural integrity even if a few locations get missed. Our structural integrity has been greatly increased," Paulo Sousa shared with the team.

"The materials in the center have all been checked and remain secure. The logistics folks did spot checks, since there was no way to do a comprehensive check on all the materials secured in the center of the Savitar. Since there are wire mesh barriers around all the materials, we feel justified in saying we are secure. The material stored outside the central sphere has also been checked," Gregor Menkowski thundered in his deep voice. He was impressed by this young-looking American's leadership and beginning to get more confident in him with his willingness to take immediate action.

"Well, little has changed in the field of science, so we feel secure. We have done some preliminary calculations as to the impact of the current welding progress. The overall structure should be at least one hundred times stronger than the original strength when we left orbit," Conrad Zepf said in a serious tone.

"The navigation team has continued to monitor the situation. We are coming in fifty per cent closer than originally planned. Were it not for the reinforcement of the new welds, we would probably be ripped apart. The welding should provide a significant safety margin," Chiang Lee informed the group.

"Well, boss our ship seems ready. I have set up a large screen in our navigation facility. It is not quite up to Star Trek specs, but it should provide a central place for us to gather and watch as we travel around the moon," Enrico finished.

"Thank you all for the quick response on the welding. Lars Mendelssohn and his group deserve some sort of recognition and reward for their super effort. Invite them to sit with us as we go around the Moon. Also, think about what we should do to recognize them and the crew after we round the Moon," Zack said as he closed the session.

The next morning as the four of them went to their breakfast, Zack noted the welding thermometer had reached the top and gushed out.

"Well, this amount of work was supposed to take us almost all the way to Mars. I am certainly glad we have been able to pull off this small miracle," Zack commented as he walked along the breakfast serving line.

It seemed everyone was up and getting breakfast.

Janet and Susan both agreed with him about it being a small miracle. Mitch who was bringing up the rear as usual, just said ditto. Janet always led the way. Zack was next. Susan and Mitch brought up the rear. This was their normal configuration when moving about.

Over coffee they all chatted quietly. Everyone was in a subdued mood as the moment for the encounter with the Moon approached.

Zack had his laptop computer with him and planned to spend his time looking ahead to what needed to happen after they made their way around the moon. There was nothing for him and his entourage to do while the Savitar got its first acceleration boost.

The trip around the Moon was anticlimactic. The Savitar went around the Moon and smoothly accelerated as planned. The structure creaked and groaned as it went around but nothing broke. The creaking and groaning was a little unnerving.

Lars relieved the tension in the room by telling stories of his younger days welding the beams of skyscrapers. He told a story about being caught in a high wind on an almost completed building. The skyscraper creaked, groaned, and swayed back and forth at least ten feet from side to side.

He claimed to have hung on with one hand as he was pulled horizontally back and forth all the time welding with his free hand. Everyone sitting in the observation room had a good laugh.

Zack was pleased to have him there.

Back at mission control the ground crew was ecstatic about the Savitar surviving the higher forces exerted by the closeness of its passage. The structural engineers were going back over their structural calculations. They had predicted disaster but celebrated like drunkards after a soccer tournament.

Craig listened to the discussion about the structural strength of the Savitar. He immediately realized Zack had somehow managed to change the game by strengthening the Savitar's structure. Zack would not have risked the lower more stress laden path around the moon unless he was sure of the capability of the Savitar.

The Savitar came around and was traveling at about fifty-six thousand miles per hour. It was speeding to a point in space where Mars would be in about ninety-two days. This additional speed had been factored in by the navigation team and the course they were now traveling was slightly different than originally planned.

Back on Earth Craig took one of the bottles of Black Label and shared a drink with the President.

"Dan, I don't know what Zack did to make it around the Moon and he is not telling us. You somehow knew from his message. I know he has concerns about other ways the Savitar might be sabotaged, and I am sure he will take the right action to overcome these attempts. Here is to his continued success," Craig said as he raised his shot glass.

"I have a great deal of trust in Zack, and we have the world riding on his success," the President toasted back.

Out on the Savitar Zack declared a day of celebration and rest. He had brought a bottle of Liebfraumilch wine and shared a glass with the entire leadership team. He invited Lars in to participate.

Chapter 18: Moon to Mars

"Team now is the time for us to establish a normal work cycle. I have talked this over with Enrico and a few others. We agreed on three work shifts and four work teams. This will allow one team to be free for a period of time. I want to set up the southern swing shift. A team will work seven days. They will then take one day off. They will then work another seven days. Then take three days off. Then they will work another seven days. Then they will take five days off.

During the five days off period, everyone will be required to participate in one or more of the seven following competitive activities: swimming, racket ball, handball, volleyball, weight training, aerobics, or track.

Everyone will also be required to select a personal hobby or self-development activity from the following list, gardening, painting, reading, playing a musical instrument, writing, learning a new skill or trade, learning to fly the shuttle, learning to navigate. If there is a hobby that I missed by all means let's get it put on the list.

Zack wanted everyone to keep in shape.

All personnel must learn self-defense and hand to hand combat." Zack said as he looked around the room.

"It all sounds good. Why the hand-to-hand combat?" one of the leadership team members asked.

"The first reason is I want to create a stronger crew. But the real reason is once we succeed, I expect there will be an attempt made from Earth to take us over. I wouldn't doubt certain countries have already started to build intercept vessels designed to come out and overtake us, and then take over this vessel," Zack said as he looked over his leadership team.

"If an attack occurs, what will happen to the Savitar crew members who are from the attacking country?" Chiang Lee asked as he studied his clasped hands. He knew his country would indeed be sending up a crew to attempt such a takeover. He had been briefed and coached to the expected support he and his counterparts were to provide.

"I hope we will have established ourselves as a close crew with a common vision of how we can best serve the Earth. I am hoping an allegiance to the Savitar will be stronger then the allegiance to the home country that we may never return to," Zack responded in a quiet but very serious way.

"Let's get the work rolling and let's develop the crew. Then we can come back to this topic in a year or so," Janet spoke up

She was sure of Chiang's position. He was between a rock and a hard place. She felt it would be best not to discuss this philosophically.

"In the next month, please talk to every person under your direct leadership and have them select the activities they want. One month from now we will begin the personal improvements." Janet finished.

"Our trip to Mars will take about three months. During this time, I would like all the welding for the current structure of the Savitar to be completed including the layers recommended by Lars. This is a change in our plans, but it should provide us with more structural strength for our Mars encounter.

Lars has recommended another layer of welding for each of the main joints. I would like to have this evaluated by the welding Engineers know how more strength this gives the Savitar.

We have estimated the strength of this small black hole, but the final figures are still being worked. Significant extra strength for the Savitar is very attractive," Zack shared with the leadership team.

"Paulo, please work with engineering and have the answer to the welding question resolved in the next few days," Zack said as he looked at Paulo DeSouza who was in charge of the welding.

"Today I am establishing the post of Internal Security and putting my three bodyguards in charge of this department. I would like them to establish a system to include laws, judges, and the procedures we will use when individuals clash. If any of you would like to participate in the development and design of this justice system, please indicate so at this time. I would like a proposal for this leadership team to review by the end of the month. Comments, Questions?" Zack said looking around the table.

After some discussion and several of the leadership team volunteering to participate in the definition of the legal system for the Savitar, business moved on to other topics.

"Paulo and his crew of two thousand welders will focus on completing the external welds and then connecting the Bucky balls inside each joint. This will take the next few months to complete and will greatly increase the strength of the forty-mile level. This will be the level to feel the greatest stresses from the black hole. It is our foundation. This is the primary focus for the next ninety days," Zack emphasized.

"I will be working with Dr. Garrity back on Earth to finalize the design of the rest of the Savitar.

However, this small black hole is giving us a problem in estimating its exact size and strength. It is very small relative to other black holes. The top scientists are arguing about its exact mass and strength. Some even question if it is a black hole in the conventional sense.

I am not sure what the disagreement means. It is clear these very intelligent folks are a little frustrated in their lack of knowledge about this anomaly we are now planning to encapsulate.

Our goal is to establish our facilities and living quarters at the one G level. Once we come around Mars and head out toward Jupiter it will be time to begin building the outer most or living level of the Savitar. All the material in the center of the Savitar is designated for this outer layer. This outer structure will be less massive than the foundation Bucky ball sphere but as you are aware it is a monumental undertaking. The diameter of the outer sphere is two hundred forty miles, and its circumference is seven hundred fifty miles. Building it in space as we travel is going to be a huge challenge. We have no experience to guide us. We will all need to review how we are going to keep people safe as we do this work," Zack continued his monologue.

"Radiation exposure is our greatest threat and many of our welders are already experiencing radiation sickness. Dr. Trimble has perfected his nano-bots to the point he feels it is ready for human testing.

The three welding crew who are suffering the most radiation damage volunteered to test the effectiveness of this technology. The nano-bots will be injected, be given time to do their work and then be deactivated. Samuel will be in to update us in the next few days on the outcome of these tests," Zack shared.

"Are there any comments, questions this morning?" Zack concluded.

There was a round of comments and questions about the safety of the nano-bots and about their effectiveness. Everyone knew without some technology similar to the nano-bots, many of the crew would perish from radiation exposure. However, it seemed somehow threatening and counter to human nature to turn some active virus like technology loose inside a person. They were all aware of the many people already beginning to feel the ill effects of the radiation.

Still, they had reservations.

Zack reassured them that the nano-bot use would progress as it proved itself.

"Beginning tomorrow, I would like us to follow a set agenda for this morning meeting. I have discussed this with Enrico, and he has a draft agenda for tomorrow. If you see any outages, please let him know. Enrico will be in charge of the day-to-day business of running the Savitar," Zack concluded as he looked around the room at his team.

"Tomorrow, I would like to begin the morning meeting using the following agenda," Enrico said as he smoothly took over as he handed out his prepared standard agenda.

"Everyone will follow the same basic process. If everything in your area meets the criteria for the area you will simply put up the green card, I am handing you and say nothing. If you have a measure out of specification or need some help or direction show the red side of the card, clearly state your area, the current measures for your area, the measure missing its target and describe the help you need. Immediate support will be identified, and action planned. Are there any questions?

This should make our morning meetings short and painless. I will run the meeting and keep things on track. Each day one of you will be responsible for taking notes and writing the summary. Your picture will be on the board in the note takers section," Enrico concluded.

He was anxious to organize this group into a smoothly operating leadership team, but he did not want to waste time in meetings. They had worked together throughout the building and launching of the Savitar. Now it was time to act as a crew to operate, maintain and improve the Savitar.

Enrico would be the one to run the Savitar directly. Zack would be in charge of the Mission. Enrico would act as captain and allow Zack the time needed to continue the development of the Savitar.

Zack and company left the morning meeting and proceeded to the break area for their morning cup of coffee. Outside the break area, they saw a new visual showing the outline of the Savitar and the welding being done externally and internally, and the percent completed. The graph stood at twenty five percent complete. This represented the welding already done on the exterior as they approached the Moon. The graph included the welding being done in the interior of the frame.

"I really like the enthusiasm of the Welding team and the visuals they generate to inform the rest of us on how they are doing. Their leadership seems to have them pumped. Let's visit them today to see how they are proceeding," Zack said as they poured themselves coffee.

"I would like to set up a cycle of review allowing me to inspect every location and work area of the Savitar. I want to know everyone and what they do. I want to talk to each of them as part of a complete cycle. Somehow, I want to know exactly what support, coaching or encouragement each person needs. I want them to know I care about them as persons.

They are the Savitar, and I want them to know it," Zack said as he looked at his three bodyguards.

"I will take on the responsibility of learning about each person we visit and what they are currently up to and let you know." Janet said. This fit her normal approach to checking out the people Zack would interact with.

"I will evaluate the work plan and help determine a good cycle to take us across the entire structure in a comprehensive and logical fashion." Mitch volunteered. Once we agree on the cycle, we can determine how often we execute it and what we want to see.

"I will work with Drs. Twillinger and McMillan to determine who is sick or having a problem. We can schedule visits with the people we identify," Susan joined in.

"Thanks, as we visit these folks and tour the Savitar, I want us to approach the visits with an attitude of trying to see how we can take the hard work out of what people are doing. Everything from how they need to prepare to do the work, the work, the environment, all these things are especially more difficult than doing it anywhere else. The work is hard, the environment unforgiving and the amount of work ahead of us is monumental. I want the minds and hearts of our crew to think of the Savitar as theirs. It is their home." Zack mused as he finished his coffee.

Zack focused on keeping the crew busy and making them feel valued. Their well-being was the most critical element of the long journey ahead. He planned to keep the crew busy for the next three months. They would be welding, getting plants growing and doing their own self development. Any extra time was to be spent as they wished. Zack wanted the crew to remain busy with little time to contemplate what might happen next.

Every other morning the four of them worked out with one of the Korean black belt Tae Kwon Do masters on the crew. On alternate days they would do the same with an Aikido master. These workouts lasted for one hour. Afterwards they all showered and went to the morning meeting. This was followed by a light breakfast.

Zack would then retire to his quarters to work on the design of the Savitar. This was a regular "discussion" with Craig. These discussions were a lot like doing discussions in chat rooms on the internet. They were slowly becoming exchanges of ideas as the communication time lengthened. The issues at hand were refinements in the basic lay out of the living areas.

The enormous size of the Savitar meant many details had been left blank. It was clear there was only enough material for a partial coverage of the outer sphere. The idea for a second outer level was abandoned. As Zack identified the amount of living space for the crew, the coverage of outer sphere was reduced to only the hexagons of the structure. Later even this was reduced.

After about three hours of design work, Zack and company would take a tour to a specific part of the Savitar and see how the work there was doing.

This served two purposes. It gave Zack firsthand knowledge of the ship and its condition. It also allowed Zack to interact with the crew members of the Savitar.

Everyone was busy, fully engaged and the mood of the crew was upbeat. In addition to the personal development activities, every Thursday was movie night, Saturday was dance and light entertainment night and Sunday was concert or band night. There was no place where everyone could get together at one time, so this was done by location and the entertainment timing was varied.

The more Zack studied the situation, the more it became clear the crew needed more room. Zack took note and adjusted the design of the Savitar in several ways. First, he planned more space where large groups could gather. Then he also added more open space for people to move about freely.

After a grueling day and evening of determining how many Bucky balls it would take to construct the outside layer of the Savitar, Zack voiced his concern.

"You know, I have been working on how the Savitar might be constructed from the materials we have. The folks back on Earth have also come up with several designs. I figure I need approximately one point two billion Bucky balls to make the outside layer of the Savitar a two-foot-thick Bucky ball shell. I will need to ask Gregor how many of the prefabricated Bucky balls are in storage. I don't think I have enough material," Zack said to Janet and Mitch.

Susan was absent tending to her new role as security chief. They all agreed Zack's protection should be reduced to two guards versus three. This would allow them to rotate into other activities so they too could enrich, grow themselves and carry out their role as security chief.

The next day in the morning meeting Zack shared the current state of the design of the Savitar.

"The center Bucky is the Savitar at the nine G level. You can see I have only sketched out the main items. This brings me to the question bugging me. I calculate to cover the one G layer with a web of Bucky balls I will need about one point two billion two-foot Bucky balls. Gregor, how many prefabricated Bucky balls are there in stock?" Zack finished.

"Well, our inventory says we have five hundred million prefabricated Bucky balls in stock. We also have two-inch stainless-steel pipe available. We have an unbelievable number of square feet of surface plating. I think Conrad and I should spend some time with you on the design. This will help us assess our current situation in terms of supplies and the effort required to do the fabrication," Gregor replied.

"I would love the help. Would you two consider taking over the design leadership. I have a lot of help on the Earth side, but they keep coming up with designs I consider impractical or on the minimal side for the good of the crew.

It seems they are worried about materials, and I am worried about maximizing the strength of the Savitar and providing more space for the crew. The answer is probably somewhere in the middle. It will take some concentrated design effort. More than I have the time for," Zack replied.

The two agreed to take the lead and organize a full formal design team. They would utilize the engineering contingent on board. Gregor would assign several of the logistics folks to the team

He had gotten just the support he was hoping to get. He would establish a project delivery team in charge of delivering construction plans for the rest of the Savitar. Zack felt comfortable having worked the overall concepts and initial estimates, but he knew the details would bore him out of his mind. He needed to get this turned over to a team willing to get into these details

During Paulo's part of the meeting, Paulo shared the additional weld pass recommended by Hans would strengthen each weld three-fold. This was so significant Paulo had immediately started the additional welding.

As Zack walked out with Enrico, he wondered out loud; "I wonder why the folks doing the design never mentioned this to us. A threefold increase in strength for the nine G level is so significant it should always have been in the plan. How many areas have been skimped on and was it on purpose or because we were rushed? I wonder if it was intentional," Zack conjectured.

Enrico nodded but did not answer. He too had wondered about where the weak spots were in the design of the Savitar. He hoped Zack and the rest of the team would continue to stay ahead of the folks who seemed bent on having the mission fail.

Enrico's mind was on the upcoming sling around Mars. They were about thirty days away. He had a picture of Mars put up in the cafeteria. A new picture was updated each morning. It was now the size of an orange. He knew this would be the next sabotage timing.

He now felt good about the structural integrity and thought they were not at risk in that area.

He knew that Chiang Lee kept a close eye on the course of the Savitar and felt it was exactly on track. The navigation team on the Savitar controlled their course. So, it probably would not be navigation.

He knew that the folks on Earth did not know of the progress of the welding process. Zack had convinced the Savitar leadership team to hold back on this information lest the saboteurs get information causing them to take action in some other arena.

Each day they reported back to Earth, on the percentage of welding the Earth expected the crew to achieve. In reality the crew had been done with most of the work before the trip around the moon and they continued for the last two plus months to weld away like mad men. They had completed ninety five percent of the second pass welding.

This was a layer with three welding beads layered across the first bead. They had already started the process of welding a third pass that would completely fill in the joint and strengthen the Savitar by three hundred percent.

"I have been wondering where the next attack on us will come from. We seem to be taking control of the situation but there are so many ways this journey could be compromised," Enrico said as they sat sharing a cup of coffee.

Zack replied, "Well, I figure each time we approach one of the trajectory acceleration points there will be some risk. We will be constantly accelerating out to Jupiter and then we will need to decelerate as we approach the black hole itself. Then at the black hole itself we will have some very risky and untried procedures to position the Savitar around the black hole. Let's look at this again once we get past Mars.

The Savitar had gone around the moon and gotten a nice doubling of speed and had been accelerating for the last three months as they approached the orbit of Mars. They were now traveling at a heady 62,000 MPH. They were hoping to achieve 112,000 MPH as they left Mars. Their speed was a critical factor in this race.

However, as they went past the orbit of Mars the biggest threat to them was the space between Mars and Jupiter. This was the orbit filled with countless Asteroids of a failed planet formation.

To go through it at the speeds they were going would be tantamount to running through a dense mine field. It was something no one should try.

As they went around Mars, they would change their trajectory upward so they would fly above the asteroid belt plain and then at some point they would point themselves back down toward Jupiter. Even then there was still a high level of risk of having an object impact the Savitar.

A straight shot across the asteroid belt would have taken one hundred fifty-five days. Taking the route, they now planned, would take one-hundred seventy-five days. Even on this longer path would present a high risk.

Their approach to Mars was the first manned flight to get this far. All telescopes and cameras were trained on the surface of Mars. The Savitar science team would get all the data that they could in the brief encounter.

They had been preparing for this event for the last month. There was an even larger team on Earth. They would get and transmitted pictures continually. This was the science team's moment and they cherished it. The analysis of the pictures would take years to complete. This information and the knowledge it would generate made a good down payment on the cost of the Savitar.

They successfully launched an instrument and telescopic satellite into orbit as they went past Mars. This satellite was equipped to examine the entire surface of Mars. Every square inch of the surface would get photographed to a one-inch resolution. The satellite would circle the planet and continue to take pictures for at least a dozen years. It had booster and positioning rockets enabling the controllers on Earth to adjust the orbit. This capability would enable specific areas to be studied more closely.

The nano-bot experiment had gone extremely well. Two, very radiation sick welders, had volunteered for the experiment. Within a day the volunteers experienced improvement. A week later, they were a little thinner but completely back to normal. One aspect of the treatment was the need to drink enormous amounts of water, coupled with the need to urinate. The urine was filled with a great deal of additional dead tissue as the nano-bots fixed some cells and totally turned others off.

Dr. Trimble was ecstatic about the outcome. He and his team monitored each individual and examined them with every instrument capable of looking in to see what was happening. The two patients resigned themselves to being, the guinea pigs. They were getting more attention than ever before in their lives.

After the success with the initial volunteers, Dr. Trimble recommended weekly, one day treatments for the entire crew. With this approach, no one needed to get as ill as the original volunteers.

His recommendations were shared with the entire crew and a voluntary program was established. The virus nano-bots were easy to produce and within a week the entire crew had been treated. The only measurable impact was the use of drinking water went up dramatically. Everyone's health improved and a secondary benefit was everyone also trimmed off some body fat. The nano-bots once they fixed radiation damage tended to remove much of the fat cells in the body. It was not long before everyone was taking part.

Back on Earth, the secondary effect of fat removal would make this a very sought-after product.

Samuel and Zack discussed how they might share this with the rest of the world. They were in agreement they would wait until after they had dealt with the black hole before deciding how to release the information about the nano-bots.

Every birthday on the Savitar was announced and the birthday person got a special meal of their choice. Their choice was of course limited to what was available on board.

Janet's birthday had been celebrated September 12th. Zack presented Janet with a silver necklace on which hung the flattened bullets that had hit him in the back. It had the day month and year carved into the lead and the lettering was filled in with silver and embedded with small emeralds.

Janet realized that Zack had arranged for this gift while he was still on Earth. She gave him a hug and whispered her thank-you.

Lisa Heming's birthday fell almost exactly on the day they were going past Mars. Zack arranged for her to receive the four coffee trees Sampson and his buddies had been growing. Zack had recruited several other people to grow a variety of plants. In all there were the coffee trees, cacao trees, cashew trees, apple trees, tangerine, orange, and mango trees. All arrived in the central cafeteria area in stainless steel pots that were filled with soil. They were a little scrawny and only about three feet high, but they were a good start.

Lisa was brought to the cafeteria after the morning meeting to have a cup of coffee. Zack's recruited farmers stood proudly in front of their plant offerings and sang happy birthday. The surprised look on Lisa's face was all any of them needed as a thank you.

"Well, this is a little like giving a bus to a bus driver but if it's the thought that counts, then the folks on this bus really think a lot about you," Zack said as he presented Lisa with yet another small envelope of wildflower seeds.

Enrico gave Lisa a bracelet with a small silver and ruby encrusted rose hanging down from it. The bracelet was designed to hang additional objects on it.

Zack was surprised at the gift and was about to make a smart aleck comment when Janet poked him in the ribs with her elbow.

"Hey, I guess I'm just not as observant as I should be," Zack whispered quietly to Janet.

It made sense. Different people were beginning to associate with one another and were pairing off.

This had been part of his selection process. The Savitar was almost exactly a 50-50 split in gender.

The Mars encounter was anticlimactic. The science team got lots of communication but in general communications with Earth was now getting to be difficult. The messages sent were in complete concepts. Dialogues, discussions, or interviews were impossible.

Craig, accessible on Earth, covered the sound bites the news media needed.

"Good luck on your journey around Mars. Emily sends her best wishes. The politics of the Savitar have taken a new twist. The space capable countries are in a race to build fast going spaceships. I will share more with you later," Craig.

"Journey around Mars was fantastic. No problems on the Savitar. Our course will take us up above the Asteroid belt. Velocity is up to 120,000 MPH. We have about one hundred thirty days to Jupiter. This is what I call speeding on the way to destiny. My regards to Emily," Zack cabled back.

Chapter 19: Mars to Jupiter

Zack was now beginning to understand the difficulties of the work going on around him on the Savitar. There was still a great deal of dangerous work ahead. The cable pulling, the construction of the living quarters, the installation of the super magnets and continued radiation exposure all posed risks to his crew.

He had personally experienced the clumsy feeling of working in his space suite. He realized working out on the surfaces of the Savitar was not very safe. He felt luck and the sensible fear of his crew was the reason no one had been lost.

A review of the process to pull in the remaining stabilizing cables from the nine G level to the one G level rang alarm bells. Each cable was tack welded at the nine G level in a prefabricated mounting block.

The cable was then to be pulled outward from the one G level by a light pull cable. These pull lines were very thin high tensile wire more than two-hundred miles long. They were taken down by the one person lifts. Once at the nine G level they were attached to the massive stabilizing cable.

The pull wire with the stabilizing cable connected to it was pulled out toward the one G level. Anyone who ever went fishing would have immediately understood the process of pulling in a cable. You pulled the fish in but always let it play to prevent breaking the line.

Ten teams in all were pulling the remaining cables.

The safety of the cable pulling crews concerned Zack. He had personally ridden the lifts down to the nine G level and had walked the entire circumference of the one G Level.

It was not safe.

He immediately had safety lines installed and he assigned a safety review team to identify and put into place all safety counter measures. All personnel were required to be tethered to safety cables added along all the exterior surfaces.

"I want every team member to review the safety practices and to discuss the safety aspects of their tasks. Once the entire team has reviewed and understands, they will be allowed to do the work," Zack instructed Paulo Souza during the morning leadership meeting.

He left the meeting to join the Savitar design team morning meeting. Every day it became clearer to Zack how important a more open environment with a mix of living space and open garden space was to the long-term well-being of the Savitar.

The Charter for the design team called for a living environment where everyone could find enjoyment, peace of mind and enough open space to relax. This team was eagerly exploring how to accomplish their charter.

There was only enough plate steel to provide a partial cover for the Savitar and to provide for building all the facilities Zack insisted on. The design covered every other hexagon and left all pentagons open.

The super magnets were at the foot of the pentagons and designed to be mechanically lifted if they ever needed repair. Leaving this area uncovered made more sense than covering it.

The living facilities were put to the back half of the Savitar giving them slightly more protection. A hydroponics garden was at the center of every one of the five living areas. A cafeteria was associated with each garden. Around the garden would be a park and then the apartment living areas. Every apartment would have a view of the park and the gardens.

Initially there would be only six living areas located on the backside of the Savitar. The front half of the sphere would be the production and work areas. The design allowed for the additional expansion. The work to complete the construction of this new design fit in the time horizon of the travel out to the black hole.

Dr. Sam Trimble continued working on his nano-bots at full swing. He had twelve researchers working with him. This continued to be the most heavily staffed single focus area after the assembly work of the Savitar itself. Even with the weekly use of the nano-bots the prolonged exposure the crew was experiencing was taking its toll.

"The weekly application is a success, however, for those working continuously outside, I recommend a prolonged use of nano-bots. I am ready for continuous use of the nano-bots," Dr. Trimble spoke up during one of the morning meetings.

"How long can the nano-bots remain in a person?" Zack asked looking around to see the reaction of his leadership team.

"I believe the time period can be indefinite. Nano-bots do have a finite length until they themselves cease to function so for now we will need to do monthly replenishments," Dr. Trimble replied.

"Do you mean we should all be using this procedure," Zack asked?

"Yes, all of us have suffered some radiation damage and continue to do so. Those who spend more time outside have more damage" Dr. Trimble replied.

Zack always helped Samuel take the next step with the crew. "OK, then I will be the first official user of this new technique," Zack replied.

The leadership team recognized what Zack was doing and they all volunteered to the new Nano-bot use.

Samuel thought of his work on the Savitar as the most fulfilling in his life and he admired Zack for the quiet but consistent way he gave his support and made things happen.

Zack continued to give weekly updates of events to Craig. Craig in turn kept Zack abreast of the latest developments on Earth. The Russians were developing a new space craft designed to fly at least as far as the moon and many suspected well beyond. The Chinese were also developing a new generation of spacecraft. Craig was totally silent as to what the US was doing in this area, but the silence told Zack all he needed to know.

He knew the President would not let the US be left behind.

The world economy was booming, and the majority of people seemed to have forgotten the doomsday object waiting ahead. In the first few months of the journey the reports Zack sent back made the news on a daily basis. After the sling around the Moon, the frequency dropped to a weekly update. Then the frequency dropped down to a monthly update. The successful sling around Mars had been reported. That was the last report Craig had been contacted about. He figured when the Savitar got to Jupiter it would make the news again.

Zack now knew all the crew by face and most by name and history. He also knew every section of the ship. There was not a nut, bolt or weld he had not inspected. The crew was amazed at his powers of observation and his range of knowledge. They were also surprised someone in his position would take the time to get intimate with the details Zack did.

Zack's routine though varied was intense and he followed a consistent cycle.

The hydroponics was expanded to almost double the capacity and provided fresh fruit and vegetables for the entire crew.

When Zack shared the seed trove with Lisa, she had been overwhelmed at the selection. She was now confident in expanding into the extra garden space being planned in the new design.

Life on the Savitar took on an energetic rhythm of work, exercise, and self-development.

Zack became known for joining various groups to get firsthand knowledge of what was happening on the ship. He became qualified to weld the joints, to tend the plants, to navigate the ship, to council the weary.

He seemed to be everywhere.

The tight security continued well beyond when he thought it should have been eliminated. He and Janet argued about this several times, but she would not relent. She was worried there would be a deep mole activated in some way that would happen when they were well into the trip.

She, Susan, and Mitch kept a close watch on Zack. They participated in everything he did, so they were as busy as he.

Their regimen was one of getting up early, practicing Tae Kwon Do or Aikido, exercising, going to the morning meeting, getting breakfast, doing a planned tour, swimming, going through one of the hydroponics sections, lunch, doing an afternoon exercise, hitting the library, light dinner, and either an evening study/reading or on weekends, a movie or discussion about some topic they had decided to dig into.

This was the pace seven days a week.

Zack used the library and evening study to continue his development of the Savitar. He and the design team made significant changes to the initial design.

Most of the changes were to improve the living quarters.

A key feature missed in the original design was in the design of moving around on the Savitar. Zack learned it would be impractical to have working personnel travel around the sphere in their space suits.

He and his team designed transit tubes running from one location to another. These transit tubes would be powered by the gravity provided by the black hole and would work like a car coasting from the top of one hill to the top of the next. Zack wanted to have the tubes on each half of the sphere installed before getting to the black hole. He also had the team make a car for each tube. The tubes crossing the two halves of the sphere would be completed after the capture.

There were seventy-five such tubes. They each connected to a transfer station at the edge of each pentagon. This allowed each pentagon to connect directly to the five pentagons surrounding it. Getting totally around the Savitar would require several transfers. Each car would be able to be programmed to go to any pentagon on the sphere.

The fabrication, construction and installation of this transport system were each a major effort. Teams to carry out the work were identified and staffed from the welding group as they completed the welding of the Savitar frame. The crew of the Savitar could begin immediately using the transport system as it was built.

Christmas was approaching as they came closer to Jupiter. They would be spending their first Christmas aboard the Savitar in close proximity of Jupiter.

There were several major religions on board, Judaism, Christian, Moslem, Hindu, and Buddhism. Each religion was allowed to practice the elements of their faith. Each was provided with facilities. These facilities were of course shared due to the lack of space. In the final design of the Savitar, each faith had its own facility.

Zack and the crew decided they would modify the custom of giving gifts and separate this practice from the religious observations. They called this event the Savitar Thanksgiving. It combined the customs from several countries and would be unique to the Savitar.

Every culture represented on the Savitar was involved in the design of this holiday. They ensured the occasion adhered to the beliefs of all the religions.

Zack had thought ahead to this occasion and had arranged for a unique gift for every person on board. Family members on Earth had been asked to give some small item for their relatives.

Zack had Craig put them in one of the many containers sent up to the Savitar. He now arranged for the gifts to be brought out and put around the various gift giving areas.

The Savitar Thanksgiving event was a huge success. The fact Zack had thought so far ahead about the crew impressed everyone. He already had the crew's solid respect and admiration. This now changed to total allegiance to him by almost all of the crew.

Shortly after the celebration day Zack was out checking the final installation of one of the forty-two super magnets. He had made it his project to participate in and inspect the installation of these super magnets forming the magnetic bottle designed to hold the black hole in the center of the sphere.

These magnets were vital and an integral part of the structure. The design was redundant. Theoretically eight magnets were sufficient to maintain the black hole at the center of the sphere. However, they were dealing with a black hole, and no one knew its exact strength. There would be fourteen magnet centers and forty-two magnets in all. The magnets would be located at the nine G level and would be very difficult to service. The goal was to make them so effective they would need little to no maintenance. The redundancy allowed for some problems and provided electrical ways to overcome the problems without the need for humans to work at the nine G level. The Magnets were designed to be raised up to the one G level when servicing was finally required.

Zack wanted to get out on his own to inspect one of the magnets. He devised a means to misdirect his bodyguards. Zack was surprised that his simple misdirection of Janet, Mitch and Susan worked. He had outwitted his ever-constant bodyguards. They were his friends and in Janet's case much more.

He just wanted space, some free time on his own so he had figured out how to get it.

After getting over his initial surprise and making sure he had not been found out he made a bee line down to the spacesuit dressing room.

He called Sampson and verified he would be down to accompany him on the magnet inspection.

He quickly went through the required routine checks. He was thorough but fast. He stripped down to put on his body glove. His six two frame was lean and tawny. He was proud of his abs. He never dreamed of having the six-pack he now sported. He was in the best condition of his life. The strenuous exercise routine and the strict diet he, Janet, Susan, and Mitch were on put them all in great shape.

Janet was a disciplinarian and kept all of them true to their exercise routine.

He stepped into his suit and made sure it was properly sealed. He skipped over the required contact with the communications center. They would immediately contact Janet.

He took the exhilarating ride down to the nine G level on one of the many lifts rigged up by the welders. The rapid acceleration and then after a few minutes the rapid deceleration, gave a stomach churning, up in the throat feeling Zack last experienced on a roller coaster ride. Though totally encased in his space suit, he could almost feel his hair blowing behind him. He was momentarily light-headed as he stepped off the lift to join Sampson for the final inspection of the number twelve magnet.

Zack apprehensively approached Sampson. They were both in full space suits talking over their radios. They exchanged greetings.

"Where are your shadows tonight," Sampson asked a little surprised Zack was alone.

He knew Janet and the rest always accompanied Zack. He looked around worried.

"Oh, I gave them the night off," Zack replied calmly as he looked over the work plan Sampson handed him. He counted on Sampson's stoic personality and hoped he would not make a big deal about the missing bodyguards.

Sampson observed him quietly not saying a word. He knew this was unusual but did not want to challenge the boss. Zack always surprised him by being such a practical guy.

"Hey," he thought, "It's none of my business." He never understood the need for the intense protection for Zack. This was Sampson's turf, and he knew it was safe. He turned and led the way out to check the grounding connections of the giant black hole bottling magnet.

The giant magnet was the twelfth primary magnet to be mounted. The magnets would hold the small black hole in the center of the sphere. Another thirty magnets would be added. Each station would have a total of three magnets. The catastrophic nature of a failure to keep the black hole centered in the containment field warranted three levels of redundancy at each mounting location.

Back in the control room, Indira's heart almost stopped when she saw Zack appear alone on her secret spacesuit changing room monitor. She watched as Zack went through his check out routine. His sharp cut physique caused her to regret her lack of success in getting him into her bed. She had tried unsuccessfully for several years. He really was a well healed specimen. She would have loved to spend more time watching. After Zack checked out his suit, she threw the switch disabling all of his suit's jet controls.

This was her chance.

She rushed to where her suit was located.

This was her chance!

She experienced an adrenaline rush.

Her heart raced as she hastened to carry out her long dormant plan.

Sampson and Zack had been working about an hour when a moving shadow or some other warning caused Zack to stand and turn around. Torpedoing toward him through the emptiness of space was a four-foot-long welding cylinder.

Instantly Zack went into motion as his adrenaline kicked in. Months of Tae Kwon Do, swimming, and running now paid off. Everything seemed to go into slow motion. He felt his leg muscles tense and then launch him into the air as he did a summersault over the torpedo cylinder. He slowly reached out and caught himself on a cable connected to the magnet structure.

The only thing he could not explain was the instant beads of sweat now trickling down his forehead into his eyes and the sharp jerk on his arm as his motion was arrested.

He turned to look around. He could smell his own sweat and what he knew was a dreadful stench of guilt.

He should have known Janet would be right.

He had made a potentially deadly mistake.

Sampson had continued on ahead of him and gone around to the other side of the huge magnet and was nowhere in sight.

Zack was alone and he knew someone was trying to kill him.

Once again, his recent argument with Janet on the need for continued tight security flashed into his mind. She had insisted he continue to be guarded until after the capture of the black hole.

She had been right, and he now knew he had been dead wrong.

He hoped he would get a chance to tell her how right she had been.

Chapter 20: Miracle

Zack was now standing on the magnet housing. Behind him at about shoulder level was the make-shift machine shop serving as a break area for the workers. There was not much else at this location but the magnet itself.

He was desperate to locate his attacker. As he turned to look toward the machine shop something hit him on the side of his helmet.

Indira had watched in amazement as Zack eluded the welding cylinder that she had launched toward him.

"How was he able to do that in a space suit? No one is that good," she thought as she picked up a large steel bar and approached him from behind. His head was about to her knees. She swung the bar with all her might and caught him on the side of the helmet. Her intention was to crack the helmet open. She had not thought about her action. Luckily for her, the resulting impact reaction launched her directly back into the welding shop. Any other direction would have launched her out into the emptiness of the Savitar.

The force of the impact snapped Zack's head whip like inside his helmet. There was a ringing in his ears, and he was having trouble focusing. He felt a warm stream run down the side of his face and tasted the salty flavor of his own blood.

Suddenly he realized he had lost hold of the magnet cable. He was slowly tumbling away from the magnet.

He looked back to the person at the entrance to the welding shop. He was astonished to see the helmet lamp turn on. The person wanted him to see and know who had attacked him. They were confident he was as good as dead. Indira held up an object and made an exaggerated motion of throwing a light switch. She then waved, turned off the helmet lamp and walked over to the lift and went zooming up the cable toward the living quarters.

Indira felt light-headed. She felt drunk as she zoomed up toward the one G level. The long-planned takeover was underway. She was confident of two things. First, Zack was doomed. There was no way for him to be saved. Second, she was now the dominant force aboard and she would soon be in control.

Sampson came around the magnet looking for Zack. He wondered what had distracted Zack and why he had not followed. It took him several moments until he spotted Zack floating toward the rear of the Savitar where the main engines were mounted.

Shock and total disbelief hit him. Sampson felt a bottomless pit in his stomach. He tried contacting Zack via the headset but could not communicate with him. His heart was now racing as he rushed toward the welding shop.

He knew exactly who to call. He realized now that he should have done so earlier. He now knew that there were bad guys on board.

The vast emptiness of the Savitar became starkly ominous. Zack was looking around and trying to figure how to maneuver to some object to which he could attach himself. Ninety five percent of the Savitar was emptiness. His momentum was taking him outward toward the back of the sphere. He tried desperately to use the small jets on his suit but none of the controls worked. He cursed Indira for being so thorough as to disable his maneuvering jets.

He reached up inside his suit to wipe off the perspiration beading on his forehead and realized he was still bleeding from his head wound.

He was slowly drifting out toward the edge of the sphere. His current path would take him by the main engine platform at the one G level. He floated slowly through the emptiness of the Savitar and was totally frustrated by his inability to do anything to save himself.

He knew that Eternity awaited him beyond the one G level.

"I am almost to the point of no return, to the point where I will not get saved," Zack thought and to his surprise his thoughts turned away from the moment and went back to a few years earlier and the beginning of his current journey.

The call from Sampson sent a cold shiver running down Janet's back. She asked Sampson to go to the rear engine and be prepared to anchor a safety line reel. She contacted Susan and Mitch and directed them to get to the rear pentagon and to take a retrieval reel and line out with them.

"You have about an hour to get there with the reel. Can you, do it?" Janet inquired.

"You bet. We will get there. Its lucky we are on this side of the structure," Susan replied.

Soon she and Mitch were scooting across the engine pentagon with a reel between them. They were using their jets and flying along the surface. A sliding safety guide wire was holding them to the surface of the Savitar. They had never done anything like this and knew their challenge would when they needed to stop. They agreed their best chance was to flip over and use their suit jets to stop their forward progress.

Sampson had used a variety of makeshift cable lifts and runs to get to the engine platform. He broke several safety rules in getting to the platform at the speed he did. He made it back to the engines in record time.

He saw the two approaching with the cable reel between them. He realized they were as crazy as he was. He was contemplating throwing himself in their path when he watched them flip over and ignite their jets.

They came to rest with the retrieval reel just shy of the edge of the pentagon. Sampson immediately went to work in securing the reel to the surface of the pentagon. He could see Zack's figure approaching.

Janet rapidly put on her suit and came out of the central control area. The engine pentagon was at the very back of the sphere. There was no way for her to get there in time if she went along the surface.

The only way was for her to jet across the inside of the sphere. This had never been done and she had never contemplated doing it. Without hesitation she jumped, turned on her suit jets and went toward the rear engine pentagon at maximum velocity. She was flying across the void inside of the Savitar. She adjusted her jets and aimed at the bottom of the engine pentagon. She hoped she would not have to dodge any of the one G support cables. It seemed the way was clear. The thought of superman or in her case superwoman came to her mind as she streaked across the internal space of the Savitar.

Though the Savitar appeared as a huge sphere, most of it was emptiness.

Janet adjusted her trajectory again so she would hit close to the edge of the engine pentagon. She flipped over to brake and landed or more truthfully crashed with a resounding thud. Luckily, she did not break anything. She worked her way over to the edge and came up exactly where Sampson was finishing securing the retrieval reel.

The three were surprised by Janet's arrival. They quickly realized what she had just done and the risk she had taken to get to the rear engine platform in time.

Janet gave them no time to comment.

"Hook me up to the cable. I need to launch immediately, or it will be too late," Janet said as she looked out to where Zack was now floating.

She immediately launched herself toward Zack. She had her jets on full power.

Zack was moving slowly out toward the edge of the sphere. He would soon be leaving the Savitar's boundary. He was looking out to the stars beyond as his peripheral vision told him he had reached the surface of the Savitar. He was coming up by the Engine pentagon. Once he went past this point, there was no returning, no getting saved. He would then float in space until his oxygen ran out.

His thoughts were taking him through the events leading to this point. It really was true about reliving all the important events of one's life in the instance before death.

Only one realization caught him by surprise.

Suddenly he was hit from behind and something encircled his waist. He could not tell what had just happened, but his outward travel had stopped, and he was slowly being pulled back to the Savitar.

He knew a miracle had occurred.

Janet's suit jets ran out of fuel as she made her desperate attempt to save Zack. She would not be able to brake as she approached Zack. Just before colliding with him, Janet snapped a safety line from herself to his belt. She then embraced him as they collided. She hoped the retrieval line would hold as the reel ran out of line and the momentum of the two tested the lines ultimate strength.

The trio at the reel saw what was happening and all were holding on to the reel and to the Savitar structure. Sampson had enough foresight to have tied of the reel to the decking. Everything groaned and the cable would have twanged if sound would have been supported by the void of space. Then the recoil resulted in loose cable coming back toward them. They quickly reeled in the slack and began a slow measured pull. Soon things steadied out and they slowly hauled Janet and Zack in.

Once the Janet and Zack were on the engine pentagon they were quickly guided into a pressurized changing room.

The next thing Zack knew he was looking into the tearful eyes of a very mad Janet Romero.

"The next time you ditch me, I am going to be the one who pushes you out into space," Janet was angrily lecturing him as she helped him get out of his suit.

She was alarmed at the blood on his face.

"If Sampson had not called me immediately, you would now be history," Janet stopped and turned around looking away from him.

"Did you get a chance to see who did this," Susan asked as she patted Janet on the back?

Mitch continued to help Zack get out of his suit.

"You were extremely lucky. Your helmet is cracked. A little harder hit and you would immediately have ceased to exist," Mitch delivered the news.

<u>Chapter 21: Apology and Evaluation</u>

Zack took a deep breath. He looked at his three bodyguards and the apologized.

"Look, I apologize to all of you.

Janet, the first thing that crossed my mind was you were indeed right, and I hoped I would get to apologize to you," Zack said as he looked down at his feet.

He felt a little like the time he had disappointed his mother by disobeying her when he knew she meant the best for him.

"And yes, I did see who ambushed me. She wanted me to know she had done this deed. I think she was sure I was a goner" Zack said as he looked at Janet who had tears in her eyes.

Even when she had saved him back on Earth, she had not responded this emotionally. Zack was taken a little by surprise. He expected her to be mad, but he did not know how to react to this.

"Do you realize you were beyond the surface of the Savitar? Another few feet and you would be history. I almost lost you because when I grabbed you, my cable pulled me backward at the same time I snapped in the safety line. Dam your innocence Zack," Janet said as she turned away again.

An awkward silence followed as Zack stood facing the three but with Janet showing her back to him. He could tell she was crying. This hurt him more than anything else he could think of.

"Susan, Mitch, would you please give me a few moments alone with Janet," Zack asked the two.

It did not escape his notice they separated, and each went out one of the two doors to the compartment. Sampson had left earlier at Susan's direction.

"Janet, I admit what I did was really stupid, and I apologize. I want you to know you were the only one to come to my mind that I felt I should have said more to. I wanted to do this for a long time, but I have been afraid of how this will change our relationship," Zack said as he gently kissed her lips.

"Oh, Zack you innocent," Janet said as she responded with the passion she had kept in control since she had first taken the job of protecting him.

Now she felt her emotions surge to a new height.

"Now who did this," Janet asked.

"It was Indira. I have been thinking. She had the role of selecting the people who came on board. This may be the start of a takeover. If she thinks she has been successful, she may activate a takeover or try some other action," Zack rattled off his thoughts.

"Susan, Mitch come in here. We need to huddle," Janet called out.

Her heart was still racing from the sudden change in her and Zack's relationship.

They decided to report the loss of Zack to see if they could draw out the hidden cell or cells aboard the ship. They sent out an old suit as a dummy. They then returned to the control center and reported Zack missing.

Zack meanwhile took a circuitous route to the hydroponics area. He would hide out there for a few days. Janet, Susan, and Mitch would play out the hand they had planned. He was met by Lisa who had quarters in one of the hydroponics gardens. He would bunk with her since she would be able to feed him, and no one would notice.

"How do you know I am not one of the subversives?" Lisa said as she escorted Zack into her quarters.

Zack noticed Lisa's decorations were some budding flowers and other plants she was nursing to life.

"Well, if you are then I will have to conclude I am on the wrong side," Zack said with a chuckle.

"You get the top bunk. I hope you don't snore." Lisa continued as she removed a few plants and other items from the top bunk. She was one of the few people with no room mates. Zack didn't know how she had pulled that off.

"These are going to be close quarters but most of the day I will be out in the gardens. Susan said she would bring over a few of your clothes. You will be able to get on my computer as me and then your clearance codes will let you monitor what is going on," Lisa said as she continued to move her plants about.

Zack was going to be the hidden monitor. He could use his code and have the computer monitor anyone he wanted. He typed in Indira's name and looked to see if she had contacted anyone.

Indeed, Indira had placed three calls, one to Earth and to two other people on board.

The call and message Indira had sent to Earth was never transmitted. It was intercepted on the Savitar and later Zack sent it on to Craig explaining what had transpired and who on the Savitar was involved.

One of the two people on the Savitar was a shuttle pilot.

This surprised Janet.

John Adams was a shuttle pilot for years before the concept of the Savitar had come about. John broke down quickly. He explained his wife, daughter and young son were all being held hostage by people in the US Army. He was told he would take command of the Savitar if a chance ever came about. He also implicated an Air Force General who had implied a group of military officers were contemplating an overthrow of President Manning if he won re-election. Janet and Zack sent this information on to Craig.

The final person who Indira called was the most disturbing because it was one of the Electrical Engineers assigned to optimize the magnetic bottle to be used to contain the black hole.

John came forward the day of Zack's simulated demise and asserted his claim to be the captain of the Savitar based on his military rank. Indira, a member of the leadership team agreed with his claim.

Enrico, second in command and in charge of the Savitar and the rest of the Leadership team disagreed. He had both put into detention until the situation could be worked out.

This surprised Indira. She could get no support from any of the other members of the leadership team.

"I smell a dead fish. I want to know what happened out on the structure and who was involved," was Enrico's reaction and order to Janet.

"Why was Zack left alone? He is supposed to be under your protection. Where were you?" he inquired of Janet.

He did not wait for an answer.

"Our mission has not changed. We will take the Savitar on to the black hole and capture it. That is our mission, and we will fulfill it. Until further notice, I will take command of the Savitar. Are there any objections," Enrico continued?

"Until farther notice Captain John Adams and Indira are under arrest and will be held in their quarters. The rest of the leadership team will go about their work as planned," Enrico said as he got up and walked out as he guided Janet out by the elbow.

Instead of explaining in the presence of the other members of the leadership team, Janet led Enrico back into the hydroponics center.

Zack walked out of Lisa's quarters to meet them.

"My friend, it seems you have been resurrected. You are a man of nine lives," Enrico said as he stepped forward and gave Zack his usual hug. "Did you plan this on purpose to test us," Enrico continued.

"No, I did not plan it this way It was my stupid actions that caused these events.

You did a wonderful job in taking control and keeping the ship on track. A lesser man may have turned over control. I would like you to take over the Captain's role permanently. I want to be an Admiral," Zack said with a smile.

"Well, sure but what does an Admiral do?" Enrico shot back.

"Well, this Admiral is going to check all the software developed to manage the black hole once we capture it. One of our moles has been responsible for the development and testing of this software. In the next several months we need to go over the software with a fine-tooth comb to ensure there are no hidden traps," Zack replied.

Zack came out of hiding a few days later when it became apparent no other personnel were involved. Relief spread throughout the ship. The crew had grown to trust Zack to see them through.

Zack announced Enrico as the permanent Captain of the Savitar.

Enrico called together a board of inquiry to look into the recent attack on Zack and any sabotage done by the three.

The board was made up of twelve people. It was a cross section of the crew. Enrico presided over the inquiry, but two lawyers were assigned to help with the process. One was assigned to protect the rights of the accused. The other was assigned to ask the questions of the accused. The twelve would decide if there was enough information for a trial to be held.

Indira not only confessed but expressed her hatred of the abominable act they were attempting. She lashed out at Zack and the journey of the Savitar. Her fanatical attitude and anger immediately convinced the board of inquire not only of her guilt but of her as a danger to the ship.

She was turned over for confinement until the day of her trial for attempted murder and sabotage.

The ship did not have a prison. This was immediately addressed by an eager construction crew.

John Adams admitted his role in trying to take over the Savitar. He explained his circumstances and apologized. He said he had nothing to do with the attack on Zack and did not realize Indira had taken such action.

The board of inquiry accepted John's statements and recommended a Captain's board take up any punishment and that Captains board would occur when he was back on Earth.

Finally, Sunny Chen, the programmer was brought before the board. He would not talk except to say they were all doomed. He joined Indira in the new prison to await trial.

The trial was set for a date two months later. Each accused was assigned a legal representative.

"Enrico, I would like you to use the law structure similar to the one in the U.S. to guide the trial. Before the trial I would like the crew to establish punishment guidelines. I would also like to understand what the ultimate punishment is to be," Zack said as they finished their dinner.

"I have taken a preliminary look at the control software for the magnetic bottle and have decided it is a rat trap. This is the most complicated programming I have ever seen. I am pulling together a team to go over every bit of code.

This is more than two years of programming. We need to go completely through it in the next six months.

I think it was lucky Indira chose to act at this time, otherwise we would most likely have found out about this sabotage as we were getting sucked into the black hole," Zack said looking around the table.

"Don't try to justify your sneaking out on us," Janet said as she poked Zack.

The group was eating in the general mess hall. There were no special officer's or leader's areas. Everyone on the crew had access to the same amenities or lack of, as was often the case.

When Zack and his team began to dissect the software program it quickly became apparent it was a mess. Zack had the team lay out the basic monitoring and control requirements. Next, they did a basic logical layout for all the potential problems. They addressed the multidimensional nature of the problems and the responses. After all of this they returned to the software. Within days they decided to totally replace what had been programmed before.

At dinner that evening Zack shared a concern.

"I have been thinking about the mess we found in the software for the magnetic bottle. We could easily be sabotaged by someone on Earth who previously planted a Trojan horse program. It could be in the capture program to control the shuttle firing. It could be in the program of the propulsion system.

It could be hidden in the operating system. What if multiple groups have set up independent failure scenarios in each of the systems?

The Trojan horse programs could also be about taking over the Savitar." Zack said looking over a cup of tea.

"My, and I accused you of being naïve," Janet joked.

"Well, you were right. I still can't believe the mess we found in the software," Zack said shaking his head.

"I suppose we should set up multiple teams to review all the systems. We have many people who selected computer programming as their careers after they got done with the construction. Thanks to you for driving everyone like crazy for the last year, we are significantly ahead of schedule in the construction area. We were just getting ready to trim the work week back by a day," Enrico replied.

"I think getting new blood into the programming group is a great idea. There are currently only three people doing specific program maintenance work. I would like to get seven people on each of the following evaluation teams:

Team 1: Operating System Evaluation
Team 2: Capture Control System Evaluation
Team 3: Navigation Control System Evaluation
Team 4: Environmental Control System Evaluation
Team 5: Hydroponics Control System Evaluation
Team 6: External Environmental Monitoring.
Team 7: Weapons control System Development.
"What weapons would that be?" both Janet and Enrico spoke up at the same time.

"Well, they would be the ones that I have concealed in containers 4076 to 4798" Zack said with a sly grin.

"And I accused you of being naïve." Janet said for the second time.

"Well, when it comes to individual people, I suppose I am. When it comes to groups of people, I always expect the worst and have usually not been disappointed," Zack replied.

"Let's assign about one hundred people to these special projects, seven teams of seven plus support. We can also start the implementation of the Savitar's defense systems. I have preliminary drawings for the construction of these defense systems. There is one set for the long-range systems, one set for the close in systems and another set for the onboard systems. We should probably set up a security force to be responsible for this. Don't you think so Janet," Zack finished with a sly smile.

"In just a few days you go from dunce to hero. I don't know how you do it, but you are always a surprise." Janet said as she got up and gave him a kiss on the forehead.

"I will see you back in the room. Mitch, Susan, make sure he finds his way back safely," Janet said as she walked out.

"It has been a hard few days for her," Susan said to the group.

She blames herself for Zack ditching her and for not having followed up on the idea of moles in our midst. Really, Zack used the lot of us to ditch us. It would have served you right if the rope had been two feet shorter," Susan said as she looked at Zack.

"OK, I repent. I should not have ditched you. It was just a moment of weakness. I just wanted a few moments alone. But I admit, I was not looking for eternity," Zack replied knowing he had not yet heard the last of this incident.

The trials for Indira and Sunny came out more or less as expected. Indira was found guilty of attempted murder and was condemned to serve twenty-five years of rehabilitation. If the Savitar made contact with Earth again, Indira would be transferred back.

Sunny was banned from working on software and received the same twenty-five years, but he would work under supervision as a permanent janitor on the Savitar. He too would be sent back to Earth if the opportunity ever arose.

It was interesting and ironic to Zack. Punishment meant being banned to Earth.

"Don't throw me into the briar patch," Zack said to no one in particular.

"What did you say," Mitch asked as he was brought out of his own thoughts.

"Oh, I was just thinking about the punishment given to our two criminals. It reminded me of Brer Rabbit. To think punishment is to be banned to Earth really says something about the mindset of the crew," Zack replied.

"I would say you picked the people on the Savitar well and you have developed them dramatically in the last couple of years," Mitch continued the conversation.

Mitch felt more alive now than ever before. He taught a Tae Kwon Do class each day. He worked on the flight simulators in the afternoon. He and Susan often painted each evening.

Life was good. In fact, they both had discussed that it was better than ever.

Everyone he knew was similarly busy and feeling valued, developed and all had the same feeling about Zack as he did.

They loved him.

"Did you wish for a different outcome?" Enrico asked as he played checkers at the next table with one of his friends.

"No, I am pleased the team charged with establishing our justice system decided against capital punishment. I believe we have just the system we need. I just find being banned to Earth an amusing punishment. I keep thinking of Great Britain and Australia.

"On a different topic, I was just thinking beyond the black hole. It will provide us not only with gravity, but we can also use it to provide propulsion. As we slow down for the black hole, we will be going through a dust cloud. If we can capture enough mass, later we can expel this mass and create the propulsion necessary to make the Savitar a spaceship in its own right." Zack put his idea on the table.

"I don't suppose you have any idea how to capture this mass? Enrico gave Zack the lead he knew was being asked for.

"Well, I thought about fishermen at sea. They would throw out a net and troll. We could do something similar. We could use our navigation system to pick a relatively dense cloud of debris. We could send out four space shuttles to pull our net out. It could be the Kevlar sails stowed onboard in some containers sent up before we left," Zack said with another of his radiant smiles.

"In other word's you have had this planned for several years. I don't suppose you reviewed this with anyone on Earth," Enrico said with a chuckle.

"Well yes as a matter-of-fact Dr. Garrity and I discussed this at length. He helped me design the matter catchers in such a way the energy of the material we capture does not tear us apart. We reviewed and got agreement of the President and he approves," Zack said earnestly.

"OK, how many people should I put working on this. And I wondered what an admiral would do. It turns out he does anything he pleases," Enrico teased.

Zack just smiled and took sip of his tea.

He hoped that Lisa was successfully growing the coffee trees.

<u>Chapter 22: Jupiter, Saturn and Beyond</u>

The crew had solidified and were now identifying with the Savitar as their home. The Savitar Thanksgiving Celebration endeared Zack to all the crew. The fact he had thought about each almost a year earlier and had arranged for a personal gift from family or friends and that he had also given each something they had identified as their favorite when he interviewed them on Earth, personally endeared him to all but Indira.

Indira refused the gifts and refused to talk to anyone. Deep inside she needed to hold on to the belief she was right. She hoped for an opportunity to restore herself. She would work to be ready. She could not accept being a prisoner on a journey she felt was wrong.

That Thanksgiving night Janet and Zack sat up talking well into the morning. He shared his vision of what lay beyond the black hole. He had a dream of using the Savitar in an exploration of the solar system. Perhaps long after his time the Savitar would venture beyond the solar system.

For the first time Janet realized Zack had thought through all the large problems and had taken action while still on Earth. He might be naïve on a one-to-one basis, but he knew the ways of politics and group thought. He indeed was superb at what he was doing. She hoped she could keep him safe for the next few years until she was sure all the moles were truly exposed.

She also knew why she was in love with him. She fell asleep thinking about when she was a young girl laying in the meadow dreaming of being a princess and marrying the prince.

It was the first night the two slept together. It was not the mad passionate affair Zack had always imagined. It was a soft gentle experience which swelled his heart and brought tears to his eyes each time he recalled it. He knew Janet was his soul mate. His heart welled with the love he now found for this person beside him.

As they went by Jupiter, the science team was once again at the center of the action. They had every monitoring resource in action.

Every moon, every ring and the surface was photographed and looked at through every media on board. The amount of information being captured and sent out kept the bandwidth full for weeks after they went past the planet.

Once again, they successfully launched a satellite to orbit Jupiter. This would happen once more when they reached Saturn. The journey out would put Hubble like telescopes and scientific analysis satellites in orbit around three planets. This would dramatically increase the knowledge of the Solar system.

The ship left Jupiter behind and was now on its way to Saturn for the last acceleration. It had been slowly accelerating and would continue to do so all the way to Saturn. Once past Saturn the Savitar would flip over and begin a deceleration as it continued outward toward the black hole.

The seven software investigative teams worked hard and carefully under Zack's tutelage. They each precisely stated the purpose of their program. Then they listed the actions the software should take for all events. Zack was insistent each team consider the normal flow of events. Then the team had to come back and develop the emergency flow of events. He had them come back a third time and develop the abnormal flow of events. Finally, each team developed the logic to be executed. Then they began checking the existing software program itself. It was amazing even when the software worked the way it should, the programming was often more complex than necessary.

The teams simplified whenever possible. Taxed and overloaded computers began to run faster and more reliably. Program response time became significantly faster significantly. Zack's early passion for computer programming and some excellent teaching had once again paid off.

Team one, Operating System Evaluation, had a great deal of trouble understanding what about twenty percent of the operating system was for. They carefully investigated each questionable program and then after backing up the system on a separate computer they would kill the section in question. They went through many such events. Each time they would hold their breath and kill the questionable program. They had a parallel team back on Earth doing similar work. Craig would send out daily communiqués of what had been found. Between the two locations the cleanup went well and fairly rapidly. Zack however had his team second check and verify all improvements sent up from Earth.

Back on Earth Craig was also taking an additional precaution with a small team he knew was loyal to him alone. He was double checking everything sent up to the Savitar. He used his connection at MIT and recruited some of the best young minds on the MIT and Harvard campuses to validate the programming being developed. He was not about to let this mission fail due lack of action on his part.

Team two, Capture Control System Evaluation, was another team with a parallel team on Earth going through the software. The original programmer was resident on Earth and immediately found several deviations in his program.

Under Zack's guidance he also participated in simplifying and enhancing the program. The bugs found in the capture program would have resulted in failure at one of the most crucial moments in the task the Savitar faced.

Team three, Navigation Control System Evaluation, found a bug allowing an external signal to switch the control of the Savitar to another location or vessel. It was a well-hidden Trojan horse and would not have been found in a normal review. However, Zack's style of doing an external logic diagram and then checking the programming uncovered these hidden packets of logic meant to allow someone else to gain control. These findings were not shared with those back on Earth. Instead, plans were put in place to monitor who tried to activate these programs.

Team four, Environmental Control System Evaluation, found similar external control logic hidden in their program. The loss of control of the environmental systems would have meant the loss of control of the Savitar. This program was modified one hundred per cent by the Savitar crew. This was necessary because the many changes in the design of the Savitar. None of these changes had been shared with the folks back on Earth.

Team five, Hydroponics Control System Evaluation, found no bugs or hidden logic. There was a good reason behind this. Zack had been working with Lisa to optimize the hydroponics control system. They had eliminated ninety eight percent of the original programming and had designed one using about fifteen per cent of the original computer space.

This change allowed for additional plant management programs and programs for the additional facilities. Since there would be six facilities the program would grow to about ninety percent of what it had been originally.

Team six, External environment monitoring, was another area where most of the programming had been done on the trip and had been done by individuals who were extremely loyal to Zack. They were eager to make improvements and to make the program more efficient. They spent a great deal of time placing camera's and monitors around the ship. Their work greatly increased the feel of the Savitar as a space going vessel with eyes and ears. They also added a radar system Zack provided to them as part of the reprogramming work. They worked with both the Navigation Team and the Weapons team to integrate the Radar into the other systems.

Team Seven, Weapons control System Development, was surprised at the number of weapons on board. Zack had the weapons hidden in a series of containers labeled as spare parts. They were almost exclusively self-propelled rockets. However, he also had some older easily obtained recoil weapons. The problem with them would be countering the reaction to their firing. They were mounted on the structure and would provide defensive capability for specific sections of the Savitar. The numerous shoulder rocket launchers were modified and mounted on pivoting holders in strategic locations around the Savitar.

The weapons team spent weeks discussing the purpose for each weapon and then figuring out how to use them. They additionally designed a group of new weapons based on what they had learned about magnetic pulsing.

It was Zack's practice not to divulge to their counterparts on Earth what they found or how they changed their programs. They acknowledged each of the Earth's findings and thanked them. The improvement ideas were used but most programs were rewritten by the Savitar teams.

Team number one was one area where the help from the Earth was essential. Zack assigned various team members to modify and eliminate the current operating system. This would be years of work. The immediate task was to find and eliminate any hidden take over programs.

All the original programs continued to run in a single isolated computer. This computer was the only computer that outside communication came to. It had a printer and a speaker system.

No other operational system on the Savitar was connected to it.

No system on the Savitar could be controlled from outside.

The goal was to learn which groups on Earth were behind these subversive actions.

The construction on the Savitar continued at full speed. The inner structure was complete. Zack had assigned thirty separate teams to inspect every weld. They were to reinforce any weld they decided needed to be improved. The goal was to have the inner welds totally inspected by the time Saturn was reached.

The decking around the five Hexagons at the back of the Savitar was being completed. As quickly as the decking was in place, construction began on the living quarters, the new hydroponics, and the remaining facilities for each hexagon area. The crew's energy skyrocketed when they were able to see the spacious design of the living areas. Everyone made a tour of the living spaces in their spare time.

Each Day Zack would go to one location on the ship to understand the condition and work being done. He constantly begged Lisa for fruits and vegetables to give to the groups he visited. He joked with Janet about conditioning the crew to salivate when they saw him coming.

The Savitar was finally approaching Saturn. It had taken four hundred eighty days for them to get this far from Earth. They were almost halfway to their destination. In a few days they would rotate the Savitar so that the engines would be pushing them in the opposite direction. This braking action would go on until they reached the vicinity of the black hole.

The work on the Savitar was changing. Life was taking on a more routine aspect. The structural welding was almost complete. As the construction work shifted to operational and system maintenance the crew shifted their work to their second or third roles. They continued their personal development and eagerly took on new assignments. The change provided new energy for the crew.

Zack made a point of checking with each person and encouraged them to continue to pursue their personal development.

He formed teams to focus on various long-term survival problems.

Dr. Trimble took the lead in this effort. He had continued the development of his nano-bot technology. He now had a strain with a specific life span of a few days. Every individual on the Savitar got weekly shots. Radiation damage or other damaged cells were routinely repaired. The health of the Savitar crew was beyond what anyone on Earth enjoyed.

The one remaining side effect was the nano-bots focus on eliminating fat tissue whenever they could not find other problems. This in itself would make it a commercial success on Earth. As it was it made everyone on the Savitar appear thin. They were in fact at the ideal body weight to fat ratio. This of course was not a serious side effect though it became a challenge to Dr. Trimble.

Dr. Trimble continued to expand the capabilities of the nano-bots. They now could find and repair not only radiation damaged cells, but they could be programmed to find and fix cells suffering from a handful of specific diseases. He had targeted several specific viruses such as the common cold and both breast cancer and lung cancer.

Zack had a group study the structural integrity of the Savitar to determine if additional strength could be added. After all he thought it will have a black hole trying to ingest it.

These teams all worked with counterpart resources back on Earth.

Communication with the Earth was a rather slow laborious process. It took four or more hours for the message to go one way.

One team was working with a high-powered laser to see if it could be used to communicate with the Earth more quickly.

After watching some tests, Zack figured if they failed to achieve their goal, they would probably develop a very powerful short-range laser weapon.

Mitch was put in charge of a group forming the Savitar defense unit. This group was in charge of the weapons and the strategy for protecting the Savitar from any physical attacks. This group worked very closely with the facilities management team in charge of maintaining the living environment.

The construction on the long-term facilities was underway in earnest. Facility to facility travel tubes were put in to ease the movement of the Savitar population. Since, these relied on having a gravitational well they would only go into full service once they had captured the black hole. For now, they provided a shielded way to go from hexagon to hexagon but required a pull cable system.

The interior of the eight-foot diameter piping making up the one G frame was put to use as a conduit through which to pass all the wiring and facility services. This provided an interior location were the maintenance work could be done without using space suits. It also provided an emergency connection around the one G level. The passageway was modified so a person could travel the entire Savitar via the inside of the service tubes. Each tube had several sealing doors to ensure structural damage in any location could be isolated. The work to put the facility support wiring and piping inside of these tubes was just beginning. These enhancements had not been shared with Earth.

Zack allocated his resources to enhance and improve the environment the Savitar crew would have to endure for their lifetime.

As they approached Saturn the science team once again staged all their equipment. They were getting very proficient at taking copious number of pictures and completely jamming the air waves. The memory brought up to store information was quickly getting full. Science would spend the next fifty years examining and studying the material being captured about each planet.

Saturn had only one major moon though there were hundreds of particles in orbit around it. The passage of the Savitar around Saturn and the path of the moon came extremely close. The pictures of this moon would be better than the pictures they had taken of Earth's moon.

They passed Saturn and the day for rotation to the braking mode approached. The work on the Savitar proceeded, with a sense of urgency.

Even though it seemed they were ahead of the schedule both Zack and Enrico were worried about unforeseen problems.

They wanted to be able to move into the new facilities as soon as the capture took place.

The command-and-control structure of the Savitar was designed with multiple backups. There would be a "forward" control center, five peripheral control rooms around the connecting section and one at the rear, near the main engines. Any of the centers would be able to manage and control the Savitar.

Only the forward control center would be staffed on a permanent basis but a team for each of the other centers would be designated and would qualify in managing and maneuvering the Savitar. This redundancy ensured problems in one part of the Savitar would not result in a catastrophe. None of these command centers were of the original design.

Zack continued to look to the future and use the resources at hand to put the improvements in place.

Everyone on board was aware of the substantial changes in the design. Many of the crew had participated in thinking of and inputting their ideas to make these changes.

Zach skillfully used the modifications to enroll the crew. For him it was his life's work, for the crew it became their Savitar.

The daily life of the crew was as full as each member desired. They each looked out for the other. The interaction required by Zack caused the crew to learn about each other, to appreciate the differences and the varied skills the members possessed.

Zack purposely put people of differing back grounds together to ensure a cross pollination of their personal values.

Zack was constantly reviewing the capture procedure, the magnetic bottle design, and the structural strength of the Savitar. The changes he and the other designers made dramatically increased the structural strength. He was worried about the ability to hold the black hole and not be slowly eaten by it.

This was a point he never voiced or shared with anyone. It was his personal nightmare.

Zack scheduled reviews with each of the programming teams to go over the programs they were responsible for.

He had inspection teams check the workings of the magnetic bottle.

He had a large fifty-foot sphere made out of steel plate. It was used to test the workings and controllability of the magnets. The magnet operators moved this ball around inside the nine G sphere. They played a multidimensional ping pong game. This was either watched or many people asked to be allowed to play the game. This became a favorite past time. It was a tremendous way to test the controls and the logic of the system. In the process of this play, several improvements to magnet control were identified and made.

The new facilities were another attraction for the crew. The living areas were assigned and though it was impossible to live there because of the lack of gravity, almost everyone went to look at their apartments. Each person would have a spacious bedroom, living room, office area, kitchen area and their own bathroom. The apartments were all built so they had a window looking into the park and the hydroponics area. This area was designed like a garden with walking paths and benches for relaxation. Everyone was now eager to get to the black hole so gravity would allow them to enjoy their new facilities.

Zack leveraged this energy to keep people on task and focused on practicing, checking, and doing it all again.

Lisa Hemming was focused on multiplying her plant treasures so she would have enough plants to seed the additional five huge new facilities she would have once the Savitar gained its gravity.

She now had a permanent crew of five hundred people and almost everyone on the Savitar was raising some plant or seedling for her in their rooms. "Where are we going to get all the materials necessary to accomplish the development of the gardens on the Savitar? Specifically, where am I going to get soil for my parks and gardens?" Lisa Hemming inquired one day.

"Well, that is another surprise I have kept secret. Each of the containers from 51198 to 81198 is full of soil. This soil will provide the material for your gardens. This will only be enough to provide enough soil to get the gardens a few inches deep but it's a start," Zack disclosed with a grin.

"I can't believe you got away with sending dirt up into space," Enrico chimed in.

"Look, we have enough material to create living centers around the Savitar. Each of these centers should be communities enjoying some common living features. We do not yet have enough materials to totally enclose the surface, but someday we will have.

We need to establish a group to manage the development of the Savitar as we travel along. This will keep the crew busy and will transform the Savitar into a small world.

We need to be totally independent from Earth and be able to produce our own goods and the food supply to sustain ourselves. About a third of us need to become dedicated farmers," Zack said as he looked around the table.

Zack then gave Lisa the rest of the seeds he had brought along.

Lisa assured everyone the moment there was gravity her crew would begin the immediate transfer of the plants to the new facilities. Each of her staff was given the responsibility for a certain number of plants, fish, or other creatures to transfer to the new facilities. Plans on how to manage during the weightless period preceding the capture were developed, reviewed, and improved upon. As anticipated, the hydroponics had become the most important of the systems needed to sustain the crew.

Lighting was a big issue. The full frequency lamps from Earth were crucial. There was no sunlight this far out. This was one of the manufacturing capabilities Zack had brought out with the ship. This lamp manufacturing facility was commissioned and began production. It would produce the lamps for the bubble structure covering the living quarters. It would also be used in the hydroponics areas.

The facility could produce fifty bulbs per day. This would allow them to produce the ten thousand bulbs needed by the time they reached the black hole. This same team would produce the interior lights to illuminate the miles of transportation tubing and other lighting needs across the facility.

These manufacturing facilities were located on the front side of the sphere from the living quarters. This allowed them to operate as many hours as needed without disturbing the living quarters.

The logistic personnel were focusing on moving the extra parts and materials into permanent storage facilities. This meant moving them from inside the center sphere out to storage sheds located on the forward hexagons. This was a huge effort. There was a little of every type of material one could think of. Eighty percent of what had been sent up to the Savitar had been used to build its' current structure. However, the twenty percent left took up most of the area of one hexagon. Since there was no gravity all of this material was put in its final location and strapped down. It was also stacked or positioned in such a fashion that when gravity was established no damage would occur. The work was tedious and hard, but it was crucial work.

The crew was developing into a multi-skilled, highly trained, and motivated crew. Their extra-curricular activities included a theater, an orchestra, several bands, and some outstanding singers. "Savitar Sings" written and recorded by one group was a best seller back on Earth.

As the journey continued, Zack encouraged the crew to think up ways they could use their skill to enhance the Savitar's environment. One group organized themselves to make furniture from plastics, metal, and glass. They were making pieces of their own design and they worked with others to make the pieces they wanted for their apartments. Since there was no need for money, the relationships established were ones of trading favors and general good will.

Mitch's security force had one hundred full time members and five hundred emergency members. This group only faced an occasional fight or minor altercation.

However, Zack pushed the group to play war games to include external ships and troops boarding the Savitar and attempting to take control.

These practices would later allow the Savitar to fend off outside efforts to take control.

Chapter 23: Events on Earth

Craig and President Lansing continued to meet on a quarterly timing. These meetings were enjoyable for both of them. President Lansing continued to see the journey of the Savitar as the center piece of how history would distinguish his period of leadership. Though many others had almost forgotten why the Savitar was on its journey, the fact of lifting this ultimate threat from Earth never escaped his thoughts.

The President hoped the Savitar would be successful in time to save his political bacon. He had used up all of his political credits with his own party as well as with the people of the country. Globally he was in good stead, but a new space race was in full swing.

The fact the special powers were still in effect, irritated the opposition. Many people questioned whether these powers were needed.

The military leaders would never forgive the President for putting Zach in command of the Savitar. They were sure this alone would cause the failure of the mission. The message about the attempt on Zack and the identity of those in the Military put the Chiefs of Staff back on their heels. They had their hands full in dealing with a few senior ranking Generals and Admirals who had crossed the line into politics. This had quieted the rhetoric coming from them.

Craig had a crew of five hundred of the leading thinkers in the world working with him. They were from almost every country in the world. Many were eager to design experiments to open up new fields of scientific studies. Many openly asked to go out to the Savitar if the opportunity ever presented itself. This group's main focus was to determine how the Black hole would behave and how it could be managed.

The other task was to organize and catalogue all the information they had collected. New information of the Moon, Mars, Jupiter and its many moons and rings, Saturn and its major moon and many other objects were coming in and being studied. Soon they would have information about the black hole. There was a lifetime of study either on Earth or on the Savitar.

Craig hoped to spend his time on the Savitar doing so.

Mary Ringhold and Jeff Mabry were not only the bodyguards for Craig and his wife Emily, but the two couples had become very close friends. A year after the Savitar's departure Mary and Jeff married. Since they lived around the clock with Craig and Emily, it was a blessing the two couples got along so well. The two couples decided to build a new home together designed to provide extra security but also to give each of them some sense of privacy. Emily complemented Craig on having chosen so well when he had selected his bodyguards. Mary was one of the few people Emily immediately took to.

At work Craig followed the activities of the Savitar as closely as possible. He was aware Zack was establishing the Savitar to be independent and was pursuing a course where Earth was a resource but not critical to survival.

He knew the design of the structure had been changed and strengthened. In general, he was aware of the living quarter redesign and of the transport system. He would have loved to get the details so his scientists could evaluate the improvements, but he knew this would risk the well-being of the Savitar and its crew. He also realized Zack would never communicate this back no matter how encrypted the airwaves were supposed to be.

The computer links to Earth seemed to be the same as when the Savitar had left. This worried Craig. He sent a cryptic message to Zack identifying his concern.

In the reply and totally buried in a theoretical discussion about personal behavior, Zack had written, "Beauty is only skin deep; the true being inside is more complicated."

Craig had almost missed this reply. He had interpreted it to mean Zack had a separate layer below the links they had with Earth. He hoped this layer was ultimately secure. Craig would have been relieved had he known the Savitar systems were totally isolated from any connection to the Earth.

The organization Craig headed had three main focuses, The Black Hole, The Exploration of the Solar System, and the study of the Universe using the Savitar as a remote sensing station.

He communicated this to Zack. To his pleasure and surprise Zack replied he had set up three mirror groups of fifty persons each on the Savitar to work with their counter parts back on Earth.

Conrad Zepf the Savitar chief science officer was put in charge of these groups and would set up communication for each of them.

The ability for Zack to staff such an effort with so many people surprised Craig. It was the single message giving Craig the most information and confidence about the progress of the work and the development of the crew.

He shared this insight with President Lansing.

"We picked the right leader for this mission. His passion, his intellect, his ability to recognize and respond aggressively to problems and his ability to bond his people to the vision he holds makes me feel comfortable on those days I get attacked by my detractors," President Lansing shared with Craig.

Craig agreed that Zack had been the right choice.

The thought of sharing in the Savitar's long range adventure kept nagging at Craig.

"You know, sometimes I feel I would give my left leg for a chance to get out there with Zack," Craig shared one evening as he and Emily sat in front of their fireplace.

"Well, I certainly wouldn't mind the adventure," Mary replied quietly. She knew Emily was not as warm to the idea of leaving Earth.

"Well, if there is a real opportunity to do so after the black hole is captured and moved, I am open to the idea of joining them. Let's talk about it then. However, if this idea fails, I would rather be here on Earth," Emily said to the surprise of everyone.

Craig now felt he knew why Emily had not wanted to go. She had always feared being away from home when a storm or other threat surfaced.

The turn-around of the Savitar after it passed Saturn made the evening news and Craig was interviewed about the journey and how the Savitar's crew was progressing. Craig used the material, pictures and information Zack and Enrico had sent him about life aboard the Savitar. It was clear to Craig the crew had become the Savitar crew and not crew members from various countries.

This interview was one of the few he did for the Savitar. Within two weeks the media no longer showed any interest.

"What is the real situation on board the Savitar and how do you feel about the chances for success," President Lansing asked at their next meeting.

"Well, everything Zack has shared with me, the way he is able to free up crew members to work in parallel with our science teams and his cryptic messages when I ask about items affecting the Savitar's security, indicates to me the Savitar, it's leadership and its crew are positioned as best as any team could be given the challenges they face.

What is also amazing is it appears the crew, contrary to early fatality estimates is totally in tack. No deaths have been reported. This by itself would make the trip a success. It is really a blessing someone like Zack was at the right place at the right time," Craig replied as he set his coffee down.

"I know the military are building a spaceship to venture out to the Savitar. I would like to ask for a berth for myself and a select group of scientists. Also, I want you to know Zack will not let the US or any country commandeer the Savitar. If I know him, he has already put in place his own defense system with the materials you provided before he left," Craig spoke bluntly.

"How do you know of the efforts of the US? Is there a leak I should know about?" the President inquired.

"No, however, I am aware of the Russian, the Chinese and Indian efforts and I have heard rumors about Japan, Israel, Germany, England, and France. I can't believe we would allow ourselves to be left behind," Craig replied.

"Well, I won't discuss what we are doing. However, if there is an opportunity, I will make sure your request is addressed," President Lansing said as he set his cup down and indicated he needed to go on to another meeting.

Craig recognized this as Dan's way of not getting into a topic he could not discuss.

That day Craig began to plan for his and a group of scientist departure from Earth. He had conversations with the individuals he thought would be a valuable addition to the Savitar. Craig was intimately aware of Zack's interest in making the Savitar self-sufficient.

This included the desire to have the ability to manufacture many of the necessities of everyday life as well as the equipment needed by such a huge endeavor. Craig began to think through and to investigate the availability of people in those fields.

It appeared the Savitar would arrive at the black hole just before the US Presidential elections. This was either going to be a positive or if things went wrong, it would be overwhelmingly negative, and the elections would matter little.

In his next message to Zack, Craig updated him of the delicate situation President Lansing was in. If possible, he suggested Zack openly praise the President.

Zack's success would be a tremendous and pivotal political boost.

Hours later he received a simple response that the president would get the Savitar's endorsement.

Chapter 24: Long Journey's End

The Savitar was on the edge of the abyss. The display showing what lay ahead was blank. Nothingness had a new meaning to all who looked out ahead of the Savitar. Their navigational calculations put the black hole about five thousand miles ahead. They were virtually on top of it.

They had continued to slow down as they approached the black hole. They were out just past the orbit of Uranus. The planet was on the opposite side of the sun at this point in time. It was hard to fathom after all this time and travel that they were still inside the Solar system.

And once again the solar system was coming in contact with the black hole.

The Savitar was now at a crawl speed of fifty miles per hour.

A probe to pinpoint the exact center of the black hole and its event horizon was getting its last-minute check over.

The Capture Control System Evaluation Team had reprogrammed the monitor probe system as part of getting rid of any attempts at sabotage. They had found several questionable packets of code and had done some stream-lining work as well.

Everyone was on edge as they waited for the launch. The countdown was proceeding and was being synchronized with the Earth. This would be the first test of the potential subversive intervention of some Earth organization.

They had practiced the capture maneuver six times over twenty-one days. They split the Savitar in two. This new approach involved each half of the sphere proceeding around alternate sides of the black hole and then closing directly toward each other. The leadership team had decided it would easier to guide the two halves toward each other if they were free to maneuver independently.

There were fifteen rods and mating holes at the nine G level to interlock the two halves when they came together. A heavy-duty auto welder was positioned at each of the mating locations. There were three longer guide pins in each half and three matching guide holes on the opposite half at the one G level. These outer three guide pins ensured alignment of the two halves. The goal was to align the three pins and guide holes as the two halves of the sphere came toward each other from opposite sides of the black hole.

Enrico had the crew practice the capture maneuver six times. Each time the maneuvering got better and the coordination of those guiding the two halves improved. Every activity including the immediate welding of the two halves was practiced. The navigation system was refined.

The magnetic control system was tuned but this would be one system that would get its true christening under fire.

Enrico was very pleased with the practices and praised all involved and declared the Savitar ready, for the capture.

Immediate welding would occur when the two halves of the sphere came together. One hundred heavy duty automatic welding machines were strategically positioned at the nine G level. These would immediately go into action when the two halves came together. Two hundred normal automatic welding machines would perform similar work out at the one G level. There would also be roughly one thousand welders doing manual welding at the one G level. These welders would be inside the structure and simultaneously weld one thousand strategically located pins linking the two one G central rings. These had been designed in as a way to ensure no rotational forces would threaten the integrity of the Savitar.

The date for the capture was set and the two halves parted and proceeded to their positions. Enrico commanded one half and Zack commanded the second half.

Zack knew he was being used to put the crew at ease. Enrico did not need him to do anything.

Enrico had overall capture command.

Everything on the ship was secured and the ship prepared for the capture. The hydroponics posed the biggest challenge, and everything had been done to allow a quick recovery. All plants and materials were prepositioned at the new facilities and secured.

The days leading up to the capture day, at times seemed to crawl and at other times they to flash by. It had been almost a month with no gravity. The crew was getting tired and at least half were fighting the nausea associated with weightlessness.

The messages sent to Earth at this time did not share the new capture approach. Craig figured out something different was happening and sent a cryptic message wishing Zack good luck.

Zack had several of the team monitoring the incoming messages and the effect each had on the programs on the isolated computer. There were words of encouragement coming in from all the countries. A message coming in from the Congo triggered the collapse of the navigation program in the isolated computer.

Zack sent an encrypted message to Craig letting him know of the collapse of the navigation system. He cryptically let Craig know the Congo message had triggered a failure in the navigation system.

It was not long afterwards the Savitar received a message expressing sympathy at the failure of the navigation system from the Iranian leadership. They wished the crew of the Savitar good luck at survival.

President Lansing sent a message wishing the crew luck and thanked Zack for his valor in the face of adversity. He hoped the crew would recover from their current problems and still make the capture of the black hole.

Zack figured Craig had translated his cryptic message to mean the Savitar was still in control and had shared this with the President. He was very much aware President Lansing had used the code word telling Zack to do everything on his own. This at least made Zack feel better. Throughout the journey he had already done so.

The capture of the black hole by the Savitar was underway. The two halves approached each other a foot per minute. The magnetic fields provided the cushioning effect allowing the two halves of the sphere to glide toward each other smoothly and come together like two down pillows softly coming together.

In a show of confidence, Zack assigned Captain John Adam to be in charge of the shuttle pilots. They provided the maneuvering to the two halves. The Captain skillfully led the shuttle pilots as they guided the pins toward the target holes. They were actually holding the two halves apart and allowing them to be pulled slowly together. This was something they had not been able to practice

Everything they had practiced now had to be done in reverse. They had talked through this reverse process a dozen times.

This time they were doing it for real.

It took a full week for the two halves of the Savitar to slowly close the distance between them and to "feel" the strength of the black hole.

The magnetic power was being adjusted to meet the conditions as the two halves went toward each other. Up to this time everything had been a theoretical estimated. Now the actual force of the black hole was being felt and measured. It was only slightly stronger in power then had been calculated. The one G level would in essence be the 1.03 G level.

This was an amazing result.

A cheer went up from all the crew as the two spheres met and the guide pins found home. Immediately the strategically positioned welders welded their thousand pins into place. The two halves of the Savitar were locked permanently together. The welders went out on the exterior and continued their welding work. The automatic welders were started and would continue for the next several weeks to make the two halves a permanent structure.

For six months, on their approach, the Savitar had collected all the space debris possible. This material had been stored in forty-foot-high bins on three of the forward hexagons. The quantity and the variety of material had overwhelmed the collection crew.

This material would now be slowly released to augment the Savitar's propulsion system. In this way, Zack felt he would be able to save the Ion engines to provide long term support. He would use the shuttles to provide defense and exploratory capability.

He was successfully extending his resources by harvesting the materials of the solar system.

The magnetic field was increased on the pushing side as the Savitar began its attempt to move the black hole. The increase of power to the magnets on the engine side of the Savitar coincided with the nudge being provided to move the black hole. For the first few days nothing seemed to be happening as the engine power was slowly increased and the magnetic bottle adjusted.

When success was totally sure, Zack sent a very simple one-word message, "Success."

Enrico followed this with "The Earth has the Sunshine for warmth, the moonlight for love and the Savitar to take the hurt away."

Next Zack addressed the crew, "Ladies and gentlemen of the Savitar, we have traveled farther and faster than we humans have ever done. We traveled a long way together. We have achieved the impossible. We have done this together. Our team, all of you, has contributed countless hours preparing, planning, and working hard.

All our efforts were focused on achieving the capture of this black hole. We will celebrate the capture together. We will all share a glass of home grown Savitar wine. This is wine made by our hydroponics' angel. There is probably only enough for one glass and one swallow apiece. Please make sure each of you gets your share. I want to thank each of you for your contribution to our success. In five minutes, we will raise our glasses together and toast our success. Please get ready."

Zack was at the jail where Indira and Sunny were being held. Janet, Susan, and Mitch as always were with him.

"Indira, Sunny, I offer you an opportunity to toast our success with us. You incorrectly chose the other side. However, even your deeds caused us to become successful. You caused us to question all previous work and caused us to check it all over. Would you care to join in?" Zack asked as he offered them each a glass of wine.

Sunny accepted a glass, but Indira just turned her back. She had tears of anger in her eyes.

Zack got back on the intercom and continued his toast.

"To our crew, to our upcoming adventures, to the contribution we have made together in the well-being of Earth. May each of us enjoy our success," Zack finished his toast.

"Except for the welding and the most necessary work to keep the Savitar operational, I declare a holiday to be known and celebrated in the future as Capture day," Zack continued.

Zack and the leadership team spent the rest of the day going to each of the operating stations, the new crew's quarters, and the recreation areas to personally thank each of the crew for their contribution.

The Savitar began a very slow acceleration toward an area known for its numerous asteroids and other debris. Unstated but critical in Zack's mind was for the Savitar to load up on the materials of propulsion and perhaps materials to be used for survival such as: ice, oxygen bearing minerals, iron, and other heavy metals.

A one hundred twenty-five-mile diameter ring held out in front of the Savitar. It was held in place by four slender buckyball poles that held the capture funnel made of a Kevlar capture funnel shaped netting. It looked like a giant butterfly net. This formed a cone guiding the material in front of the sphere down the throat to a capture bin.

The material from this bin was guided down two delivery shoots falling toward the black hole. At the last moment, downward falling material was redirected toward the back of the sphere and a forward thrust occurred. The propulsion exhaust went through the same pentagon on which the thrust engines were located.

This exhaust was the same pentagon were Janet had rescued Zack. She joked that if he were determined to repeat his transgression this would be the time. His slide down the chute would aid the progress of the Savitar.

Of course, most of space was empty but whenever the ship could, it would scoop up and add to the propulsion system material. A crusher and grinder reduced all the propulsion material to particles about the size of a grain of sand. The initial material for this propulsion system had been captured during the deceleration period. An amount well beyond what Zack had hoped for was captured and available for use. This allowed him the option of saving the liquefied oxygen and hydrogen that had been sent up from Earth. This was something Zack had sought to achieve. Additionally, he had the material being sorted to provide soil supplements and to screen out specifically defined materials.

There was a team of almost a thousand strong continuing to weld the two halves of the Savitar together. The welding at the nine G level being done by especially designed computer-controlled welding robots was a continuous cycle of the robots coming up for reloading and then going back down to do the welding. The welding at the nine G level would take much longer than the rest. The welding was much heavier and took longer than what was being done at the one G level.

Zach had recruited the "Boss" and Sampson to lead the nine G work.

There were a host of workers activating the transportation system and completing the link at the mid joints.

The remaining crew was activating the hydroponics systems.

The personal moves happened as each person went to their new quarters to rest and recover. There was a massive move going on even as the Savitar began its initial movement.

The congratulation messages from Earth piled up. Zack anticipated this and had set up a screening team to review and organize all the messages.

Janet, Susan, and Mitch had set up a parallel message inspection system designed to identify calls to subversion or to trigger some sort of action.

Messages for Indira had come in from the US. Sunny had several messages also from the US. Five other people got suspicious messages, but it was impossible to follow up on them. Almost every person on the ship got a personal message. All would be reviewed but this would take some time.

Meanwhile several program hits came in, but these were not traceable. They did confirm the intent of some outside force to take control sometime in the future. These hits were on the environmental controls and the navigation controls.

Zack reviewed these first. It appeared the parties were just trying to determine if their specific program hooks were still in place. Zack was happy the Savitar's internal computers were totally isolated from the outside.

Running and attending to this extra layer of computing had eaten into the excess computing power the Savitar originally enjoyed but it provided a screen behind which the Savitar and its crew could hide. They had regained a significant amount of computer capacity by making the programs they were using much more efficient.

A few days later, Zack and the leadership team finally sat down to go through their messages. They had established a protocol for the leadership team to work together to answer all the messages.

Zack and Janet answered all the head of state messages. Questions about the capture and the workings of the various systems were split up among the leadership team. All of these special interest questions would be answered in general but no specific details were to be shared. They figured those who had planted the various sabotage routines and efforts were wondering how the Savitar had survived.

Zack send out an open message,

"To President Lansing of the United States, the Savitar team wants to thank you for all you have done from the beginning and through the intervening time to make this capture successful. Your inspired leadership and untiring support almost single handily made this venture a success.

The people of the United States have the right leader in the right place at the right time. I know they are smart enough to put you back in office for another term. The same dynamic leadership you provided to make the Savitar a success is what the US needs to guide it for the next four years. You have my vote, and I am sure the votes of all aboard the Savitar qualified to vote in the US.

Thank you, your valor in the face of all our challenges has been un-questionable."

He knew the entire world would see it and he hoped it would help the President win his re-election. He also enjoyed using the code word shared between the two.

Messages of thanks and recognition were sent to each of the heads of state for the countries supporting the Savitar. The messages to each country highlighted their crew members in the message. Even, Indira's and Sunny's names went out.

After eight hours of sending messages the team was finally over the first hurdle. There were still a series of messages needing answering or addressing but the bulk had been handled.

Zack was on the encrypted line with Craig and President Lansing. He shared the events of the capture. Then he highlighted the surfacing of the Trojan horse programs. One Trojan horse program in the environmental and the guidance system was apparently from the US government.

"I want both of you to know the intentions of the crew of the Savitar are benign towards the Earth. I also want you know no single country will be allowed to gain control of this craft. It will remain a global starship with all information and knowledge it discovers open and available to all on Earth. If this is counter to your desires, please let me know now," Zack shared.

"Zack, would you allow the US to contribute a long-range transport as an additional feature of your vessel," the President asked in reply.

"Yes, but each of the offering countries will also be allowed to contribute a similar vessel. So far there are four offers. I anticipate some of these vessels will try to take over the Savitar. Be aware we are prepared for this and will counter any attempt at take over. No one will succeed." Zack replied openly.

"Let me assure you our intentions are entirely altruistic. After talking with Dr. Garrity, we have decided some additional astronomers, mathematicians and other key specialist may be beneficial. Dr. Garrity has also indicated he and his family would like to come out and join you on your journey. We also think you would benefit by having some new computers and other technical equipment, such as long range and larger telescopes. Let me know if there are any other specific things useful to your continuing success," President Lansing replied.

"It will be a pleasure to have Craig and his family aboard. Please make sure Captain John Adam's family gets a berth as well." Zack concluded.

He knew this request would free the Adam's family from their captors and would let the Captain act in a full capacity aboard the Savitar.

Zack had similar conversations with the other countries offering a ship. After these conversations, Zack sent out a message to the crew asking for them to identify any supplies they thought should be requested of Earth.

The responses back from the crew should not have surprised him but they did. There were many things they were doing without. The most pressing one was the crew desire for computer time. Books for reading and enriching oneself were available but access to the materials was difficult. Also, many of the crew requested large flat viewing screens for their new quarters.

A few days later Zack requested four thousand personal computers and an equal number of large flat viewing screens for the crew. He also requested the equipment to manufacture computers. Zack was very eager to establish the Savitar as an independent entity capable of sustaining itself.

To this end he had already stocked it with every plant life he had been able to get seed for, but he asked for more.

He had made sure the Savitar could fabricate almost any type of equipment. He was intent on shoring up the areas he had previously overlooked. To this end he had established several teams to determine what type of self-production equipment and systems to request from the Earth.

The teams worked on this and put in lists of materials and equipment they would like as these new ships were brought out to the Savitar.

The speed of the Savitar slowly crept up. In the first week they only moved ten feet. The second week they moved twenty feet. This slow exponential climb kept up until in the twenty-first week the Savitar had reached almost 25,000 mph. This speed relative to the solar system would be sufficient to move the black hole far enough out of Earth's path so its effects would be minor.

Once they had moved the Savitar out, so they were no threat to Earth, they matched the speed of the debris field they were approaching. This provided the Savitar a way to pick up a huge amount of material from the asteroid belt with little risk. The screen in front acted like a giant scoop directing all the materials into a chute directing the materials to a holding area where it was processed. Large pieces were blasted with a laser beam to ensure they would not damage the Savitar's structure. These lasers were the result of the failed communication experiment. They were excellent and very accurate short-range weapons.

The materials being captured included a variety of minerals, iron, ice, and materials containing large amounts of hydrogen and oxygen. The processing of these various elements became a primary endeavor.

Zack made sure this area was appropriately staffed with the resources necessary to make the capture of materials a primary focus for the Savitar.

He continued to have his eye on the long-term journey of the Savitar. He was now thinking that this journey would continue beyond his lifetime.

Chapter 25: Craig Gets His Wish

It was election year in the US. The success of the Savitar and the message of gratitude from Zack on behalf of the Savitar did wonders for President Lansing's political standing. He had used all his political clout and connections to ensure the Savitar was a success. He sold the Savitar's mission to the people.

However, the length of time the journey took and the problems on Earth had eroded the confidence of many people. Now only a month from the election, the message from the Savitar sent to all on Earth sent his ratings through the roof.

His competitors all knew it would be futile to oppose him.

He was a shoe in for his second term.

"Well, I don't know exactly how Zack managed to overcome all the barriers to achieve the capture of the black hole, but he seems to have anticipated, and counter acted the various attempts our adversaries made. I will say his rouse during the final capture worried me. I know you assured me he had everything in control but none the less those were tense days," President Lansing shared with Craig.

"I want you to know one of my first actions will be to announce the position of ambassador to the Savitar. I thought you might be interested in such a position.

Of course, it would mean you would have to go out and live aboard the Savitar," President Lansing said as he watched his friend's reaction.

You bet I am interested. My wife and I have talked it over and we are ready. I suppose this means the US indeed has a vessel capable of going out to the Savitar," Craig replied.

"Of course, we do. I will arrange for you to get a tour. We will send over one hundred people out on this vessel. At least three quarters will be the scientists, engineers, and entrepreneurs you have identified.

There will be a contingent of twenty-five of the most capable and deadly commandos we have. Their role will be to counter act any attempts by other powers to take over the Savitar. Here again I am fighting my military advisors who want to send up a full one hundred commandos to secure the Savitar.

I have informed them that the Savitar has declared themselves as an independent entity similar to any other country in the world and that they will welcome us, but they will rule themselves and remain independent.

I however have been listening to you and Zack. The two of you have earned my trust. I believe Zack will ably defend the Savitar and keep it neutral.

So, I am loading the ship up with the items he is requesting versus military equipment and ammunition. I have taken a clear, very unpopular, stand with the chiefs of staff," President Lansing continued. "They will be happy to see me go after this term."

"Well, I want to support your position. It is the right one. I have every confidence in Zack. He has matured and grown as a leader. I would stand by his view no matter what anyone presents as arguments against it. When will the departure for the Savitar take place?" Craig responded and inquired.

"The timing will depend on when the Soviet, Chinese, and Indian ships depart. However, I am currently planning for the departure to take place after the inauguration," the President replied.

Craig's evening conversation with Emily, Mary and Jeff centered on this upcoming opportunity.

They all looked at Emily and waited for her reaction. They knew this was the moment they would find out whether they would really go.

"Well, I must be in the spotlight because you are all looking at me. I guess you are all awaiting my reaction. I still have mixed emotions but everything I have learned about the Savitar in the last few years, makes it seem like a place of wonder and adventure. Our good friend Zack has performed a miracle. Yes, I am willing to go. I certainly don't want to be left here by myself," Emily replied when Craig shared the news.

It was only a few days later when Craig got a visit from Ben Samuelson, the head of NASA.

"Hello, Craig, I hope you aren't upset about not having been included in the development of this new space vessel. The President did not want to distract you from the primary mission of supporting the capture of the black hole. Even my wife does not yet know about it. This has been a very closely guarded secret. However, the President tells me you will be one of its first passengers. I thought I would come and invite you to tour the ship. It will be capable of atmospheric as well as space travel. This will make it versatile in the exploration it might participate in. I understand Zack has accepted the offer of having the ship assigned to the Savitar," Ben said as he met with Craig.

"Well, I have to say I knew about the Russian, Chinese and Indian efforts in this area. The fact not a word was heard about our efforts pretty well let me know we were doing something. I am pleased you were leading this effort. You did a great job getting all the loads out to the Savitar," Craig replied.

"Yea and you did a great job sending up at least twice as much pay load as we thought we were capable of. I hope Zack appreciates what you pulled off. I am not sure what all the extras were, and I purposely turned a blind eye. It seems it was the right stuff. I think what he has pulled off is as close to a miracle as we will see in our lifetime," Ben replied.

"I almost put a stop to all the extras being hoisted to the Savitar. It was an off comment from my wife that stayed my hand," Ben continued.

She said, "I hope you are making sure that young man gets everything he needs. I would hate to learn he failed because he ran out of fuel or did not have enough of something we should have provided. After all, his failure would mean our doom."

I stopped my brooding about all the extras being hoisted by you and decided to make sure you got all the space you needed.

"Well, the next time I see your wife, I will have to thank her and yes, I am sure Zack is grateful. I am looking forward to seeing what he has done with the resources we provided. He has been and continues to be very secretive about the design modifications he has made. I think once we make contact with him and the various factions get over trying to take over the Savitar, the relations between the Savitar and Earth will be a very productive one," Craig continued.

It was the following week when Craig and Jeff flew to an undisclosed location for a tour of the ship. It was very much like a fat version of the Stealth Bomber but with much smaller wings and a much longer fuselage. One might have mistaken it for a flattened wingless 757. The "wings" if you could call them wings ran the length of the fuselage. There was no tail.

There were two large after thrust engines and various smaller navigational engines positioned along the fuselage. Clearly the various rocket thrusters were to maneuver in the vacuum of space.

The interior was a combination of sleeping compartments, living quarters, exercise areas and storage compartments. It was immediately obvious it was not going to be a luxury trip out to the Savitar. It would however be a much faster journey then experience by the Savitar. Where the Savitar had taken several years to make the trip, this ship would make the journey in less than six months.

The two spent several hours on the tour. They talked about the personnel planning to make the trip. The military would be in charge of the ship and planned to keep it in military hands.

Upon his return home, Craig began to confirm who wanted to go and to arrange for the various things Zack had asked for. His team of long standing now became very active and began to make the arrangements for the next group of people going out to the Savitar aboard the US spaceship. Those selected went through an intense screening process. There was still concern about those trying to cause harm to the mission.

Craig got in communication with the Russian and Chinese leaders and gained space for twenty-five non-military personnel on each of their vessels. The Indian government agreed to take seventy-five scientists. There was no additional space available on any of the other vessels.

At home, he and Emily spent a great deal of time discussing the trip out to the Savitar. They also discussed if they would return to Earth any time soon or even in their lifetime. Emily wrestled with the concept of never coming back to Earth. She had some misgivings, but she could see how important this was to Craig. They did not have to face the issue of leaving anyone behind.

Mary and Jeff were eager to make the journey. Mary was very close to Emily and the two would talk through various scenarios Emily was concerned about. Emily went through cycles of concern.

"You know what scares me the most, is out there we could run out of oxygen," Emily confided one day as the group was discussing the upcoming journey.

"Well, we are taking several oxygen generators capable of breaking down a variety of compounds and yielding oxygen.

Zack has also let us know the space material he is capturing to help fuel the Savitar has a wide range of elements including oxygen. He has already processed enough oxygen to provide air for five very large living spaces. Running out of oxygen will probably be one of the least problems. I am more worried on how the Savitar will use the excess low-grade heat that will be generated." Craig informed her.

Emily had no clue why Craig was worried about heat. However, the fact oxygen would be plentiful seemed to help her reduce her fears. She was slowly becoming more engaged and interested in the upcoming trip out to the Savitar. She hoped to overcome the boredom of the six month trip out by reading all the great classics.

Chapter 26: New Quarters

As the Savitar ever so slowly began to move the black hole, the activities on board took place like a hoard of bees feverishly working to get the honey in from the fields. To someone unaware of the detailed planning preceding this point in time, the activities would have seemed random and disconnected. However, everyone knew their part of the plan and carried their part out in a timely and organized manner. It was moving day. Everyone was eagerly moving into their new quarters.

The move to the new quarters was an emotional event even though everyone had visited their quarters several times before the capture of the black hole.

Zack had made a point of getting the work done before the capture. He had wanted all of the crew to have the confidence they would be successful, and they would survive. It had worked.

This time the crew brought their belongings and unpacked. This time they did not need to wear their space suits in their quarters.

Zack's quarter had special security access and was a bit more spacious since it was expected he would have visitors to his quarters. However, Janet, Susan and Mitch's quarters were the same as everyone else's and were strategically positioned around Zack's.

The living quarters were almost immediately occupied by their assigned personnel. Every apartment had the basics provided and each occupant quickly brought their meager but personal items they had accumulated. The move was done by the individuals themselves working together with those who they would be sharing the new living quarters.

The increase in space each person enjoyed actually caused an anxiety reaction. This was shared with the leadership team. Many people felt vulnerable because they were not surrounded by shipmates the way they had been for the last several years. They felt more vulnerable and exposed.

This malady jokingly came to be referred to as the Milton syndrome because Zack had made all the extra space available.

The hydroponics areas were quickly reestablished, and plants were distributed based on the specific environmental needs of plant groups.

The limited amount of grass was planted in patches in what would become a park at each compound location.

Grape seedlings were organized into vineyards.

Various fruit, ornamental trees and bushes were planted around the gardens.

A wide variety of flowers were planted in the gardens designed by various volunteer groups on the Savitar.

Everyone had a part in getting the gardens in place, started, and then doing the maintenance of part of the grounds. Those who wanted could have a plant for their apartment. These activities helped relieve the stress built up during the months leading up to the capture of the black hole.

The transport tubes were activated and became an instant success. They required almost no power and provided a flexibility the members of the Savitar had almost forgotten existed. Now they were getting around in their "subway" system as smoothly or maybe more so then their counter parts in the Boston or the London subway system. Certainly, the Savitar's system was newer and cleaner and had no graffiti. The real benefit was personnel did not have to don spaces suites to make the trip to various places on the Savitar.

A new way to manage the location and use of space suits was set up. The general suits not custom fit to a person were assigned to strategic locations. These could be checked out for short periods of time if needed and then checked back in after use. Those with fitted suits would use specially designed carriers on the transport tubes to bring the suits out to the location as needed. This provided much greater flexibility when work on the exterior needed to get done.

The majority of the work aboard the Savitar was now done within the confines of the structure and living spaces. Only a small contingent of personnel had work requiring them to be on the exterior of the Savitar.

The dramatic change in the living environment was enjoyable, exciting and had the crew of the Savitar experiencing an almost drunken exhilaration. The space in everyone's living quarters had increased to the point their living space resembled normal sized apartments. A person would have their own bed, bath and personal living room or area. There was a small kitchenette as well. Full meals would still be served in a cafeteria centrally located in the living complex. However, individuals could choose to prepare their meals in their small kitchenettes.

After all the time in confined quarters, the ability to go for a walk in a garden and have a running brook with flowers and trees was a surreal experience. It was easy to forget they were in the depth of space, moving an object of extreme danger.

The parks and gardens were almost always populated by a host of people walking, talking, laughing, and playing. What was more remarkable was the existence of five very different garden environments. Each had a huge park with different trees and plants meant for enjoyment.

They also each had the hydroponic garden meant to the grow tomatoes, squash, watermelons, grapes, corn, lettuce and a host of other fruits and vegetables. These gardens were planned carefully and timed so the Savitar's crew would always have a good mixture of fruits and vegetables. All the gardens were planted, and the farming portions were fully activated. Being self-reliant in feeding the crew was of critical importance. Everyone was required to spend a minimum of an hour a day to help with the gardening.

The layout of one hexagon facility would hold about one thousand people. There were five such facilities. There of course was room to build many more facilities but more materials to build them would need to be obtained. The current design allowed for the additional growth Zack felt would occur naturally. Some of these additional people would come from Earth. The rest would be the children Zack could foresee. The population of the Savitar would need to be managed and controlled.

Random growth would not be allowed to happen.

The living area under roof was about an acre for each person on the Savitar. Each facility was in the shape of the hexagon on which it sat. This huge area had metal sides and top. This design and need for materials caused Zack to cancel any plans for floors between the one G level and the nine G level.

Getting the oxygen for this amount of space was a major effort and could be called a small miracle. All the oxygen sent from Earth was only enough for one or maybe two enclosures. The material the Savitar was successfully scouring from space yielded the additional oxygen and other needed gases. The few oxygen generators brought along had been working full time as the Savitar approached the black hole. Their maintenance was of utmost concern and had been carefully attended to. Additionally, Zack commissioned a team to design and build new oxygen generators.

Of course, the Savitar was a closed system and recycled one hundred percent of its waste. This included the gases being used and released. This recycling system was constantly being improved and expanded as the structure grew. The gardens, the hydroponic tanks, the oxygen generators, the waste management all were designed to work together to create and recreate the materials and gases needed by the crew aboard the Savitar. This system was greatly expanded as part of the redesign of the living areas.

Each pentagon facility featured a few apartments larger than the rest. The leaders of the Savitar each enjoyed one of these. Each leader was assigned to a different hexagon location.

Zack proposed marriage to Janet after the Savitar successfully demonstrated its ability to move the black hole. He knew she was his soul mate and he wanted her to be with him for the rest of his days. He, Janet, Mitch, and Susan were working in the garden outside of their apartment when he proposed.

"We can now look forward to a long life. I would like to ask you to share it with me. You have been my bedrock and I will always need your love and support," Zack said as he held out a large diamond ring to Janet.

There was a moment of silence as Janet took in her surroundings. She would not see Hawaii on her honeymoon, but she would be among the stars. There were tears of happiness as Janet gave Zack a hug, followed by a passionate kiss.

"Nothing would make me happier," Janet said as she let Zack put the engagement ring on her finger. She suddenly realized Zack would have had to have this ring since they had left Earth. Her heart swelled again with the love she felt for him.

She realized that he had thought of this day for their entire trip.

"Well, I cannot be out done," Mitch said as he proposed to Susan and presented her with an engagement ring as well. He had earlier thanked Zack, who had made sure he had the ring before leaving Earth.

"This is wonderful, let's go in and celebrate with a bottle of the new Savitar wine Lisa gave me. She only had enough grapes to make two bottles," Zack said as he and Janet walked in together.

They called Lisa and Enrico to share in the celebration.

"I would like to have the wedding when Craig and Emily arrive. I would like him to be the best man," Zack said once they were inside.

Janet and Susan were talking excitedly about their wedding and what they planned to do for it.

Similar situations were occurring throughout the Savitar. When Zack informed Enrico he would like to have him be the person to marry he and Janet as well as Mitch and Susan, Enrico replied he would be pleased to do so.

He let Zack know there were at least 100 requests and inquiries about getting married. The various priests and religious leaders had all cornered him trying to find out whether this was now allowed.

"Yes, I think it's time we think about the future. We will need to control the population of the Savitar but certainly we should think of the happiness of our crew," Zack responded.

Chapter 27: Next Steps

The anticlimactic nature of the capture and the ease with which the crew switched to a new focus was all part of Zack's careful conditioning of the crew.

Now with Savitar underway and successfully moving the small black hole Zack began to work with the leadership to develop new goals and new purpose for the Savitar.

Zack envisioned the Savitar traveling with the solar system in its journey around the edge of the Milky Way. The Savitar would serve as an advance warning system for Earth. It would conduct the myriad of experiments to develop man's knowledge of the Universe. This could only be done from a platform such as the Savitar. The Savitar would be able to take the various journeys to investigate the anomalies and interesting points in the solar system.

On a daily basis Zack was addressing the crew sharing his vision of the mission ahead. Zack saw the Savitar as Earth's spaceship capable of going out to explore and develop the knowledge which before had eluded the human race. It allowed man to overcome the weightless nature of space.

He also knew once the danger to Earth was eliminated the support of the Savitar would quickly become secondary. There were many dark, uncharted, dangerous miles ahead for Earth. This would be lost in the jubilation of the moment. There were millions of potential objects waiting ahead in the darkness of space capable of obliterating the Earth.

The Savitar could act as an escort and provide for safe passage for the Earth by acting as an interceptor of threatening objects.

Zack envisioned the Savitar escorting the Earth through its journey around the edge of the Milky Way. This escort service would allow wide latitude in the actual location of the ship. The Savitar would become a platform of scientific enquiry and research. It could explore the solar system and investigate the many scientific curiosities. The Savitar would need to be developed and maintained through an infinite length of time.

Zack called his leadership team together to outline the plans for the continued transformation of the Savitar. He highlighted the expansion of the outer surface of the Savitar. He especially focused on the manufacturing facilities, the science and research facilities, and the farming areas. The team was amazed at the scope Zack had in mind. They immediately recruited folks with the necessary background and training to begin detailed planning and execution.

The work began immediately. A new energy could be felt on the Savitar. The crew embraced the concept of developing the Savitar into a self-sustaining world. The survival of the crew had always been an unasked and seldom discussed topic. Never-the-less it had gone through everyone's mind. This topic was now discussed openly and in a positive and constructive way.

It freed the Savitar personnel to look forward.

Zack outlined the ongoing mission to everyone.

On a daily basis he methodically made the rounds until every person had direct discussions with him. He wanted the hearts and minds of every individual and he worked hard to get them.

The small security group led by Mitch was now expanded to include all personnel. Everyone was trained to serve in this security force, and they rotated through the force every three months for a month of renewal training. This renewal training included hand to hand combat, use of the facilities to isolate sections to trap people, weapons operation, and use.

Mitch and Susan were in charge of the security force and the small police force used to maintain order.

Everyone thought of and spoke of the Savitar as the Switzerland of space. The Savitar would remain neutral and would ensure its protection by enrolling all of its citizens in keeping this neutrality. This was just what the Savitar needed to totally enroll everyone. The crew liked the concept of a neutral spaceship focused on the good of the Earth.

Back on Earth, President Lansing was re-elected by a landslide. And as anticipated, the politics of Earth looked inward once more. The Savitar all but vanished for the common lay person. Only the military of several countries and the scientific communities paid the Savitar any attention. And in all cases this attention took the form of how the Savitar could be brought under their control.

Craig was in constant communication with Zack. He coordinated a group of scientist running various tests and experiments via the Savitar. Many scientific experiments had been set up on the Savitar's journey out to the black hole. These were continued and other project packages sent out more recently were erected and started up

At least a third of the crew got involved in these experiments and developed themselves into scientist in various fields. Many had already earned their bachelor's degree in their new fields, and some were working on advanced degrees. This scientific link was one of the strongest and most positive relationships the Savitar enjoyed with those remaining back on Earth.

Meanwhile the military was linked to the Savitar by John Adam. His family was on the way out to the Savitar. John and Zack had become close friends, and both had a similar worry about the intent of even the US military leaders. China, Israel, France, Germany, India, and Russia all were deemed threats in the sense they wanted a military presence on board the Savitar.

Britain and the US argued that the Savitar should be a military free zone similar to Antarctica.

Five spaceships designed for space travel were going to become attached to the Savitar. China, Russia, and the US were sending, spaceships with crews of close to one hundred people. Israel was sending a twelve-person ship and Britain was sending a ten-person ship.

The Leadership on the Savitar decided the best initial use of the larger ships was as freight carriers to and from the Savitar to Earth. The two smaller ships would serve as exploration and retrieval vehicles.

The discussion between Zack and Craig was constant and detailed as the negotiation for the use of the vehicles were discussed and agreed on. Russia, China, and the US all agreed the ships would be used to supply and ferry goods and people to and from the Savitar. Israel and Britain agreed to have their ships assigned directly to the Savitar. The current crew was to stay with these ships. The other three ships would remain under the control of each of the mother countries.

"Well, it is good to have this ship question out of the way. I hope the intentions of the larger countries are just of supplying and aiding the Savitar. I have my doubts. I believe Britain and Israel will send spies and expect first-hand messages back. This is not so much of a worry to me initially. However, I believe the larger ships will bring more than just crew members. They are capable of bringing out as many as one hundred people. This means a powerful commando group could be put together and brought out to the Savitar," Zack shared with his leadership team.

"We will plan for a takeover attempt by the countries providing the three larger ships. I have a way to verify the intentions of the US vessel. We will prepare for all three, but we need to worry mostly about the Chinese and the Russians.

The crew of the Savitar has practiced hand to hand combat. We have developed a variety of weapons to be used against any attack or insurgency. The internal environment has been set up to be used offensively if it becomes necessary," Janet continued the discussion.

She was proud of how the Savitar crew had progressed in becoming a powerful force. She, Susan, and Mitch had worked hard at getting the crew combat capable.

The construction work on the Savitar went on night and day. Zack wanted to make as much progress as possible before the arrival of the spaceships from Earth. Each living area was also a defense zone. Each of the hexagons had weapons located on them.

Zack was especially happy with the newly designed magnetic projectile launchers. These weapons would launch a projectile by pulling it magnetically along its barrel. It could be aimed and followed a straight-line path to its target

The super powerful communications lasers had become what Zack called an unique weapon. These weapons went from some handheld versions to full three-inch guided lasers. The guidance systems had cost the Savitar a number of their computers, but they increased the capability of the lasers. These lasers had been tested and were capable of taking out a missile in flight.

The development had been a huge resource expense for the Savitar, but Zack prevailed, and these projects got the resources it needed.

The Savitar spent nine months, moving the black hole out of Earth's way, and then lining itself up to a parallel course to the Solar system. The sun was a distant star point. Establishing this course had taken all of the maneuvering skill of the crew and help from astrophysicists on Earth.

It became obvious guiding the Savitar with the black hole at its center was comparable to the maneuverability difference of an aircraft carrier and a ski boat.

In the nine months since capture, the Savitar had undergone a dramatic transformation. There were now five identical major living centers on the surface. The priority for the work had been living quarters, defense systems and the training and health facilities. The gravity well tube transport systems were commissioned and travel to and from each center took only minutes. Travel bubbles would get on the rail at one end and then fall steeply down toward the center. This would give it the energy to take it back up to the next center. Each center connected to the five centers around it. Travel to the front five hexagons was by the same style of transport but a station was located at each pentagon. The entire system formed a very efficient personnel and equipment transportation method requiring very little additional energy.

Several of the magnetic technicians got together and developed a generator using the same principle to generate the electricity and these supper efficient generators provided the electrical power for the entire Savitar population. This was a major breakthrough allowing the Savitar to save its precious oxygen and fuel for special use. The black hole was yielding value in spite of its dangerous nature.

The shuttles underwent a transformation to spacecraft making them more maneuverable. Special small steering jets were positioned in specific locations giving the shuttles three-dimensional steering control. They also sported missiles, lasers, and magnetic rail launchers. They maintained their capacity for large scale transport. This ability to move large volumes of materials would always be required when they were close to various asteroid belts to be mined.

Though the shuttles were more than thirty years old, Zack felt comfortable the updated shuttles could tackle the oncoming group of newly designed space craft.

The events and progress on the Savitar surprised everyone. The progress in the short period of under a year was phenomenal. Lisa recruited people to transport the required soil and grow the plants to make each of the five communities independent for their basic needs. Each had a hydroponics facility, and growing gardens capable of yielding enough vegetables to feed the entire Savitar population.

The Savitar now had excess food growing capability. This included the making of wines and spirits from the various crops. Wheat, corn, and rice were grown as was a variety of beans. The rabbit population was now large enough to provide a large portion of the crew's protein needs. Salmon, red snapper, crab, oyster, clam, mussels, and shrimp farming produced an abundance of sea food. Mussels were becoming a favorite specialty.

Chickens and ducks were raised in all the facilities as well. Their eggs were still in short supply, but the chicken and duck population were growing, and eggs would soon become an everyday staple.

This independence in its ability to feed themselves allowed the leaders of the Savitar to have a very confident position when it came to dealings with the various countries back on Earth. Several times the governments back on Earth had reminded the Savitar leadership they would always ensure the Savitar would have sufficient food to feed the crew. These were veiled reminders that the Savitar was dependent on the Earth for survival.

This was no longer true.

Zack made a point of sharing only a fraction of the capability growth of the Savitar with the leaders back on Earth. He wanted to have the element of surprise for the first visitors. He figured this would give him a needed edge in his first encounters with the oncoming group of space travelers.

His discussions with Craig continued on a daily basis and he felt well connected to the American craft. It was clear the craft had a small but deadly contingent of military on board. Craig seemed reassured the intentions of the American military personnel were in helping the crew of the Savitar.

In one of the recent conversations, President Lansing once again used the secret code word to let Zack know he might have some issues with the American craft as well as the rest, but he felt sure it was relatively manageable. His biggest concern was for the intentions and orders Russian, and Chinese crafts might have.

Zack now spent time with the Chinese and Russian contingent on the Savitar. It was time to determine his success in creating a new allegiance to the Savitar. He got their assurances they were Savitarians through and through.

As the Savitar awaited the visitors, India launched a ship. It was coming out last, but it was coming out much faster than the rest. Their intermediate size craft was extremely fast. They operated on the same engines as those of the Savitar. They were a high-powered version producing at least three times the thrust of previous designs. This was of great interest to the Savitar. Was there more they could do with the engines they already had? Could the Savitar generate the fuel for this new version coming out?

Zack made contact with the Indian government and was assured the team coming out was made up of scientists and engineers who were eager to contribute to the journey of the Savitar. They reminded Zack the Savitar was named after an Indian god. This had been a signal to the Indian government to build the Savitar an auxiliary ship.

They had named the ship the Rama. This meant protector against harm or evil. They made it clear the ship would be under the control of those in charge of the Savitar.

"Well, this is one I did not expect however there are almost three hundred Indians aboard the Savitar, and they have done a great job," Zack said as he finished his conversation.

He still had not mentioned to the Indian government the role that Indira had played nor of her incarceration and her punishment of having been banned back to Earth. He was waiting to do this until after the arrival of all the spaceship.

The Savitar's Indian population was jubilant when they heard the news their country was sending up a vessel for the Savitar. They celebrated for days, held dinners and in general carried on as if they had just won the World Soccer tournament.

Chapter 28: First Contact with Earth

The approaching vessels painted their paths on the large radar screen. The larger ships were in the lead, but three smaller ones were only a few weeks behind them. It was interesting to watch the Indian craft quickly closing the gap. Zack was sure the governments on Earth were all wondering what the Indian's had done to their drive system. He was wondering what they could learn to improve the current engines on the Savitar

Japan, at the last moment revealed the existence of their craft. It was a six person craft made by the Toyota-Honda-Nissan consortium. It was the only non-government owned craft of the group. They were by far the most believable, trustworthy craft approaching.

They made no bones about wanting to use the Savitar strictly as homeport from which to explore. They negotiated living space, food, and water from the Savitar. The forty-two strong, Japanese contingent aboard the Savitar were delighted their country was one providing a space craft. The pride they showed the day Zack shared the news with them was evident on all their faces. Their partying was subdued but they were extremely proud of the accomplishment of their homeland. Lisa Hemming provided Savitar Sake to help them celebrate the occasion.

It was decided each of the population centers would host one or more of the spacecraft. The assignment of the ships to the population centers was done at random. The Savitar population had purposely been distributed randomly. Zack did this to ensure the Savitar crew learned to live with each other and did so independent to their country of origin. Each country group was encouraged to share their culture and practices and each group was given space where they could show this cultural element through art, writings or plays and movies. The Savitar crew had indeed grown very close. Friendships spanned all the cultures and crossed all the country boundaries.

The gravity well for the Savitar was only a few miles up from the center. This meant the approaching craft would need to park in space and then come down in a craft or some other mechanism such as one of the eight shuttles the Savitar possessed.

Zack reached agreement with the first three approaching craft to use the shuttles to bring the passengers down.

When the lead spacecraft were about a week away, signals activating the various control programs on Savitar's isolated computer began to come in. The Savitar's programs gave no hint they no longer controlled anything. The interrogators had no clue they were talking to programs doing absolutely nothing.

The Savitar programs instead, sent back signals containing programming to build a connection from the computer aboard the Savitar to the sender's computer. The programs sent back were designed to give the Savitar information from the data banks aboard the approaching craft. Zack was extremely proud of the hacker development classes he had sponsored and whose programming weapons immediately began to yield information to the Savitar leadership.

The Savitar had successfully sent back undetected Trojan horse programs.

It was in this way the Chinese intentions became clear. Though they had scientists aboard, they also had a contingent of 75 commandoes to be used to take control of the Savitar.

The Russians had a similar arrangement.

The Indian crew remained a mystery since they did not interrogate the computer aboard the Savitar but only interacted in the voice communication mode. It did not appear they had any military at all.

The US carried only 25 commandoes and it seemed they were less sure of which way to go but they were focusing on the actions of the Chinese and Russians.

Zack began holding drills on the Savitar to test his crew's readiness for the upcoming confrontation. He hoped by being prepared he could avert an actual battle which could damage the Savitar. He had shielded the supper magnet generators from direct attack. He knew this was the Savitar's Achilles' heel. The shields were designed after the shields put up on tanks and other vessels to reduce the chance of stray bullets from passing into a tank enclosure. It consisted of six rows of staggered rebar and then a thick steel plate. This plate, with the six layers of rebar was lowered down the pentagons above the magnets. Zack was willing to go to this extend because it also provided the magnets with protection from space debris.

The three hundred strong Chinese crew members left no doubt they loved their country, but they had developed a love for the Savitar beyond their country allegiance. They agreed to work with the Chinese representatives and to persuade them to set aside any takeover plans. Without reservation, they all aligned themselves to a free Savitar. They felt they could persuade the Chinese contingent not to engage in military action.

The contingent of each of the approaching ships would be housed in specially constructed holding areas. These areas could be isolated, and the environment controlled. Their environments were part of the Savitar defense system.

When the three craft were a day out, signals began testing the control they thought they exerted over various Savitar capabilities. The Savitar programs were modified to respond in the affirmative in all actions commanded and to send the appropriate variation in the speed, or the environmental controls. This gave the oncoming crafts the impression they had some sort of control. Unknown to them, the reverse infection was happening.

The Savitar hackers had infiltrated the controls of all three on coming vessels. The Russian and Chinese both had subroutines in the environmental control systems. The US had one in the communications control and power control programs. Without exception, none of the oncoming vessels had protected themselves from the very technique they were using in an attempt to control the Savitar.

The leadership of the Savitar was overjoyed with the success of their hackers.

"I will have to commend the hacker team for their work. It really gives us the edge in dealing with these ships," Enrico commented in the morning meeting.

The day arrived when all four larger craft hovered in space near the Savitar. They appeared like small moons to the members of the Savitar crew.

All eight of the space shuttles were positioned between the oncoming craft and the Savitar. They were fully armed and were in the defensive position they had practiced hundreds of time. If any aggressive action was initiated, the team of defenders on the shuttles had orders to defend the Savitar.

The position and the stance of the shuttles were noticed by all of the oncoming craft. This was a surprise and caused some hesitation.

It was clear the Savitar was prepared.

Arrangements were made to ferry the members of each ship to the surface. Two shuttles were sent to each spacecraft. They would ferry the passengers down thirty or forty at a time. The two extra shuttles stood by in a defensive position.

The new arrivals were all ferried to similar arrival rooms but to different living centers. These facilities were being controlled by the external infected computer on the arriving ships. Whatever happened would happen to the members of the invading personnel. Ironically, it would be their own leadership who would inflict whatever harm they planned to inflict on the Savitar, but it would be applied to their own personnel.

Zack worked with Craig to segregate the scientists from the military personnel and as they came on board, they moved the scientists to a separate arrival area. This was done as the personnel were escorted down a hallway and turned a corner. The scientists were taken through a side door.

It was clear to the American military group they had been separated from their civilian counterparts.

"Welcome to the Savitar. This is the common room and around and down the hallways you will find your quarters. Please make yourself at home. Relax and enjoy the refreshments. I understand you are here to help. Be assured if we need the help, we will call you," Zack said as he greeted the twenty-five commandos entering the common room.

The signal to take control came down when about three quarters of the personnel were down, and the last load was on a shuttle.

Then both the Chinese and the Russian ships in an almost simultaneous communication, hailed the Savitar.

"We are in position to take control of the Savitar. Our personnel will position themselves in the control center. Zackary Milton and his team will put themselves in our protection," the Chinese ship announced. The Russian countered they would take control and the Chinese were to stand down or face the consequence.

"We thank both of you for your concern but as guests on the Savitar you have no authority here. Any hostile action will immediately be countered and amplified. You do not know the capability of the Savitar, but it is much superior to anything you have with you. In fact, the eight shuttles facing you have the capability to annihilate your vessels," Enrico replied calmly

The signals to take control of the environment came immediately afterwards. These signals locked the respective crews of the attacking space vessels into the spaces to which they had been escorted. They were experiencing the effects dictated by their own commands. The communication from each group back to their respective ship was immediate and clear in requesting a truce.

The US craft had not taken any aggressive action. They had instead turned to have better aim at the two other spacecraft.

Three Savitar teams, each monitoring the spacecraft took the counter actions they had practiced. Both the Chinese and Russian spacecraft came under the control of the Savitar. The weapons system of each ship was disabled.

The Chinese and Russian commandos attempted to break out of their containment. However, they did not have the tools or the time. The actions of their ships had started a purge of the air from the compartment in which they were located.

Zack informed both the Chinese and the Russians of this situation and pointed out the only people being attacked were their own crew members by their ship's actions.

The American contingent was listening in. They asked if the Savitar needed their help. When Zack thanked them and declined, the commandos relaxed and continued to enjoy the assortment of refreshments laid out for them. Their leader had been coached by Craig to expect the Savitar to be well prepared for any contingency.

This leader had been impressed at how effortlessly his team had been stripped of their civilian crew members. The American contingent felt relieved that they would not face a battle.

In short order the Chinese and Russian ceased their aggressive actions. They were unprepared for the comprehensive, absolute, and effortless way the Savitar overcame their takeover attempt. They replied there had been a misunderstanding and they were only trying to protect their people.

Zack put each country in touch with the Savitar group organized to communicate to their arriving countrymen. He watched as the Chinese contingent went through a series of heated debates. Chiang Lee, senior navigator on the Savitar was the spokesperson. He engaged in a quiet but forceful discussion with the Chinese commander.

He was a very different person than the one who had left China to join the Savitar.

It was clear to the arriving Chinese leadership; they would get no support from their countrymen in any action taken against the Savitar.

A day later the arriving Indian contingent came down to the Savitar and had a jubilant reception. Their only thoughts were on the amazing opportunity a ship like the Savitar provided their scientists.

They came in eagerness and with an earnest desire to be part of what they saw as the next great adventure for Earth. They had a jubilant reception and the discussions they held with their countrymen was about life on board the Savitar.

An arrival dinner was planned for Craig, Emily, and John Adam's family. Enrico and Lisa rounded out the dinner guests. John introduced his wife Joanne and his daughter and son. He thanked everyone for their help in getting the family back together and up to the Savitar.

"Well let me toast our two youngest arrivals. Lisa has brewed our first batch of ginger ale for this occasion, so everyone please take their glasses and welcome our two youngest Savitar members, William, and Melanie." Zack said as he handed a glass to the two young members.

"I will talk with the American military group and make sure they understand the situation on board," John said as he hugged his children and kissed his wife.

Craig updated the group on the American contingent. It had been sent heavily armed to prevent a takeover by either the Russians or the Chinese. At least their initial actions would be benign.

"It's great to have all of you here. I hope to have the idea of a takeover put to rest in a very short time. It just won't happen," Enrico said confidently to everyone at the table.

The next day at a meeting of the leaders of the various countries Zack brought this point up.

"Now that I have your attention, let me inform you the Savitar will not give itself over to any country's control. The Savitar will remain an international vessel representing the Earth in its entirety. I recommend you cease your takeover attempts and enjoy our hospitality," Zack sent the message to the leaders of the arriving contingent.

After a few moments, both the Russian and Chinese responded they would be pleased to be the guests of the Savitar.

Zack had gotten this assurance the day before from the US contingent.

The US craft had been monitored. They had activated and aimed their weapons at the Russian and Chinese spacecraft. The Savitar teams monitoring these vessels through the computers kept to the background. It was the Savitar's leadership intentions to keep quiet and in the background. The longer they could keep the depth of their control of these vessels a mystery the better it would be for them.

Zack was pleased with the initial interaction, but he knew the battle was not yet over. He, Enrico, and the leadership team had discussed this at length.

They had decided to have a mini-Olympics where the capability of the Savitar could be displayed. This would be followed by an elaborate celebration dinner.

They scheduled the Olympics event after the arrival of the three smaller ships from Israel, Britain, and Japan. Each ship would be able to enter members in the Olympics in whatever sport they felt they had representation. Boxing, pole vaulting, shot put, discus and javelin throw, various races, archery, Tae Kwon Do and shooting all were in the mix.

The Savitar team had anticipated doing such a thing and had their personnel training these events for months. This gave them a tremendous advantage in matching the competition from the arriving spacecraft.

Those on the arriving spacecraft were the best specimen each country could field. However, they had traveled almost six months to reach the Savitar. The Savitar leadership knew this would take a toll even with the conditioning they had done on the way. Meanwhile the Savitar folks had gravity to use in strengthening their runners, jumpers, and throwers.

Their real secret weapon was the nano-bots. These had the health of the Savitar crew at a level previously unknown to mankind. Everyone on board had the ideal muscle to fat ratio. To those just arriving from Earth it seemed the Savitar crew was under nourished when in fact they were all almost at the ideal body to fat ratio and were healthier than anyone on Earth could dream of being.

The ensuing contest was very lopsided. The Savitar personnel consistently won the competition. There were a few bright spots for the Chinese, Russian, Indians, and Americans but very few. The Israeli, Brits and Japanese were few and they did not show up well. It was overwhelmingly obvious the Savitar crew was in great shape, very capable and demonstrated superior capability in all the contests.

The banquet was planned for the day after the competition. It was to celebrate the occasion of the first visit by each country. The dinner had been carefully planned and prepared for by all of the Savitar crew. Nothing was left to chance. The seating arrangement ensured those arriving got to talk to their own countrymen and also to other members of the Savitar.

The banquet was in the number one hexagon facility where Zack lived. It had a huge banquet hall able to house all the people of the Savitar. Everyone was there with the exception of key personnel who remained on watch and a few crew in each of the visiting vessels.

"Ladies and Gentlemen, I know some of you have been sent out with the mission, to take control of the Savitar. I want to let you know this will not happen now or any time in the future. The actions of your personnel have been observed. You tried to take control from your ships and learned the hard way you cannot do so.

Your personnel have continued to attempt taking control since they have landed. This will cease and you will desist otherwise we will put you back on board your ships and send you back to Earth with a do not return message. Are there any questions," Zack said as he looked around the room at the Captains and political leaders who had identified themselves?

"I am pleased to let you know the US contingent, all volunteers, would like to join the crew of the Savitar. President Lansing has sent his congratulations and commends you on the valor of the Savitar crew. We have also brought a number of distinguished scientists. I trust they will integrate easily into the fabric of the Savitar. I must commend you on the extraordinary transformation of this vessel. What I see amazes me and I am sure you have not yet shared all with us. You and your crew will be interested in the cargo aboard the Sprite," Adrian Moffit the Captain of the US vessel the Sprite offered as a reply to Zack.

"Thank you, Captain Moffit, we will be pleased to tour you and all our other guests through the entire facility and share with you the future vision for the Savitar. We are very interested in the cargo you bring with you," Zachary replied as he once again heard through the words used by Captain Moffit, President Lansing giving him the OK to act as he saw fit.

"We mean no negative action against the Savitar. We were misinformed our personnel were being mistreated but it is obvious this is in error. We wish to correct the poor beginning of our visit and contribute to the success of the Savitar," Lin Sin Pao the captain of the Chinese vessel, the Star Seeker said quietly.

He had been surprised how dedicated to the Savitar the Chinese contingent had become. To the last man and woman, they had informed him he would get no support from them in any action taken against the Savitar or against Zackary Milton.

This was unheard of for the people of his culture.

He would heed their advice.

"Thank you, then perhaps you will ask your commandos to stop trying to break into our computers. They have made six hundred or more attempts since their arrival. We will interpret the next attempt as an unfriendly act," Zack said evenly as he gave a slight bow.

"These actions shall be stopped immediately," Lin Sin Pao said as he turned to an aid and gave her some orders.

Again, he was surprised at the capability existing on the Savitar. His crew did not know they were being so closely monitored. In all their attempts they had not been able to gain one bit of control or to get any information.

His programmers claimed to be in the computer and have total control.

"We of India only wish to share in the benefits of having the Savitar out in space. We have brought up all the things you requested and additionally things our scientist thought would aid in maintaining the Savitar. Our most prized contribution on this trip is a hive of honeybees. Their care has proved to be very difficult." Captain Adrinath Rajkumar of India spoke up.

There was no way he could describe how difficult it had been to bring the bees and to keep them alive. His beekeepers had brought the bees down with them when they had embarked to the Savitar. They had been immediately introduced to Lisa Hemming who eagerly helped them get the bees to an area where they could acclimate to their new surroundings.

She had thanked them and made sure that they all understood that the bees were a treasure of extreme importance.

"The bees are an outstanding gift. Let me thank you for this gift and send back a dozen bottles of Golden Spumanti wine from the vineyards of the Savitar. With bees to do the pollinating perhaps we will be able to have more wine and other crops," Zack responded.

Lisa had eagerly shared the good news about the bees when they had first arrived. She was working with the Indian beekeepers to get the bees acclimated to their new homes on board the Savitar. The lighting system was already being re-programmed to provide the bees with the orientation the sun provided them on Earth. The bees were a new challenge for the scientist aboard the Savitar.

Zack had not thought about bees. This made him conscious of possibly having missed many other critical items he would later need.

"We are pleased to be here aboard the Savitar and hope to enjoy your hospitality and become partners in your journeys and adventures," Hamasura Tokura of the Japanese craft, Hoshi-no-ma-de, spoke next.

"We have brought some small gifts. We have Fuji apple seedlings, a dozen small food oysters and some oysters for the production of pearls, some green tea plants, and a variety of sea grasses. We hope these will be a welcome addition to the collection of the Savitar," Hamasura said as he gave a slight bow.

"This is wonderful. Your countrymen are extremely proud to have you here. I am pleased with these gifts. We will be able to cultivate and enjoy these gifts for years to come," Zack said as he accepted the offered gifts.

The Israel contingent had also brought a gift. They had brought the necessary equipment to produce computers and other electronic equipment.

This capability had been one that Zack had greatly desired. It would be crucial for the Savitar to increase their computing capability. He thanked the Israeli leaders.

A very serious Commander Elena Stanislav of the Stremitel'noye took her failure very hard. She expected an easy take over and had only worried about the Chinese and American contingents. The excellent conditions on the Savitar, the attitude of the Russian people on board all were counter to what she had been told she would find. Her countrymen had informed her that a fight with the Savitar meant a fight with them. There was no room to negotiate or for her to convince them otherwise.

This had been unexpected and unnerving.

"We from Russia have also brought out supplies and we have brought out several machining and plastic molding production facilities. We will be proud to contribute to the success of the Savitar. There is an attitude of excellence, a confidence from the crew of the Savitar which speaks to the continued success of this effort," Elena said as she looked around at the leaders of the Savitar with her new-found respect.

She had studied Zack Milton's dossier and had found nothing in it to indicate the dynamic nature of his leadership.

She now knew what was on paper could fall extremely short of what was found in real life.

"We are pleased to greet each of you as valued individuals. We understand the political pressures some of you face and the mission you may have been sent here on. We welcome you to the Savitar, a vessel belonging to all the Earth but to no nation. Let us begin again, in friendship, with respect for each other and for the independent nature of the Savitar. Servers, please bring in the food," Zack ended his brief speech.

The dinner consisted of a starter of frog legs, mussels, and a large garden salad. The main course was Shrimp, Salmon, Chicken, duck, or Rabbit. Each was accompanied with potatoes, or rice with broccoli or cauliflower depending on the choice of the main dish. Special vegetarian meals for those who followed a vegetarian regime had also been prepared. The three Savitar chefs and their trainees had spent almost a month getting ready for this event.

This was their moment in the spotlight, and they intended to please.

This offering astounded all the new arrivals. They had not yet grasped the extent of the Savitar's resources and capability. It was also the best meal the Savitar crew had enjoyed. The leadership team decided to make this a meal to remember. Lisa assured them the gardens and their animal population could support this one extravagance and still be supporting the crew on a normal basis in the immediate future.

Enrico made sure all the crew members received the same meals even if they were on duty. Even Indira and Sunny received the same meal.

The table arrangement had been planned to make sure a Savitar member sat on each side of the arriving guest. This provided the newcomers talk partners who could share the current situation and attitude aboard the Savitar.

The dinner went on well into the evening as the new arrivals and the crew of the Savitar exchanged stories and small talk.

The Olympics and the dinner changed the attitude of all concerned.

Zack and the leadership team had the impact they had hoped to achieve.

Chapter 29: Savitar's New Lifestyle

The goods from each of the arriving ships were off loaded to the appropriate locations.

Gregor Menkowski made sure each batch of manufacturing equipment was logged and appropriately located as close to the final location as possible. He wanted to minimize later rework.

The crew of the Savitar had each been asked what they wanted to do for the long run. They were offered a variety of business opportunities such as being barbers, hairdressers, bakers, nail shop owners, restaurant owners, farmers, equipment repair specialists, doctors, dentists, nurses, optometrists, furniture makers, plumbers and many more. Those making a specific choice had studied their field and came up with a list of goods they would need to get them started.

As the goods came off the arriving vessels these entrepreneurs were given the goods they had ordered on consignment. Later as they got their businesses started, they would pay back this initial loan from the Savitar Bank.

Gregor took an instant liking to Elena and the two spent most evenings walking and talking in one of the five major gardens on the Savitar.

This of course did not go unnoticed but after a discussion between Mitch and Zack they both decided it could indeed be a mutual attraction and they would err on the side of letting Gregor have a run at the attractive Russian commander.

They had developed a very high level of trust in Gregor and did not fear any issues to do with his work.

The scientists brought up by the Indian, American, and Japanese were quickly integrated into the fabric of the Savitar staff. They provided the new energy, eyes, and brains to bolster the work the Savitar had started.

To the last they were amazed at the facilities and the equipment the crew of the Savitar enjoyed in the science labs. From the beginning the science labs were Zack's and the Savitar leadership team's pride and an area they focused on making the best and as spacious as they could possibly afford.

The remaining American crew commanded by Adrian Moffet requested permission to accompany the Savitar on its journey. The tour provided to them by Zack had impressed Captain Moffet and inspired him to seek membership in the crew of the Savitar.

Zack and Enrico agreed to have Adrian on board with the condition he agreed to adhere to the rules of the Savitar. He would retain control of the Sprite but when it was docket on the Savitar, he would be under Enrico's command. This was agreed upon and communicated back to the US military.

The response of agreement came directly from President Manning. He commented that the valor shown by Savitar leadership had earned them a powerful new vessel in the USS Sprite. It was to be the Savitar's flagship.

Adrinath Rajkumar agreed to similar terms, only his orders were to be at the disposal of the Savitar leadership. He would in the future always be at the disposal of those commanding the Savitar. He was quickly and eagerly becoming a member of the Savitar. The treatment his fellow countrymen extended to him made him feel like a hero.

Zack welcomed Adrinath into the Savitar's expanded leadership team. This expanded team would be made up of the captains of each space vessel, Enrico, and himself.

The Israeli ship would support the Savitar but would be run by its current Israeli crew. It would carry out the scientific programs that had been assigned to them upon their Earth departure. They would respect the Savitar command and adhere to its rules.

This team was very proper, but Zack did not sense the same "join the Savitar on its wonderous journey" attitude that the other new arrivals displayed. He decided to employ patience and move slowly to make the crew feel welcome.

Britain's ship, the Fortune, would be under Enrico's command and he retained Marcus Langley the captain, and kept him in charge of the Fortune.

This arrangement finalized the new capabilities the Savitar now commanded.

Zack and Enrico discussed how each vessel could be used in the near future.

The new arrivals took a grand tour of the ship. Not one among them expected the ship to be so advanced. Its construction and the capability of the vessel and its people surprised everyone. They were astounded by the space, convenience, and beauty of the five living areas. The gardens at the center of each, the lake, the lighting all contributed to a feeling of wonderment. The transportation tubes and the ease of getting around on the Savitar was the biggest surprise of all.

How could the Spartan vessel, leaving Earth just four years ago, have undergone such a dramatic transformation?

Elena was especially conscience of her disbelief that a quiet person like Zack Milton would be the catalyst for such dramatic improvement. The more she observed and listened, the clearer it became, he was the spirit behind all the gains.

She herself was quickly being swayed to his call.

Zack took in the surprise that the tour elicited. He kept praising the massive amount of work the crew of the Savitar had pulled off.

Craig and Emily chose an apartment in the same hexagon Zack was in. Emily was especially pleased with the gardens and hydroponics. She, Mary, and Lisa Hemming immediately became friends. The three toured the hydroponics areas and discussed how to maintain and expand the work.

Emily inquired about utilizing her skills as a chef. She was immediately pulled into the group that had become the chefs on board. She was well known by reputation, and she was asked to become one of the trainers of chefs to be.

She shared with Craig that she had made the right decision in coming to the Savitar.

Craig was relieved to see Emily immediately engaged in the workings of the Savitar. He had worried about what she would do once they arrived. He had not foreseen the transformation Zack had orchestrated. He was overjoyed to be working with Zack once more. It was obvious Zack had matured dramatically and become a great leader and in total control.

Craig was especially conscious of the total dedication of the crew.

The group was sitting around living room when Zack shared his proposal of marriage to Janet. He let everyone know that the two of them had waited for the arrival of Craig and Emily to be at their wedding. He asked Craig to be best man and Janet asked Emily to be matron of honor.

Emily agreed to the role if Janet would let her bake the wedding cake and decide on the menu for the wedding dinner.

The women all began planning the wedding.

Zack immediately offered the men a Savitar beer and a walk in the garden. He knew the wedding plans would now take over the discussion for weeks to come.

The Russian Captain Elena and Gregor let it be known she wanted to give up her position as the captain of the Stremitel'noye and stay on board the Savitar. Gregor had proposed to her, and they decided the Savitar would be home.

Elena did not relish the return to a disappointed and angry Russian leadership that would make her life a hell back on Earth.

Zack was pleased that Gregor had found his other half. He welcomed Elena and suggested she spend her time to decide what she wanted to do on board the Savitar.

These events and similar other ones throughout the ship set the stage for the long-term positive environment on the Savitar.

Enrico spent time with the various religious leaders to ensure the message to the newly paired couples was that for near future there was a one child limit on children.

The discussion on this topic was still going on. Zack had decided that the one child message needed to go out early. The final resolution to this issued depended on how fast living space on the Savitar could be developed.

Chapter 30: Continuing Journey

The Savitar now took on its escort and exploration role. It slowly transformed from a rescue mentality to a scientific research and escort mentality.

The three transport ships were scheduled back to Earth about six months apart. This would ensure a cycle where each ship visit was about once every eighteen months. This would give the Savitar a six-month production window. They would produce goods to be sold to Earth and to identify the most wanted items to be brought up from Earth.

Zack and the Savitar leadership team intended the Savitar to be a major trading partner and to pay for itself as it went along. This capability to produce a variety of goods and services would serve to keep the Savitar independent. It would also go a long way in paying back the world for the resources spent in getting the vessel built.

The initial goods from the Savitar were wine, rare minerals and gases, and samples of meteors and space rock. These would all be extremely valuable to the scientists back on Earth. More important of course was the tremendous amount of information and digital pictures going back to Earth. This information was put into memory chips since it was prohibitively large in volume to send via the radio signal.

Zack sent President Lansing a special sampling of fruit and vegetables grown on the Savitar.

Now with the Savitar moving along its maiden journey as guide out in front of the Earth, Zack and Craig once again looked out ahead searching for any objects posing a threat to the well-being of Earth. They hoped to never find another black hole.

The Astronomers set up several new and very powerful telescopes and were drowning in new views of the universe. These telescopes providing a new reference allowing the astronomers to measure distance more accurately to far objects and to determine the speed of expansion of the Universe. This sharpened the view of and the measurement accuracy of the size and distances in the Universe. There was a constant stream of data being sent back to Earth to be analyzed and studied. This data was already revolutionizing the understanding of distance and time.

Savitar

Painters, Poets, musicians, and writers aboard the Savitar were busy as well. The songs and stories written by Savitar personnel were popular and being sold back on Earth. This was a stream of unexpected but welcome revenue for those aboard the Savitar.

The relationship between the two spaceships in the sky was slowly taking shape. It was different than either ship anticipated.

On the Savitar, the fact some people could earn Earth incomes and then ask for privileges based on this, surfaced, and needed to be managed.

The fact the Savitar could almost exist without the help of Earth caused some consternation for the leaders back on Earth.

These situations were handled one at a time. Each case was handled with the governments in question.

On the Savitar, a government similar to the US was established. Every hexagon got one representative selected from those who lived there. These five people made up the Senate. Every hundred people selected one representative. This group of forty made up the House of Representatives and one person was elected by popular vote to be President. The President led the Savitar's social system. The judicial system was also established.

This government was separate from the business of managing the Savitar as a spaceship.

Zack became the first President of the Savitar. He proposed the names of the first three judicial justices. One was Chinese, one was Russian, and one was Indian. They were ratified by the Savitar Congress and took their positions. This justice system was to insure, the constitution, developed by the elected leaders in the house and senate and ratified by the entire Savitar population, would be adhered to.

The mixture in the other two branches of government also reached across all the races represented on board. This balance reflected the growth the people of the Savitar. Everyone took these roles seriously and studied their roles as they were carried out on Earth. As they learned they adapted it to the good of the Savitar and its' population.

A currency of exchange was established to enable the interface with the various businesses doing business with the Earth. It was decided one Savitar dollar would equal one US dollar and this money was to be used only for things not directly provided by living on and being a member on the Savitar. Education, medical care, food, shelter, and basic clothing would be provided to all members equally and as needed. The rest would be purchased with the salaries linked to each role on the ship.

There was a tax on the money made by the businesses trading with the Earth. This tax was used to pay for specific goods that would benefit the Savitar as a whole.

Indira was sent back to the US as her punishment had dictated. Since she was a US citizen, her acts landed her a five-year sentence in prison. She implicated a high ranking general in the Air force who was charged and met a similar fate.

Indira continued to hold to the belief Zack's accomplishment was a slap to the face of God. This illogical belief somehow helped her face the fact she had used her tremendous intellect for something as horrific as trying to kill someone.

Zack felt the punishment was sufficient and put that incident behind him. He was too, happy in his own world to be thinking about past events.

Sunny appealed his sentence. He requested to stay on board the Savitar and to be allowed to be one of the hydroponics farmers. He was granted this request and put on five years' probation.

Zack orchestrated his wedding so he could share it with his family. Janet sent Zack's mother the message that she had been to care of Zack, and she would now do so for the rest of his life.

Zack arrange with Lisa to have palm trees and a beach set up in one of the gardens. The wedding was held with water splashing up on the beach.

Janet once again was surprised at Zack's attention to her words. She had shared this scene with him back on Earth.

She got to walk the beach with the person she loved.

The End

Preview: Confluence

Chapter 1: Astounding Discovery

The Savitar was now functioning as an Earth escort and a science project platform. Zack had been elected the first president of the Savitar. It was a neutral entity considered to be the Switzerland of Space. The relationship between Earth and the Savitar was evolving and various countries desired to have formal ambassadors and staff on the Savitar.

Zack and his leadership team decided that an Ambassador might be appropriate but the staffing for that ambassador had to come from the people were already on the Savitar.

This approach caused several countries to withdraw their request for an ambassador.

Zack and the leadership team were pleased with the withdrawal of most of the ones that were pulled. They were not seeking formal recognition from any specific country.

Except for the fact that living space on the Savitar was limited and managing the Savitar to remain a viable entity was a task that kept all inhabitants totally engaged.

Life was as good as it was for those people on Earth.

Zack was proud of the active engagement his team had with various teams on Earth. These teams were critical in bringing the critical skills and capabilities up to the Savitar.

One of his teams asked to give the leadership team an update on a new discovery. They showed him a series of pictures indicating that a previous intelligence had traveled the solar system They displayed a series of pictures taken by the Savitar on its journey out to the blackhole that were being studied in detail.

Craig then let the leadership team know that he and his team had kept it under wraps until they were absolutely confident of their findings.

He then said that he wanted to put in a request.

"Gentlemen, we are sharing what my team and I feel very certain that we have discovered. We have found signs of a previous intelligence. There are indications on Mars, on a moon of Jupiter and most clearly on a moon of Saturn.

The request that I am making is to utilize the equipment of the Savitar to scrutinize the moon of Saturn and determine if an full project expedition should be sent to investigate it more closely," Craig said as he put the pictures with the evidence in front of Zack and Enrico.

"Such a discovery would be astounding. It is hard from these pictures to conclude this is the case. What am I missing," Zack asked as he took in Craig's request?

"Here, see the rows along the wall of this deep canyon. This is a picture taken of a deep mantle canyon on Mars. This seems to suggest there are multiple floors cut into the mantle.

Now look at the picture of Europa a moon of Jupiter. See this huge post. It appears to be some sort of giant anchor with a ring at the top. It is almost totally buried in the ice, but we were able to enhance the picture to see it more clearly. It appears to be fabricated and put there for some purpose we have not yet determined.

Finally, look at the ruins of some giant structure on Titan the largest moon circling Saturn. We did not see it until we were able to screen out the thick cloud cover.

This picture seals my belief of some intelligence traveling our solar system in the distant past." Craig said as he explained the pictures to group.

"Let's agree to the exploration of Titan as our first scientific investigation. I am not sure I am bought into Craig's interpretation of the pictures but investigating and learning about our solar system is what we are about." Zack commented to the leadership team.

Enrico made the official proposal to travel in toward the orbit of Saturn. The leadership team agreed and the first scientific journey for the Savitar was put into swing.

Enrico suggested that the Savitar would move part of the way toward Saturn, but it had to stay far enough away to prevent any undesired effects their presence might have. Having a captive black hole worked well to provide the Savitar with an almost perfect one G gravity but it still exerted its presence on the paths of the various objects in the solar system.

Captain Rajkumar of the Rama eagerly volunteered his ship as the perfect match for the task at hand.

The leadership team agreed and suggested that the team that would do the exploration decided what they needed and start to prepare the Rama for its first excursion.

The journey to Saturn was much slower than the journey out to the black hole. They were now moving carefully and staying away from the orbits of the planets. And moving the Savitar meant determining where they might be going next.

Currently the Savitar's travels was synchronized to the match the speed that the Solar system was moving. It chose to slow down just a bit and move toward the Saturn just a bit. A bit was the best they knew how to communicate what a slight deviation was to be. They were still in the learning process on pushing the black hole in the direction they desired.

The Rama was made ready for the exploration of Titan.

The Indian crew was excited to be the ship to be named to be engaged in the first exploratory mission. Their community had several celebratory gatherings to celebrate with the crew.

The leadership team had agreed that Craig would lead this first expedition.

The Rama was capable of landing on the surface and taking back off from Titan. This would allow for firsthand exploration.

As the Savitar got closer to Saturn they verified earlier analysis of the makeup of the atmosphere and the seas of Titan to be a methane-ethane mixture.

It was in essence a sea of gasoline. This was an obstacle to the plans of landing on to the surface.

The Rama would not be able to land after all. Their engines would potentially ignite the atmosphere and the seas.

The powerful telescopes scouring the surface of Titan. The ability to filter out much of the cloud cover allowed Craig and his team to examine the surface of Titan. They spent almost a month meticulously examining the surface.

The day the scene of the surface revealed a ring in the surface ice of the moon a cheer went up from Craig and his entire team.

They took a series of pictures and then compared it to the picture of the other ring that they had. The ring was a duplicate of the one found on the moon Europa.

Craig brought it to the leadership morning meeting and made the point that the second ring confirmed the existence of a previous intelligence.

Zack complemented Craig on his teams thorough and correct analysis.

"You would have to have a mighty big dog to hook his chain to that ground ring," Janet joked as she stared at the ring.

Her comment caused Zack to jump up in excitement.

He pointed at Janet and said that she was a genius. She had just escribed a ring to hook a space elevator to the moon. It is the anchor point of a cable. We of all people should recognize it. The Savitar is held together by cables. We rode up and down on the welding elevators for several years. There were huge rings at the ends of those cables.

How could I have missed it when Craig first showed me the pictures?"

It made sense. The previous visitors would not be able to land their space craft, but they would be able to hook up and set up a space elevator and then visit the surface.

They could not chance using the existing ring since they did not know its true condition.

Analysis of the atmosphere and the gravitational attraction showed that the Savitar would be able to land a glider near the existing ring.

They would design a similar anchor to which the Rama would connect. The expedition would then go down to the surface on the elevator. The solution was simple but executing it would be a new experience.

The crew of the Rama promised that they would be able to hold the elevator line stable. They simulated keeping the Rama in place as the various forces they were able to measure affected them.

They practiced as they traveled out to Titan. As they approached that declared that they were ready.

The news about the discovery when it hit the Earth was electrifying. The data sent back by the Savitar was now poured over as the various experts looked for additional evidence.

Every University and research department wanted access to the data and began to scrutinize it and scouring it for indication of a previous civilization.

The satellites, placed around Jupiter and Saturn as the Savitar went out to the black hole, were now programmed to examine the larger moons. Each of the major moons would have every square foot examined in multiple frequencies.

The Mars satellite began to examine the cliffs more closely on the deep canyons. They began to provide additional evidence of this previous intelligence.

The exploration of the exterior structure on Titan was carefully examined. The structure appeared to have been an enclosure designed to shield those inside from the atmospheric pressure. Titan's atmospheric pressure was sixty times greater than Earth's. The expedition going to the surface of Titan would require suits capable of withstanding this pressure and providing a suitable internal environment for the individual.

An exoskeleton design was selected. The person essentially became encompassed like a turtle.

Getting to the surface would not be as difficult as initially anticipated. Gravity was weak enough that a human could almost fly by beating their arms.

However, the concept of an elevator was more practical. The concept of a space elevator was not new. It had never been tried because of the extreme length of cable required for an Earth space elevator. The one for Titan would still be very long but the Savitar had already broken the mold on the size limits. They also had the two hundred forty- mile long pull cables used to pull the Savitar full size cables into position. These were the right length and tensile strength required for an elevator to the surface of Titan.

The fact that the Savitar had several spare cables that could be used greatly shortened the preparation time for the team to get the surface.

Craig decided this was an expedition that energized him. But he wanted to be the technical leader. He realized that someone else should be he mission leader.

One of the young marine lieutenants reporting to Captain Moffett was selected to be the mission leader. He would be responsible for the logistics and safety of the team when on the ground. He would take his direction from Craig about the actual investigation.

Craig would guide the scientific aspects of the mission. The team consisted of a four-person camera crew, three scientific analysts, four support personnel, Craig, and the mission leader.

The final design of getting the cable to the surface of Titan was labeled the Harpoon. From synchronous orbit the Rama shot the harpoon to the surface of Titan.

The force and the heated tip drove the harpoon forcefully in to the ice. Spikes shot out in radial direction from the shaft to lock the harpoon in the ice. Two of the team members glided down on the thin pull cable. They carried six additional anchors down with them.

Once on the surface they permanently positioned the initial anchor by retracting the radial spikes and sinking the main shaft to its maximum depth. They then reset the radial spikes. The six additional anchors were positioned in a circle around the harpoon anchor and sunk at an angle with their tops coming together near the Harpoon anchor. The pull cable was threaded through the eyes of the anchors and the end was sent back up to the Rama.

The team back on the Rama fed out the line until they had the end back. They then began to feed down the elevator cable to be attached to the anchor point.

Craig waited impatiently for this activity to be completed. He was anxious to get to the surface. The atmospheric cover made it impossible to get a good view of what was on the surface.

Finally, the elevator was ready.

The team would descend together except for two of the support members who would bring down the additional equipment and supplies.

The structure was within five minutes walking distance from the ancient anchor. Walking was not really the right word. It was more of a skating motion. If too much energy was put into a step the person would launch themselves off the surface. It was much more of a motion like cross country skiing.

Craig had often engaged in cross country skiing and spent some time training his team.

Soon everyone was moving smoothly toward the ancient structure and the anchor.

They approached the ruins of the immense structure carefully so that they would not disturb any of the surrounding debris.

They stood outside of the structure and carefully took pictures. The part of the team back on the Rama and viewing the pictures commented that there seemed to have been rooms inside the structure.

There was a feeling of extreme age. The pyramids felt young as compared to what Craig felt as he walked around what he surmised was the interior.

He was carefully making his way around what seemed to be the perimeter of the structure when what he saw made him stop in his tracks. Directly ahead of him was a twenty-foot diameter circular area on the floor that seemed to be a cover.

He approached it and carefully examined it. He could see no way to open it or go down around it.

They would need to bore down and see if they could go around, it to see what was below.

Next Craig led the team to the anchor just outside of the structure. It indeed was exactly that. The material was not metal. It appeared to be a highly stable and structurally sound type of ceramic. It was pitted, and it seemed and felt to be extremely old. On one side of the ancient anchor was what appeared to be hieroglyphic symbols. And just below the writing was a small, sealed chest of the same material as the anchor. Craig did not know the contents of the chest, but he imagined the contents were intended to communicate with the finder of the chest. The chest had a black spot in one corner. The spot appeared to be a seal to a hole.

He immediately called for a container that could be vacuum sealed so that he could send the chest up to the Rama. He had the person that would handle the chest sterilize his gloves before touching the chest and putting into the container. Once it was ready it was sent up to the Rama. He would take it back to the Savitar and use all the technology available to examine the interior. In the near future, he could envision himself carefully opening the chest in the confines of a sterile clean room.

He and the team returned to the structure and the circular cover to what he imagined would be a tunnel descending vertically down into Triton. He had the team examine the area around the cover.

There had to be a way around it or perhaps at one time the cover was lifted from above. There did not appear to be any exterior connections for lifting. Craig thought about it and decided it was probably designed with a failsafe mentality. This would mean the cover would be lifted from below and upon failure of the lifting system would seal itself from its own weight.

He decided trying to get past the cover should wait until the equipment to get past the cover without contaminating the interior could be brought out on a future trip. He had his team take measurements and pictures but instructed them not to move or disturb anything.

He decided that needed some archeologists to take charge of this project.

After three days on Triton the team had a complete map of the structure and precise measurements. It was time to leave. The anchor set up by the Rama was left in place. Future expeditions would be able to send down their connection cable and utilize the anchor.

Zack was waiting when Craig returned. He watched as Craig escorted the container with the ceramic chest to the clean room in the science lab.

"We will need to design and review the process to be followed in opening the chest. Here is what I believe we will find.

The black ceramic spot has material inside to allow us to establish the age of the chest.

The chest itself will have ceramic discs or other materials with the information about the race leaving the message. It may also have some sort of high-density information media. That is what I would leave behind if I was permanently leaving the solar system." Craig shared with the Savitar leadership team.

"President Lansing has sent up a message saying he would like to send up a team to study the Triton site. Your theory of life on Mars seems to have been verified by additional passes of the satellites over the area where you found the cliff dwellings. There is now a massive effort on Earth to send a team to Mars.

The satellite around Jupiter is now examining the three largest moons to see if there is any indication of visitors on them." Zack said speaking to Craig.

"It seems we will be busy for the foreseeable future studying the artifacts of the race that made it out here ahead of us."

Once again Zack's world had changed.

It was hard to believe that in his lifetime he had captured a blackhole and put it to use.

Now the Savitar had discovered an ancient set of visitors or perhaps the first intelligent beings in their Solar system. Had this intelligence developed on Mars as Craig was now proposing?

He knew that somehow the blackhole that now was part of the Savitar had been involved in what had happened to these ancient beings.

He held Janet's hand as they walked around the garden and knew that he would be going out in search of these previous space travelers to learn more about the history of his home world and its solar system.

Neither of them had envisioned this as the next adventure but both of them were committed to finding out if such solar system history existed.

Chapter 2: Visit to Mars

Zack and Janet established a research team to dig into the history of the Solar system. This after all had been the thesis for Zack's PhD thesis. His original focus had been on catastrophic occurrences that had affected the Earth. All the research and study that had been done to document the catastrophic events in Earth's past all took on a new perspective.

The fact that the black hole might have influence the events on Earth as well as Mars and the missing fifth planet had to now be considered. Zack knew that his thesis might be partly incorrect because he had not even considered the possibility of a black hole affecting the events on Earth.

Zack had not looked at the solar system as a whole and he had not considered the presence of a black hole. That presence could in fact have been the cause of many of the catastrophes that plagued the Earth.

Zack got support from President Lancing and reconstituted the Pathfinder analysis program that had been discontinued when the Savitar plans dominated and consumed the globe and its resources. Now it made sense to look again at the data they had previously gathered.

Zack suggested that the black hole that he had captured might be the reason that Mars was in the terrible shape it was in. Perhaps the black hole and the planet had in the distant past interacted. He asked the analysis team to determine the time that it took for the solar system to go one time around the edge of the Milky. He wondered whether every two hundred million years the black hole interacted with the solar system. It perhaps was the culprit for many of the solar systems ailments.

The answer to the time around the milky way was roughly two hundred and twenty million years.

Alex, Craig, Janet, Susan, and Mitch looked at each other and then they once again looked at the time frame they were discussing.

The possibility that the solar system had spawned two intelligent species was mind blowing.

It was hard to believe, and it was humbling to know that an intelligence had potentially developed space travel more two hundred million years before the human got down from the trees and took their first steps.

This meant that Mars would have developed intelligence during the first age of the dinosaurs!

Mitch commented that he wondered what would have happened if the black hole had not existed and had not interacted with the Martians, would the Martians be in control of the Earth and its people?

Zack was certain that the small black hole that was now the center of the Savitar had been the reason for the dramatic damage that Mars exhibited. It was clear that Mars had suffered an earlier dramatic impact that had cracked its mantle.

One of the team members postulated the theory that the destruction of the fifth forming planet was disrupted by the black hole and this had sent a piece out that was large enough that when it hit Mars it cracked the mantel. The impact also affected Mars core and its magnetic field.

Craig and most of the analysis team thought it was a miracle to have intelligent life arise to in such an environment. They also thought that the beings would have had to have been a tough lot to escape and survive in space.

Craig asked Zack to organize and plan the effort of discovering what was sealed in the ceramic time capsule.

He said that if as he thought, it was more than two hundred and twenty million years old, then it should not be opened unless those opening it were sure that they would not destroy the information that was sure to be inside.

Janet immediately volunteered to be part of the effort. Mary and Jeff both volunteered as well. All three of them had been working with Dr Garrity on the investigation of the ceramic box.

Janet said that there was some strong pull about the box that she was not sure she understood but she definitely wanted to be on the team to investigate it.

Zack in discussion with President Lansing established a team that had numerous Earth-bound scientists and the team aboard the Savitar working together. This was an arrangement that ensured keeping Earth engaged in a positive and constructive manner.

This team would have multiple goals.

One goal was to plan how to proceed in learning what was in the ceramic chest and what was below the gigantic circular seal down on Titan. This on its own was a monumental task.

The second goal was to set up an expedition to Mars and get boots on the ground and determine if there had indeed been a civilization there in the past. This activated the exploration support part of the effort to learn about the Martians.

The third goal was to plan for the exploration of each of the other moons that had evidence of previous Martian visits. This would be a separate group from those studying the ceramic box.

Janet became the project leader for the Savitar contingent that would go to Titan and explore what was below the circular seal.

Dr. Garrity would lead the direct examination of the ceramic chest with a goal to learn what was inside.

Zack was going to be involved in all three efforts, but he did not have full time to invest. He was the first President of the Savitar and was involved in the politics of getting the Savitar government fully functional and dealing with the interface to Earth.

Dr. Garrity was the ambassador from Earth and Zack had to constantly remind him of that fact. He suggested that Mary Ringhold and Jeff Mallory should take on a greater role in the investigation of the Ceramic box.

Craig grudgingly acknowledged this fact and did as suggested.

Craig reviewed what needed to be done to get the box examined and eventually opened. He made the point that he did not know if the box would be opened in his lifetime.

He stressed the fact that the team had to take all precautions to insure that they would not damage what was in the ceramic box.

He, Mary, and Jeff developed a draft investigation plan that entailed using all the available non-invasive technology that they could think of.

This plan was reviewed with their Earth counter parts and with the Savitar leadership.

The Rama was assigned once again to be the ship that would go to the Triton and tie to the anchor.

Zack had requested that the sea be tested to see if the Savitar could utilize it for fuel. If it were feasible, he wanted to create a fuel reservoir on the Savitar. This would ensure that they would have a supply for their engines. He asked Conrad Zepf to lead this effort.

The ceramic Bucky ball production system was producing two thousand Bucky balls a day. These were being used to create the floor for another of the many open pentagons that made up the Savitar's one G level.

Sampson had been one of the people that had saved Zack's life. He now got to do whatever he wanted.

Zack asked to Sampson take charge of utilizing each day's production of bucky balls and get another section of the Savitar covered.

Zack had rewarded the "Boss" and his team of workers by giving them the work they desired. This had been the group that had developed the self-propelled, computer driven welders that had saved the Savitar from destruction when they went around the moon on their departure from Earth.

The "Boss" was an excellent supervisor and the people working for him respected and had become his supporters. They excelled in the work they did for him.

The "Boss" was in charge of the construction of the facilities on the ceramic pentagon. He had all the required materials. The majority of what he was responsible to build was to be built of the ceramic sheet, bars, and planking. He however had the full range of plumbing, electrical and air conditioning that took a mix of materials.

The ceramic pentagon as it had come to be called was being built in record time.

Zack had expected such an outcome. He had the two best people leading the efforts.

He had plans to isolate the housing and equipment for opening the ceramic box in the middle of the newly ceramic covered hexagon.

He thought it appropriate that the Ceramic treasure box left by the mystery space travelers would be isolated in the middle of a totally ceramic based part of the Savitar that was made from the materials gathered by the Savitar.

Craig and Janet became an inseparable team as together they planned the investigation of the Ceramic container and the facility on Triton.

They engaged a full range of experts to figure out how to get around the seal at what they thought would be a shaft going vertically into the ground. They worked together to identify all the equipment needed to get around the seal.

They worked with another set of experts to determine how to handle the ceramic box. This team faced a monumentally challenging task. No one knew how they were to handle the chest if the chest was as old as it was thought to be.

Though Zack had all the burners on high it still would take a significant time to get the Triton team ready and supplied with the equipment needed. Some of the equipment was coming from Earth and that took more than six month just in transit time.

The team to examine the Ceramic box faced the same issue. They had a cat scan, a pet scan, and a wealth of other equipment also being sent out from Earth.

President Lancing had said that several specialists were also coming to the Savitar and were planning to stay for the duration that it took to examine the box and solve the mystery of who had transited the solar system in the long past.

Zack had a laugh when the several was close to one hundred scientists. The Savitar could handle the increase in population, but he realized that it would continue to get requests for additional people to come to the Savitar.

Zack studied the photos taken of the deep chasm on Mars. As he studied additional photos, he became convinced that the beings that had traveled the solar system originated on Mars. He was sure they had faced the black hole now at the center of the Savitar.

They had apparently left the solar system after their inability to establish themselves on the various moons.

He asked Janet if she were interested in seeing firsthand the origin of the beings that had most likely drilled a shaft down on Triton. The two of them decided to take a ride on the Sprite when it returned to Earth to ferry the people from Earth to Mars.

This would give Zack an opportunity to visit his family and once again put his feet down on Earth.

Janet insisted they also go to Hawaii where she wanted to walk the beach with him.

Zack kissed her and said he would love to and asked if she would marry him once again when they walked the beach in Maui.

Craig heard about the plans and decided to join as well. Emily was ecstatic. She knew that she of all people was truly bound to the planet of her birth. She had become quiet famous as a Chef on the Savitar and was immediately sought after by a wide following back on Earth when word got out of her visit.

The four of them estimated that their time away would give the project to examine the contents of the box and to visit the Triton facility the time it would need to get ready.

Space aboard the Sprite was reserved for them and the plans for their arrival on Earth were underway.

President Lancing was on his last year of his second term. He planned to honor Zack with a parade and a formal dinner event. This was something that he had not anticipated when Zack and the Savitar had departed some six years prior.

Now that his term would soon be over he was eager to meet face to face with both Zack and Dr. Garrity and discuss the possibility to immigrate to the Savitar. He, his wife, and the rest of the family had discussed this and come to the conclusion that for him it would be a great new venture.

Zack and Craig each spent time studying every picture from Mars. A robot had been landed and was making its way along the chasm. The photos from it immediately convinced both of them that they were looking at a vertical city built into the mantle.

They were now impatient to get there.

They convinced the President to allow the Sprite to make a brief stop on Mars before coming to Earth.

The President's approval meant they would be the first humans on Mars and the first to examine the ancient artifacts that were there.

Zack, Craig, and Janet were ecstatic. Emily told everyone that she was not sure she wanted to go down to the surface of Mars. She was sure they would be visiting a tomb where many people had died.

She had no idea how right that was, but she also had no idea what two hundred and twenty million years would do to any tomb.

The trip to Mars, drove home that the current design of spaceships were of an inadequate and ancient design. The designers of the current generation of spaceships were planet and gravity oriented.

The gravity orientation needed to be ship oriented.

He and Craig discussed this in great detail and decided they would sponsor a rotating structure design that would simulate gravity inside the spaceship.

The trick would be to get their design to feature ships with gravity like forces in a small structure and to do it in a practical, economical way.

They conferred with a design team back on the Savitar as they journeyed toward Mars.

On their arrival to Mars, Zack had the Sprite position itself over the area in the cracked mantle and slowly move along its length.

The Captain Moffet, Zack, and Craig all let out a yell as their telescope showed a hole in the ground.

Image enhancement revealed another anchor deep within what seemed to be a missile launch tube. This once again was evidence of a Martian race of beings.

It was an intoxicating learning beverage. The talk constantly went to what these being might have been like. What was their body structure? How did they think? Did they walk erect similar to a human. Where they bigger than Earthlings.

The discussions and questions seemed endless.

Zack requested permission to go to the surface of Mars to verify the presence of an anchor and whether the Sprite could utilize it.

Captain Moffet chuckled as he declined Zack's request. He apologized but said he could not let the President of the Savitar go gliding down to the surface. It would be much too risky.

He instead named three of his people to go down and plant a new anchor for the Sprite to use. Once the anchor had been planted and the Sprite had a functioning space elevator down to the surface Zack and his contingent could descend. He went on to state that Zack and each of the three would have two of the Sprite's crew members be their support personnel.

Janet knew Zack well enough to know he was super energized about getting to the surface to determine if their indeed had been intelligent life so long ago.

She was just as excited and could barely wait but she also sensed that their findings might haunt them. She anticipated the history of the place was a history that at its final moment had a multitude of death associated with it.

She made a joke about the fact that wisdom came with time but the amount of time that they were involved in was beyond comprehension and maybe they would find themselves to be senile before they unraveled their two hundred-million-year mystery.

Zack agreed and said that he was not going to wait until he was that old and planned to find the Aliens or their remnants in his lifetime.

Zack and Craig conferred with the rest of the team members to plan what they would do when they got to the surface.

They all agreed that they would descend into the tube where the ancient space anchor was located. They would then see if they could go beyond that point.

Janet stopped the discussion and made the point that airports and missile centers on the Earth were usually initially positioned outside of city centers where the population was the lowest. This would mean the anchor location they were contemplating might be far removed from the high-density location. She suggested that they place the anchor as close to the edge of the crack in the mantle as possible.

Zack and Craig agreed with her logic and thanked Janet for her suggestion. They once again examined their pictures and decided that the location of the anchor was a fair distance from the crack in the mantle.

They requested a change to where the Sprite's anchor would be located. It was agreed that the location would be several hundred yards from the edge of the crack in the mantle.

They asked Janet to pick the spot she had in mind. Janet carefully examined the rim of the mantle crack and zeroed in on a spot that seemed to have been created by something more than nature would have done.

Little did she know that she had selected the spot that had been the favorite location for the person that had led the Martian Survival after their confluence with the black hole and would soon become Janet's obsession

About the Author

Ronald E. Mueller
remwriter95@gmail.com

Ron grew up in what is now Flint River State Park in Southeast Iowa. The 170-year old house Ron lived in is built into a hillside. It faces a 125-foot high cliff towering over the little Flint River. The house and the land talked to him about; the passing of time, the struggle to conquer the land, the struggles people faced and the wonder of nature.

He climbed the cliffs, crawled into the caves, dove from the swimming rock, collected clams from the bottom of the pond, gigged and skinned frogs for their legs. He trapped muskrats for fur, hunted raccoon in the dead of night, and with only a stick hunted rabbits in the dead of winter.

His young life was outdoors, and nature tested him.

He walked to a one room stone schoolhouse uphill both ways. A stern but warm-hearted teacher, Mrs. Henry was instrumental in shaping his character as she shepherded him from the fourth to the eighth grade. A Montessori before its time. It was a great way to grow up.

His experiences inter-twined with snippets of fantasy lend themselves to the adventures he leads the reader through.

Characters in Book

First Name	Family Name	Role
Adinath	Rajkumar	Captain of the Indian Vessel.
Adrian	Moffet	Captain of the USS Sprite
Andrew	Pennington	Zack's first bodyguard, initial assassin
Benjamin	Samualson	NASA director
Bill	Masterson	FBI director
Chiang	Lee	the senior navigator
Conrad	Zepf	Science manager
Daniel	Lansing	President of the US
Dr. Craig	Garrity	Prof of Astronomy-MIT Zack's mentor and friend
Elena	Stanislav	Captain of the Russian Vessel
Emily	Garrity	Craig's wife
Enrico	Hidalgo	2nd in command. Becomes captain of the Savitar
Fred	Mathews	FBI chief, Janet's boss
Gregor	Menkowski	Logistics officer
Indira	DeSouza	Chief of Personnel. Leader of the takeover group
Janet	Romero	Zack's bodyguard, later love interest.
Jeff	Mallory	bodyguard for Craig Garrity.
Jennifer	Mitchel	Dr, Primary care
John	Adam	Shuttle pilot. Reluctant take over partner.
Lars	Mendelssohn	welding guru and unofficial leader of the welders
Lisa	Hemming	Agriculturalist in charge of the Hydroponics
Marion	Twillinger	Ship doctor
Mary	Ringhold	bodyguard for Craig Garrity.
Melanie	Baker	Samuel Trimble's business manager
Merriam	Lansing	President's wife
Mitch	Kennedy	Replacement bodyguard
Ned	McMillan	Ship doctor
Paulo	Souza	Welding manager
Quang	Nguyen	Welder - one of Zacks Farmers
Raymond	Walker	General that gets Indira onto the Savitar
Sam	Petroski	Welder - one of Zacks Farmers
Samson		Large black man that saves Zack
Samuel	Trimble	Nano bot inventor.
Sunny	Zhao	scientist, part of the takeover network
Susan	Sanderson	Replacement bodyguard
Victor	Marquis	Facilities Manager
Zack	Milton	Main Character
	Sprite	the name of the US spaceship Captain Moffit
	Star Seeker	the name of the Chinese spaceship Lin Sin Pao the captain
	Rama	the name of the Indian spaceship

	Captain Adrinath Rajkumar
Hoshi-no-ma-de	the name of the Japanese spaceship
	Hamasura Tokura
Stremitel'noye	the name of the Russian spaceship
	Commander Elena Stanislav
Fortune	the name of the British spaceship
	Marcus Langley Captain

Ron Mueller

Published by: Around the World Publishing LLC.

QR Links to

ATWP.US web site